BEAST OF MAGIC

The mage whirled, whipping out the dagger on the right, and thrust, hard, at the bane-wolf's throat.

It went through the throat as if through air. Not a true beast, then, but a magical one ... Lythande dropped the right-hand dagger, and snatched, left-handed, at the other, the dagger intended for fighting the powers and beasts of magic; but the delay had been nearly fatal; the teeth of the bane-wolf met, like fiery needles, in Lythande's arm, then in the knee thrust up to ward the beast from the throat.

As Lythande's struggles weakened, the thought came, unbidden:

Have I come this far to die in a dark cellar in the maw of a wolf, not even a true wolf, but a thing created by the filthy misuse of sorcery at the hands of a thief?

LYTHANDE

Marion Zimmer Bradley

With a story by Vonda N. McIntyre

SPHERE BOOKS LIMITED

SPHERE BOOKS LTD

Published by the Penguin Group
27 Wrights Lane, London W8 5TZ, England
Viking Penguin Inc., 40 West 23rd Street, New York, New York 10010, USA
Penguin Books Australia Ltd, Ringwood, Victoria, Australia
Penguin Books Canada Ltd, 2801 John Street, Markham, Ontario, Canada L3R 1B4
Penguin Books (NZ) Ltd, 182–190 Wairau Road, Auckland 10, New Zealand

Penguin Books Ltd, Registered Offices: Harmondsworth, Middlesex, England

This collection first published in the USA by Daw Books, Inc. 1986
Published by Sphere Books Ltd 1988

The Secret of the Blue Star copyright © 1979 by Marion Zimmer Bradley
The Incompetent Magician copyright © 1983 by Marion Zimmer Bradley
Somebody Else's Magic copyright © 1984 by Mercury Press, Inc.
Sea Wrack copyright © 1985 by Mercury Press, Inc.
The Wandering Lute copyright © 1986 by Mercury Press, Inc.
Looking for Satan copyright © 1981 by Vonda N. McIntyre

Made and printed in Great Britain by
Richard Clay Ltd, Bungay, Suffolk

Contents

Introduction to
Secret of the Blue Star:

*I remember first hearing Bob Asprin talk about a new
concept that he referred to as THIEVES WORLD—I
think it was at the Brighton Worldcon, which was in
1978 or thereabout. Bob described the concept enthusi-
astically and it sounded like fun, so I said, "Okay, I'm
in," without thinking much about it . . . which is how
writers get into trouble. A few months after I got back
from England I received in the mail a fascinating packet
of stuff from Bob and others who had agreed to join in
this business of writing connected stories in a common
shared background. There were maps, a basic description of the gods and customs of this place, and so forth.
We were asked to contribute a sketch of our basic
character or characters, and I obliged with a few para-
graphs about the mysterious Lythande, about whom
nothing is known, not even gender. . . .*

*All this sort of thing is fun to play with, but when it
got down to having to do some serious writing, that was
something else. I wasn't the only one who was perfectly
willing to share in the planning of the initial stages; but
as to actually getting down to the typewriter and turning stories in—well, in his original (the Ace edition of
volume one, not the super hardback reprint of the first
volumes), Bob tells about his near-nervous-breakdown;
because at least half of us, having thought it was a fun*

7

idea, proved to think we were too busy to do actual writing. When Bob said he had to have the story, I was about to fly to Phoenix, then New York, and from there to fly to England for research on a project which eventually turned out to be the most lucrative of my life's work; but Bob persuaded me, so I wrote the story on the plane and in my hotel room in Phoenix, borrowed Margaret Hildebrand's little typewriter and typed it, then left it with my secretary to be proofread, corrected, and mailed off to the Asprins. It's the only story I wrote in longhand after my seventeenth year, and I hope the last. I gave it to the Phoenix con committee (the original handwritten version, that is) to auction off for the benefit of their convention, and I have no idea who has it or what they did with it. But they have a unique item—the only MZB handwritten manuscript of a professional story ever.

As for Lythande, she is as much a mystery to me as she is to the inhabitants of Sanctuary/Thieves World. When I first conceived this character, I did not know that she was a woman; I thought her an eccentric male. When I wrote Poul Anderson's Cappen Varra (the only honest man Sanctuary) into my story, it was a simple plot device; but Cappen Varra's saying, "You are like no other man I have ever met," made me wonder: but what about women? From there it was only a little step to saying; of course, Lythande is a woman cursed to conceal her true self forever.

The antecedents of Lythande are simple—Fritz Leiber's Fafhrd, and C.L. Moore's Jirel of Joiry—but I also attempted, in making Lythande a musician and magician, to bring out something of Manly Wade Wellman's Silver John, whose silver-stringed guitar is a potent weapon against sorcery. Besides, even in a thieves-world of magic, practicing no art but magic is a thin living, or, as Lythande would say, "puts no beans on the table." A minstrel can always get a good supper for a song.

All of Lythande's songs in these works are paraphrases of Sappho, a subtle key to a side of her character which I chose not to emphasize overmuch. I have no political point to make by Lythande's eccentricities; it is simply, I think, one more stress on a woman whose life must be already overcomplicated. I have often been urged to write about lesbian women; unfortunately, the audience for this kind of thing is usually confined to the unhealthily curious male, and I choose not to cater to this kind of interest. Lythande is as she is, and even the characters in a book deserve some privacy. I wouldn't mind other people writing about Lythande—people who write, and people who read, are my kind of people and they can have anything I have. In any case, here is my Lythande and her world. Welcome to it.

For the many people who have asked me:

Lythande is pronounced (by me, at least) as Lee THOND.

THE SECRET
OF THE BLUE STAR

On a night in Sanctuary, when the streets bore a false
glamour in the silver glow of full moon, so that every
ruin seemed an enchanted tower and every dark street
and square an island of mystery, the mercenary-magician
Lythande sallied forth to seek adventure.

Lythande had but recently returned—if the mysterious comings and goings of a magician can be called by
so prosaic a name—from guarding a caravan across the
Grey Wastes to Twand. Somewhere in the Wastes, a
gaggle of desert rats—two-legged rats with poisoned
steel teeth—had set upon the caravan, not knowing it
was guarded by magic, and had found themselves fighting skeletons that howled and fought with eyes of flame;
and at their center a tall magician with a blue star
between blazing eyes, a star that shot lightnings of a
cold and paralyzing flame. So the desert rats ran, and
never stopped running until they reached Aurvesh, and
the tales they told did Lythande no harm except in the
ears of the pious.

And so there was gold in the pockets of the long,
dark magician's robe, or perhaps concealed in whatever
dwelling sheltered Lythande.

For at the end, the caravan master had been almost
more afraid of Lythande than he was of the bandits, a
situation which added to the generosity with which he

11

rewarded the magician. According to custom, Lythande neither smiled nor frowned, but remarked, days later, to Myrtis, the proprietor of the Aphrodisia House in the Street of Red Lanterns, that sorcery, while a useful skill and filled with many aesthetic delights for the contemplation of the philosopher, in itself puts no beans on the table.

A curious remark, that, Myrtis pondered, putting away the ounce of gold Lythande had bestowed upon her in consideration of a secret which lay many years behind them both. Curious that Lythande should speak of beans on the table, when no one but herself had ever seen a bite of food or a drop of drink pass the magician's lips since the blue star had adorned that high and narrow brow. Nor had any woman in the Quarter ever been able to boast that a great magician had paid for her favors, or been able to imagine how such a magician behaved in that situation when all men were alike reduced to flesh and blood.

Perhaps Myrtis could have told if she would; some of her girls thought so, when, as sometimes happened, Lythande came to the Aphrodisia House and was closeted long with its owner; even, on rare intervals, for an entire night. It was said, of Lythande, that the Aphrodisia House itself had been the magician's gift to Myrtis, after a famous adventure still whispered in the bazaar, involving an evil wizard, two horse-traders, a caravan master, and a few assorted toughs who had prided themselves upon never giving gold for any woman and thought it funny to cheat an honest working woman. None of them had ever showed their faces—what was left of them—in Sanctuary again, and Myrtis boasted that she need never again sweat to earn her living, and never again entertain a man, but would claim her madam's privilege of a solitary bed.

And then, too, the girls thought, a magician of Lythande's stature could have claimed the most beauti-

ful women from Sanctuary to the mountains beyond
Ilsig; not courtesans alone, but princesses and noble
women and priestesses would have been for Lythande's
taking. Myrtis had doubtless been beautiful in her youth,
and certainly she boasted enough of the princes and
wizards and travelers who had paid great sums for her
love. She was beautiful still (and of course there were
those who said that Lythande did not pay her, but that,
on the contrary, Myrtis paid the magician great sums to
maintain her aging beauty with strong magic) but her
hair had gone grey and she no longer troubled to dye it
with henna or goldenwash from Tyrisis-beyond-the-sea.

But if Myrtis were not the woman who knew how
Lythande behaved in that most elemental of situations,
then there was no woman in Sanctuary who could say.
Rumor said also that Lythande called up female demons
from the Grey Wastes, to couple in lechery, and certainly Lythande was neither the first nor the last magician of whom that could be said.

But on this night Lythande sought neither food nor
drink nor the delights of amorous entertainment; although Lythande was a great frequenter of taverns, no
man had ever yet seen a drop of ale or mead or fire-
drink pass the barrier of the magician's lips. Lythande
walked along the far edge of the bazaar, skirting the
old rim of the governor's palace, keeping to the shadows in defiance of footpads and cutpurses, that love for
shadows which made the folk of the city say that
Lythande could appear and disappear into thin air.

Tall and thin, Lythande, above the height of a tall
man, lean to emaciation, with the blue star-shaped
tattoo of the magician-adept above thin, arching eyebrows; wearing a long, hooded robe which melted into
the shadows. Clean-shaven, the face of Lythande, or
beardless—none had come close enough, in living memory, to say whether this was the whim of an effeminate
or the hairlessness of a freak. The hair beneath the

hood was as long and luxuriant as a woman's, but greying, as no woman in this city of harlots would have allowed it to do.

Striding quickly along a shadowed wall, Lythande stepped through an open door, over which the sandal of Thufir, god of pilgrims, had been nailed up for luck; but the footsteps were so soft, and the hooded robe blended so well into the shadows, that eyewitnesses would later swear, truthfully, that they had seen Lythande appear from the air, protected by sorceries, or by a cloak of invisibility.

Around the hearthfire, a group of men were banging their mugs together noisily to the sound of a rowdy drinking-song, strummed on a worn and tinny lute— Lythande knew it belonged to the tavern-keeper, and could be borrowed—by a young man, dressed in fragments of foppish finery, torn and slashed by the chances of the road. He was sitting lazily, with one knee crossed over the other; and when the rowdy song died away, the young man drifted into another, a quiet love song from another time and another country. Lythande had known the song, more years ago than bore remembering, and in those days Lythande the magician had borne another name and had known little of sorcery. When the song died, Lythande had stepped from the shadows, visible, and the firelight glinted on the blue star, mocking at the center of the high forehead.

There was a little muttering in the tavern, but they were not unaccustomed to Lythande's invisible comings and goings. The young man raised eyes which were surprisingly blue beneath the black hair elaborately curled above his brow. He was slender and agile, and Lythande marked the rapier at his side, which looked well handled, and the amulet, in the form of a coiled snake, at his throat. The young man said, "Who are you, who has the habit of coming and going into thin air like that?"

"One who compliments your skill at song." Lythande flung a coin to the tapster's boy. "Will you drink?"

"A minstrel never refuses such an invitation. Singing is dry work." But when the drink was brought, he said, "Not drinking with me, then?"

"No man has ever seen Lythande eat or drink," muttered one of the men in the circle round them.

"Why, then, I hold that unfriendly," cried the young minstrel. "A friendly drink between comrades shared is one thing; but I am no servant to sing for pay or to drink except as a friendly gesture!"

Lythande shrugged, and the blue star above the high brow began to shimmer and give forth blue light. The onlookers slowly edged backward, for when a wizard who wore the blue star was angered, bystanders did well to be out of the way. The minstrel set down the lute, so it would be well out of range if he must leap to his feet. Lythande knew, by the excruciating slowness of his movements and great care, that he had already shared a good many drinks with chance-met comrades. But the minstrel's hand did not go to his sword hilt but instead closed like a fist over the amulet in the form of a snake.

"You are like no man I have ever met before," he observed mildly, and Lythande, feeling inside the little ripple, nerve-long, that told a magician he was in the presence of spellcasting, hazarded quickly that the amulet was one of those which would not protect its master unless the wearer first stated a set number of truths—usually three or five—about the owner's attacker or foe. Wary, but amused, Lythande said, "A true word. Nor am I like any man you will ever meet, live you never so long, minstrel."

The minstrel saw, beyond the angry blue glare of the star, a curl of friendly mockery in Lythande's mouth. He said, letting the amulet go, "And I wish you no ill; and you wish me none, and those are true sayings too, wizard, hey? And there's an end of that. But although perhaps you are like to no other, you are not the only wizard I have seen in Sanctuary who bears a blue star about his forehead."

Now the blue star blazed rage, but not for the minstrel. They both knew it. The crowd around them had all mysteriously discovered that they had business elsewhere. The minstrel looked at the empty benches.

"I must go elsewhere to sing for my supper, it seems."

"I meant you no offense when I refused to share a drink," said Lythande. "A magician's vow is not as lightly overset as a lute. Yet I may guest-gift you with dinner and drink in plenty without loss of dignity, and in return ask a service of a friend, may I not?"

"Such is the custom of my country. Cappen Varra thanks you, magician."

"Tapster! Your best dinner for my guest, and all he can drink tonight!"

"For such liberal guesting I'll not haggle about the service," Cappen Varra said, and set to the smoking dishes brought before him. As he ate, Lythande drew from the folds of his robe a small pouch containing a quantity of sweet-smelling herbs, rolled them into a blue-grey leaf, and touched his ring to spark the roll alight. He drew on the smoke, which drifted up sweet and greyish.

"As for the service, it is nothing so great; tell me all you know of this other wizard who wears the blue star. I know of none other of my order south of Azehur, and I would be certain you did not see me, nor my wraith."

Cappen Varra sucked at a marrow-bone and wiped his fingers fastidiously on the tray-cloth beneath the meats. He bit into a ginger-fruit before replying.

"Not you, wizard, nor your fetch or doppelganger; this one had shoulders brawnier by half, and he wore no sword, but two daggers cross-girt astride his hips.

His beard was black; and his left hand missing three fingers."

"Ils of the Thousand Eyes! Rabben the Half-handed, here in Sanctuary! Where did you see him, minstrel?"

"I saw him crossing the bazaar; but he bought nothing that I saw. And I saw him in the Street of Red Lanterns, talking to a woman. What service am I to do for you, magician?"

"You have done it." Lythande gave silver to the tavernkeeper—so much that the surly man bade Shalpa's cloak cover him as he went—and laid another coin, gold this time, beside the borrowed lute.

"Redeem your harp; that one will do your voice no boon." But when the minstrel raised his head in thanks, the magician had gone unseen into the shadows.

Pocketing the gold, the minstrel asked, "How did he know that? And how did he go out?"

"Shalpa the swift alone knows," the tapster said. "Flew out by the smoke-hole in the chimney, for all I ken! That one needs not the night-dark cloak of Shalpa to cover him, for he has one of his own. He paid for your drinks, good sir; what will you have?" And Cappen Varra proceeded to get very drunk, that being the wisest thing to do when one becomes entangled unawares in the private affairs of a wizard.

Outside in the street, Lythande paused to consider. Rabben the Half-handed was no friend; yet there was no reason his presence in Sanctuary must deal with Lythande, or personal revenge. If it were business concerned with the Order of the Blue Star, if Lythande must lend Rabben aid, or the Half-handed had been sent to summon all the members of the Order, the star they both wore would have given warning.

Yet it would do no harm to make certain. Walking swiftly, the magician had reached a line of old stables behind the governor's palace. There was silence and secrecy for magic. Lythande stepped into one of the little side alleys, drawing up the magician's cloak until no light remained, slowly withdrawing farther and farther into the silence until nothing remained anywhere in the world—anywhere in the universe but the light of the blue star ever glowing in front. Lythande remembered how it had been set there, and at what cost—the price an adept paid for power.

The blue glow gathered, fulminated in many-colored patterns, pulsing and glowing, until Lythande stood *within* the light; and there, in the Place That Is Not, seated upon a throne carved apparently from sapphire, was the Master of the Star.

"Gretings to you, fellow star, star-born, *shyryu.*" The terms of endearment could mean fellow, companion, brother, sister, beloved, equal, pilgrim; its literal meaning was *sharer of starlight.* What brings you into the "Pilgrim Place this night from afar?"

"The need for knowledge, star-sharer. Have you sent one to seek me out in Sanctuary?"

"Not so, *shyryu.* All is well in the Temple of the Star-sharers; you have not yet been summoned; the hour is not yet come."

For every adept of the Blue Star knows; it is one of the prices of power. At the world's end, when all the doings of mankind and mortals are done, the last to fall under the assault of Chaos will be the Temple of the Star; and then, in the Place That Is Not, the Master of the Star will summon all of the Pilgrim Adepts from the farthest corners of the world, to fight with all their magic against Chaos; but until that day, they have such freedom as will best strengthen their powers. The Master of the Star repeated, reassuringly, "The hour has not come. You are free to walk as you will in the world."

The blue glow faded, and Lythande stood shivering. So Rabben had not been sent in that final summoning.

Yet the end and Chaos might well be at hand for Lythande before the hour appointed, if Rabben the Half-handed had his way.

It was a fair test of strength, ordained by our masters. Rabben should bear me no ill-will. . . . Rabben's presence in Sanctuary need not have to do with Lythande. He might be here upon his lawful occasions—if anything of Rabben's could be said to be lawful; for it was only upon the last day of all that the Pilgrim Adepts were pledged to fight upon the side of Law against Chaos. And Rabben had not chosen to do so before then.

Caution would be needed, and yet Lythande knew that Rabben was near . . .

South and east of the governor's palace, there is a little triangular park, across from the Street of Temples. By day the graveled walks and turns of shrubbery are given over to predicants and priests who find not enough worship or offerings for their liking; by night the place is the haunt of women who worship no goddess except She of the filled purse and the empty womb. And for both reasons the place is called, in irony, the Promise of Heaven; in Sanctuary, as elsewhere, it is well known that those who promise do not always perform.

Lythande, who frequented neither women nor priests as a usual thing, did not often walk here. The park seemed deserted; the evil winds had begun to blow, whipping bushes and shrubbery into the shapes of strange beasts performing unnatural acts; and moaning weirdly around the walls and eaves of the Temples across the street, the wind that was said in Sanctuary to be the moaning of Azyuna in Vashanka's bed. Lythande moved swiftly, skirting the darkness of the paths. And then a woman's scream rent the air.

From the shadows Lythande could see the frail form of a young girl in a torn and ragged dress; she was barefoot and her ear was bleeding where one jeweled earring had been torn from the lobe. She was struggling in the iron grip of a huge burly black-bearded man, and the first thing Lythande saw was the hand gripped around the girl's thin, bony wrist, dragging her; two fingers missing and the other cut away to the first joint. Only then—when it was no longer needed—did Lythande see the blue star between the black bristling brows, the cat-yellow eyes of Rabben the Half-handed!

Lythande knew him of old, from the Temple of the Star. Even then Rabben had been a vicious man, his lecheries notorious. Why, Lythande wondered, had the masters not demanded that he renounce them as the price of his power? Lythande's lips tightened in a mirthless grimace; so notorious had been Rabben's lecheries that if he renounced them, everyone would know the Secret of his Power.

For the powers of an Adept of the Blue Star depended upon a secret. As in the old legend of the giant who kept his heart in a secret place outside his body, and with it his immortality, so the adept of the blue star poured all his psychic force into a single Secret; and the one who discovered the Secret would acquire all of that adept's power. So Rabben's Secret must be something else . . . Lythande did not speculate on it.

The girl cried out pitifully as Rabben jerked at her wrist; as the burly magician's star began to glow, she thrust her free hand over her eyes to shield them from it. Without fully intending to intervene, Lythande stepped from the shadows, and the rich voice that had made the prentice-magicians in the outer court of the Blue Star call Lythande "minstrel" rather than "magician," rang out:

"By Shipri the All-Mother, release that woman!"

Rabben whirled. "By the nine-hundred-and-ninety-ninth eye of Ils! Lythande!"

"Are there not enough women in the Street of Red Lanterns, that you must mishandle girl-children in the

Street of Temples?" For Lythande could see how young she was, the thin arms and childish legs and ankles, the breasts not yet full-formed beneath the dirty, torn tunic.

Rabben turned on Lythande and sneered, "You were always squeamish, *shyryu*. No woman walks here unless she is for sale. Do you want her for yourself? Have you tired of your fat madame in the Aphrodisia House?"

"You will not take her name into your mouth, *shyryu!*"

"So tender for the honor of a harlot?"

Lythande ignored that. "Let that girl go, or stand to my challenge."

Rabben's star shot lightnings; he shoved the girl to one side. She fell nerveless to the pavement and lay without moving. "She'll stay there until we've done. Did you think she could run away while we fought? Come to think of it, I never did see you with a woman, Lythande—is that your Secret, Lythande, that you've no use for women?"

Lythande maintained an impassive face; but whatever came, Rabben must not be allowed to pursue *that* line. "You may couple like an animal in the streets of Sanctuary, Rabben, but I do not. Will you yield her up, or fight?"

"Perhaps I should yield her to you; this is unheard of, that Lythande should fight in the streets over a woman! You see, I know your habits well, Lythande!"

Damnation of Vashanka! Now indeed I shall have to fight for the girl!

Lythande's rapier snicked from its scabbard and thrust at Rabben as if of its own will.

"Ha! Do you think Rabben fights street-brawls with the sword like any mercenary?" Lythande's sword-tip exploded in the blue star-glow, and became a shimmering snake, twisting back in itself to climb past the hilt, fangs dripping venom as it sought to coil around Lythande's fist. Lythande's own star blazed. The sword was metal again but twisted and useless, in the shape of

21

the snake it had been, coiling back toward the scabbard. Enraged, Lythande jerked free of the twisted metal, sent a spitting rain of fire in Rabben's direction. Quickly the huge adept covered himself in fog, and the fire-spray extinguished itself. Somewhere outside consciousness Lythande was aware of a crowd gathering; not twice in a lifetime did two adepts of the Blue Star battle by sorcery in the streets of Sanctuary. The blaze of the stars, blazing from each magician's brow, raged lightnings in the square.

On a howling wind came little torches ravening, that flickered and whipped at Lythande; they touched the tall form of the magician and vanished. Then a wild whirlwind sent trees lashing, leaves swirling bare from branches, and battered Rabben to his knees. Lythande was bored; this must be finished quickly. Not one of the goggling onlookers in the crowd knew afterward what had been done, but Rabben bent, slowly, slowly, forced inch by inch down and down, to his knees, to all fours, prone, pressing and grinding his face farther and farther into the dust, rocking back and forth, pressing harder and harder into the sand . . .

Lythande turned and lifted the girl. She stared in disbelief at the burly sorcerer grinding his black beard frantically into the dirt.

"What did you—"

"Never mind—let's get out of here. The spell will not hold him long, and when he wakes from it he will be angry." Neutral mockery edged Lythande's voice, and the girl could see it, too, Rabben with beard and eyes and blue star covered with the dirt and dust—

She scurried along in the wake of the magician's robe; when they were well away from the Promise of Heaven, Lythande halted, so abruptly that the girl stumbled.

"Who are you, girl?"

"My name is Bercy. And yours?"

"A magician's name is not lightly given. In Sanctuary they call me Lythande." Looking down at the girl, the magician noted, with a pang, that beneath the dirt and dishevelment she was very beautiful and very young. "You can go, Bercy. He will not touch you again; I have bested him fairly upon challenge."

She flung herself on to Lythande's shoulder, clinging. "Don't send me away!" she begged, clutching, eyes filled with adoration. Lythande scowled.

Predictable, of course. Bercy believed, and who in Sanctuary would have disbelieved, that the duel had been fought for the girl as prize, and she was ready to give herself to the winner. Lythande made a gesture of protest.

"No—"

The girl narrowed her eyes in pity. "Is it then with you as Rabben said—that your secret is that you have been deprived of manhood?" But beyond the pity was a delicious flicker of amusement—what a tidbit of gossip! A juicy bit for the Streets of Women.

"Silence!" Lythande's glance was imperative. "Come."

She followed, along the twisting streets that led into the Street of Red Lanterns. Lythande strode with confidence, now, past the House of Mermaids, where, it was said, delights as exotic as the name promised were to be found; past the House of Whips, shunned by all except those who refused to go elsewhere, and at last, beneath the face of the Green Lady as she was worshiped far away and beyond Ranke, the Aphrodisia House.

Bercy looked around, eyes wide, at the pillared lobby, the brilliance of a hundred lanterns, the exquisitely dressed women lounging on cushions till they were summoned. They were finely dressed and bejeweled— Myrtis knew her trade, and how to present her wares— and Lythande guessed that the ragged Bercy's glance was one of envy; she had probably sold herself in the

23

bazaars for a few coppers or for a loaf of bread, since she was old enough. Yet somehow, like flowers covering a dungheap, she had kept an exquisite fresh beauty, all gold and white, flowerlike. Even ragged and half-starved, she touched Lythande's heart.

"Bercy, have you eaten today?"

"No, master."

Lythande summoned the huge eunuch Jiro, whose business it was to conduct the favored customers to the chambers of their chosen women, and throw out the drunks and abusive customers into the street. He came—huge-bellied, naked except for a skimpy loincloth and a dozen rings in his ear—he had once had a lover who was an earring-seller and had used him to display her wares.

"How we may serve the magician Lythande?"

The women on the couches and cushions were twittering at one another in surprise and dismay, and Lythande could almost hear their thoughts;

None of us has been able to attract or seduce the great magician, and this ragged street wench has caught his eyes? And, being women, Lythande knew they could see the unclouded beauty that shone through the girl's rags.

"Is Madame Myrtis available, Jiro?"

"She's sleeping, O great wizard, but for you she's given orders she's to be waked at any hour. Is this—" no one alive can be quite so supercilious as the chief eunuch of a fashionable brothel—"*yours*, Lythande, or a gift for my madame?"

"Both, perhaps. Give her something to eat and find her a place to spend the night."

"And a bath, magician? She has fleas enough to louse a floorful of cushions!"

"A bath, certainly, and a bath-woman with scents and oils," Lythande said, "and something in the nature of a whole garment."

"Leave it to me," said Jiro expansively, and Bercy looked at Lythande in dread, but went when the magician gestured to her to go. As Jiro took her away, Lythande saw Myrtis standing in the doorway; a heavy woman, no longer young, but with the frozen beauty of a spell. Through the perfect spelled features, her eyes were warm and welcoming as she smiled at Lythande.

"My dear, I had not expected to see you here. Is that yours?" She moved her head toward the door through which Jiro had conducted the frightened Bercy. "She'll probably run away, you know, once you take your eyes off her."

"I wish I thought so, Myrtis. But no such luck, I fear."

"You had better tell me the whole story," Myrtis said, and listened to Lythande's brief, succinct account of the affair.

"And if you laugh, Myrtis, I take back my spell and leave your grey hairs and wrinkles open to the mockery of everyone in Sanctuary!"

But Myrtis had known Lythande too long to take that threat very seriously. "So the maiden you rescued is all maddened with desire for the love of Lythande!" She chuckled. "It is like an old ballad, indeed!"

"But what am I to do, Myrtis? By the paps of Shipri the All-Mother, this is a dilemma!"

"Take her into your confidence and tell her why your love cannot be hers," Myrtis said.

Lythande frowned. "You hold my Secret, since I had no choice; you knew me before I was made magician, or bore the blue star—"

"And before I was a harlot," Myrtis agreed.

"But if I make this girl feel like a fool for loving me, she will hate me as much as she loves; and I cannot confide in anyone I cannot trust with my life and my power. All I have is yours, Myrtis, because of that past we shared. And that includes my power, if you ever should need it. But I cannot entrust it to this girl."

"Still she owes you something, for delivering her out of the hands of Rabben."

Lythande said, "I will think about it; and now make haste to bring me food, for I am hungry and athirst." Taken to a private room, Lythande ate and drank, served by Myrtis's own hands. And Myrtis said, "I could never have sworn your vow—to eat and drink in the sight of no man!"

"If you sought the power of a magician, you would keep it well enough," said Lythande. "I am seldom tempted now to break it; I fear only lest I break it unawares; I cannot drink in a tavern lest among the women there might be some one of those strange men who find diversion in putting on the garments of a female; even here I will not eat or drink among your women, for that reason. All power depends on the vows and the secret."

"Then I cannot aid you," Myrtis said, "but you are not bound to speak truth to her; tell her you have vowed to live without women."

"I may do that," Lythande said, and finished the food, scowling.

Later Bercy was brought in, wide-eyed, enthralled by her fine gown and her freshly washed hair, softly curling about her pink-and-white face and the sweet scent of bath oils and perfumes that hung about her.

"The girls here wear such pretty clothes, and one of them told me they could eat twice a day if they wished! Am I pretty enough, do you think, that Madame Myrtis would have me here?"

"If that is what you wish. You are more than beautiful."

Bercy said boldly, "I would rather belong to *you*, magician," and flung herself again on Lythande, her hands clutching and clinging, dragging the lean face down to hers. Lythande, who rarely touched anything living, held her gently, trying not to reveal consternation.

"Bercy, child, this is only a fancy. It will pass."

"No," she wept. "I love you, I want only you!"

And then, unmistakably, along the magician's nerves, Lythande felt that little ripple, that warning thrill of tension which said: *spellcasting is in use*. Not against Lythande. That could have been countered. But somewhere within the room.

Here, in the Aphrodisia House? Myrtis, Lythande knew, could be trusted with life, reputation, fortune, the magical power of the Blue Star itself; she had been tested before this. Had she altered enough to turn betrayer, it would have been apparent in her aura when Lythande came near.

That left only the girl, who was clinging and whimpering, "I will die if you do not love me! I will die! Tell me it is not true, Lythande, that you are unable to love! Tell me it is an evil lie that magicians are emasculated, incapable of loving woman . . ."

"That is certainly an evil lie," Lythande agreed gravely. "I give you my solemn assurance that I have never been emasculated." But Lythande's nerves tingled as the words were spoken. A magician might lie, and most of them did. Lythande would lie as readily as any other, in a good cause. But the law of the Blue Star was this: when questioned directly on a matter bearing directly on the Secret, the adept might not tell a direct lie. And Bercy, unknowing, was only one question away from the fatal one hiding the Secret.

With a mighty effort, Lythande's magic wrenched at the very fabric of Time itself; the girl stood motionless, aware of no lapse, as Lythande stepped away far enough to read her aura. And yes, there within the traces of that vibrating field, was the shadow of the blue star. Rabben's; overpowering her will.

Rabben. Rabben the Half-handed, who had set his

will on the girl, who had staged and contrived the whole thing, including the encounter where the girl had needed rescue; put the girl under a spell to attract and bespell Lythande.

The law of the Blue Star forbade one adept of the Star to kill another; for all would be needed to fight side by side, on the last day, against Chaos. Yet if one adept could prise forth the secret of another's power . . . then the powerless one was not needed against Chaos and could be killed.

What could be done now? Kill the girl? Rabben would take that, too, as an answer; Bercy had been so bespelled as to be irresistible to any man; if Lythande sent her away untouched, Rabben would know that Lythande's secret lay in that area and would never rest in his attempts to uncover it. For if Lythande was untouched by this sex-spell to make Bercy irresistible, then Lythande was a eunuch, or a homosexual, or . . . sweating, Lythande dared not even think beyond that. The Secret was safe only if never questioned. It would not be read in the aura; but one simple question, and all was ended.

I should kill her, Lythande thought. *For now I am fighting, not for my magic alone, but for my secret and for my life. For surely, with my power gone, Rabben would lose no time in making an end of me, in revenge for the loss of half a hand.*

The girl was still motionless, entranced. How easily she could be killed! Then Lythande recalled an old fairy-tale, which might be used to save the Secret of the Star.

The light flickered as Time returned to the chamber. Bercy was still clinging and weeping, unaware of the lapse; Lythande had resolved what to do, and the girl felt Lythande's arms enfolding her, and the magician's kiss on her welcoming mouth.

"You must love me or I shall die!" Bercy wept.

Lythande said, "You shall be mine." The soft neutral voice was very gentle. "But even a magician is vulnerable in love, and I must protect myself. A place shall be made ready for us without light or sound save for what I provide with my magic; and you must swear that you will not seek to see or to touch me except by that magical light. Will you swear it by the All-Mother, Bercy? For if you swear this, I shall love you as no woman has ever been loved before."

Trembling, she whispered, "I swear." And Lythande's heart went out in pity, for Rabben had used her ruthlessly; so that she burned alive with her unslaked and bewitched love for the magician, that she was all caught up in her passion for Lythande. Painfully, Lythande thought; *if she had only loved me, without the spell; then I could have loved . . .*

Would that I could trust her with my secret! But she is only Rabben's tool; her love for me is his doing, and none of her own will . . . and not real . . . And so everything which would pass between them now must be only a drama staged for Rabben.

"I shall make all ready for you with my magic."

Lythande went and confided to Myrtis what was needed; the woman began to laugh, but a single glance at Lythande's bleak face stopped her cold. She had known Lythande since long before the blue star was set between those eyes; and she kept the Secret for love of Lythande. It wrung her heart to see one she loved in the grip of such suffering. So she said, "All will be prepared. Shall I give her a drug in her wine to weaken her will, that you may the more readily throw a glamour upon her?"

Lythande's voice held a terrible bitterness. "Rabben has done that already for us, when he put a spell upon her to love me."

"You would have it otherwise?" Myrtis asked, hesitating.

"All the gods of Sanctuary—they laugh at me! All-Mother, help me! But I would have it otherwise; I could love her, if she were not Rabben's tool."

When all was prepared, Lythande entered the darkened room. There was no light but the light of the Blue Star. The girl lay on a bed, stretching up her arms to the magician with exalted abandon.

"Come to me, come to me, my love!"

"Soon," said Lythande, sitting beside her, stroking her hair with a tenderness even Myrtis would never have guessed. "I will sing to you a love-song of my people, far away."

She writhed in erotic ecstasy. "All you do is good to me, my love, my magician!"

Lythande felt the blankness of utter despair. She was beautiful, and she was in love. She lay in a bed spread for the two of them, and they were separated by the breadth of the world. The magician could not endure it.

Lythande sang, in that rich and beautiful voice; a voice lovelier than any spell:

Half the night is spent; and the crown of moonlight
Fades, and now the crown of the stars is paling;
Yields the sky reluctant to coming morning;
Still I lie lonely.

Lythande could see tears on Bercy's cheeks.
I will love you as no woman has ever been loved.

Between the girl on the bed, and the motionless form of the magician, as the magician's robe fell heavily to the floor, a wraith-form grew, the very wraith and fetch, at first, of Lythande, tall and lean, with blazing eyes and a star between its brows and a body white and unscarred; the form of the magician, but this one triumphant in virility, advancing on the motionless woman, waiting. Her mind fluttered away in arousal, was caught, captured, bespelled. Lythande let her see the image for a moment; she could not see the true Lythande behind; then, as her eyes closed in ecstatic awareness of the touch, Lythande smoothed light fingers over her closed eyes.

"See—what I bid you to see!

"Hear—what I bid you hear!

"Feel—only what I bid you feel, Bercy!"

And now she was wholly under the spell of the wraith. Unmoving, stony-eyed, Lythande watched as her lips closed on emptiness and she kissed invisible lips; and moment by moment Lythande knew what touched her, what caressed her. Rapt and ravished by illusion, that brought her again and again to the heights of ecstasy, till she cried out in abandonment. Only to Lythande that cry was bitter; for she cried out not to Lythande but to the man-wraith who possessed her.

At last she lay all but unconscious, satiated; and Lythande watched in agony. When she opened her eyes again, Lythande was looking down at her, sorrowfully.

Bercy stretched up languid arms. "Truly, my beloved, you have loved me as no woman has ever been loved before."

For the first and last time, Lythande bent over her and pressed her lips in a long, infinitely tender kiss. "Sleep, my darling."

And as she sank into ecstatic, exhausted sleep, Lythande wept.

Long before she woke, Lythande stood, girt for travel, in the little room belonging to Myrtis.

"The spell will hold. She will make all haste to carry her tale to Rabben—the tale of Lythande, the incomparable lover! Of Lythande, of untiring virility, who can love a maiden into exhaustion!" The rich voice of Lythande was harsh with bitterness.

"And long before you return to Sanctuary, once freed of the spell, she will have forgotten you in many other lovers," Myrtis agreed. "It is better and safer that it should be so."

"True." But Lythande's voice broke. "Take care of her, Myrtis. Be kind to her."

"I swear it, Lythande."

"If only she could have loved *me*"—the magician broke and sobbed again for a moment; Myrtis looked away, wrung with pain, knowing not what comfort to offer.

"If only she could have loved me as I am, freed of Rabben's spell! Loved me without pretense! But I feared I could not master the spell Rabben had put on her . . . nor trust her not to betray me, knowing . . ."

Myrtis put her plump arms around Lythande, tenderly. "Do you regret?"

The question was ambiguous. It might have meant: *Do you regret that you did not kill the girl?* Or even: *Do you regret your oath and the secret you must bear to the last day?* Lythande chose to answer the last.

"Regret? How can I regret? One day I shall fight against Chaos with all of my order; even at the side of Rabben, if he lives unmurdered as long as that. And that alone must justify my existence and my secret. But now I must leave Sanctuary, and who knows when the chances of the world will bring me this way again? Kiss me farewell, my sister."

Myrtis stood on tiptoe. Her lips met the lips of the magician.

"Until we meet again, Lythande. May She attend and guard you forever. Farewell, my beloved, my sister."

Then the magician Lythande girded on her sword, and went silently and by unseen ways out of the city of Sanctuary, just as the dawn was breaking. And on her forehead the glow of the Blue Star was dimmed by the rising sun. Never once did she look back.

Introduction to
The Incompetent Magician

When I was given the chance to edit my first anthology (Greyhaven, a series of stories showcasing the other members of my extended family who had become writers, more or less under my auspices and/or following my example), I realized that I must, of course, include one of my own stories, and since the publisher asked for original stories without reprints, I knew I must write one especially for this anthology.

The reason for two non-original stories in the Greyhaven anthology was simple; Robert Cook had died, and could not write an original story for this anthology except perhaps by medium of an Ouija board—and contractual negotiations for such a story would be too complicated—while Randall Garrett's state of health did not permit his contributing anything. So Robert, and Randall, were repesented by published works which had not been published yet in this country.

When I realized that I must simply sit down and turn out a short story (I do not think of myself as a short story writer—I tend to think in terms of 80,000 words and up. I mean, when you have a good idea why waste it on 5,000 words?)
But Lythande had haunted me since the first story,

so I decided to write another of her adventures. Besides, I was fascinated with the concept of an incompetent magician, and Rastafare and his "bag of holding" which the stammerer realistically named "not Carrier, but Ca-ca-carrier," struck me as an amusing concept. I don't write funny material that often and I didn't want this one to get away.

THE INCOMPETENT MAGICIAN

Throughout the length and breadth of the world of the Twin Suns, from the Great Salt Desert in the south to the Ice Mountains of the north, no one seeks out a mercenary-magician unless he wants something; and it's usually trouble. It's never the same thing twice, but whatever it is, it's always trouble.

Lythande the Magician looked out from under the hood of the dark, flowing mage-robe; and under the hood, the blue star that proclaimed Lythande to be Pilgrim Adept began to sparkle and give off blue flashes of fire as the magician studied the fat, wheezing little stranger, wondering what kind of trouble this client would be.

Like Lythande, the little stranger wore the cloak of a magician, the fashion of mage-robe worn in the cities at the edge of the Salt Desert. He seemed a little daunted as he looked up at the tall Lythande, and at the glowing blue star. Lythande, cross-belted with twin daggers, looked like a warrior, not a mage.

The fat man wheezed and fidgeted, and finally stammered "H-h-high and noble sor-sor-sorcerer, th-this is embarras—ass—assing—"

Lythande gave him no help, but looked down, with courteous attention, at the bald spot on the fussy little fellow's head. The stranger stammered on:

"I must co-co-confess to you that one of my ri-ri-rivals has st-st-stolen my m-m-magic wa-wa-wa—: he exploded into a perfect storm of stammering, then abandoned "wand" and blurted out "My p-p-powers are not suf-suf-suf—not strong enough to get it ba-ba-back. What would you require as a f-f-fee, O great and noble ma-ma-ma—" he swallowed and managed to get out "sorcerer?"

Beneath the blue star Lythande's arched and colorless brows went up in amusement.

"Indeed? How did that come to pass? Had you not spelled the wand with such sorcery that none but you could touch it?"

The little man stared, fidgeting, at the belt-buckle of his mage-robe. "I t-t-t-told you this was embarrass-as-as—hard to say, O great and noble ma-ma-magician. I had imbi-bi-bi—"

"In short," Lythande said, cutting him off, "you were drunk. And somehow your spell must have failed. Well, do you know who has taken it, and why?"

"Roy—Roygan the Proud," said the little man, adding, "He wanted to be revenged upon m-m-me because he found me in be-be-be—"

"In bed with his wife?" Lythande asked, with perfect gravity, though one better acquainted with the Pilgrim Adept might have detected a faint glimmer of amusement at the corners of the narrow ascetic mouth. The fat little magician nodded miserably and stared at his shoes.

Lythande said at last, in that mellow, neutral voice which had won the mercenary-magician the name of minstrel even before the reputation for successful sorcery had grown, "This bears out the proverb I have always held true, that those who follow the profession of sorcery should have neither wife nor lover. Tell me, O mighty mage and most gallant of bedroom athletes, what do they call you?"

The little man drew himself up to his full height—he

reached almost to Lythande's shoulder—and declared, "I am known far and wide in Gandrin as Rastafyre the Incom-comp-comp—"

"Incompetent?" suggested Lythande gravely.

He set his mouth with a hurt look and said with sonorous dignity, "Rastafyre the *Incomparable!*"

"It would be amusing to know how you came by that name," Lythande said, and the eyes under the mage-hood twinkled, "but the telling of funny stories, although a diverting pastime while we await the final battle between Law and Chaos, puts no beans on the table. So you have lost your magic wand to the rival sorcery of Roygan the Proud, and you wish my services to get it back from him—have I understood you correctly?"

Rastafyre nodded, and Lythande asked, "What fee had you thought to offer me in return for the assistance of my sorcery, O Rastafyre the incom—" Lythande hesitated a moment and finished smoothly "incomparable?"

"This jewel," Rastafyre said, drawing forth a great sparkling ruby which flashed blood tones in the narrow darkness of the hallway.

Lythande gestured him to put it away. "If you wave such things about *here,* you may attract predators before whom Roygan the Proud is but a kitten-cub. I wear no jewels but *this,*" Lythande gestured briefly at the blue star that shone with pallid light from the midst of the high forehead, "nor have I lover nor wife nor sweetheart upon whom I might bestow it; I preach only what I myself practice. Keep your jewels for those who prize them." Lythande made a snatching gesture in the air and between the long, narrow fingers, three rubies appeared, each one superior in color and luster to the one in Rastafyre's hand. "As you see, I need them not."

"I but offered the customary fee lest you think me niggardly," said Rastafyre, blinking with surprise and faint covetousness at the rubies in Lythande's hand, which blinked for a moment and disappeared. "As it may happen, I have that which may tempt you further."

The fussy little magician turned and snapped his fingers in the air. He intoned "Ca-Ca-Carrier!"

Out of thin air a great dark shape made itself seen, a dull lumpy outline; it fell and flopped ungracefully at his feet, resolving itself, with a bump, into a brown velveteen bag, embroidered with magical symbols in crimson and gold.

"Gently! Gently, Ca-Ca-Carrier," Rastafyre scolded, "or you will break my treasures within, and Lythande will have the right to call me Incom-comp-competent!"

"Carrier is more competent than you, O Rastafyre; why scold your faithful creature?"

"Not Carrier, but Ca-Ca-Carrier," Rastafyre said, "for I knew myself likely to st-st-stam-that I did not talk very well, and I la-la-labelled it by the cogno-cogno—by the name which I knew I would fi-find myself calling it."

This time Lythande chuckled aloud. "Well done, O mighty and incomparable magician!"

But the laughter died as Rastafyre drew forth from the dark recesses of Ca-Ca-Carrier a thing of rare beauty.

It was a lute, formed of dark precious woods, set about with turquoise and mother-of-pearl, the strings shining with silver; and upon the body of the lute, in precious gemstones, was set a pallid blue star, like to the one which glowed between Lythande's brows.

"By the bloodshot eyes of Keth-Ketha!"

Lythande was suddenly looming over the little magician, and the blue star began to sparkle and flame with fury; but the voice was calm and neutral as ever.

"Where got you that, Rastafyre? That lute I know; I myself fashioned it for one I once loved, and now she plays a spirit lute in the courts of Light. And the possessions of a Pilgrim Adept do not pass into the

hands of others as readily as the wand of Rastafyre the
Incompetent!"

Rastafyre cast down his tubby face and muttered,
unable to face the blue glare of the angry Lythande,
that it was a secret of the trade.

"Which means, I suppose, that you stole it, fair and
square, from some other thief," Lythande remarked,
and the glare of anger vanished as quickly as it had
come. "Well, so be it; you offer me this lute in return
for the recovery of your wand?" The tall mage reached
for the lute, but Rastafyre saw the hunger in the Pilgrim Adept's eyes and thrust it behind him.

"First the service for which I sought you out," he
reminded Lythande.

Lythande seemed to grow even taller, looming over
Rastafyre as if to fill the whole room. The magician's
voice, though not loud, seemed to resonate like a great
drum.

"Wretch, incompetent, do you dare to haggle with
me over my own possession? Fool, it is no more yours
than mine—less, for these hands brought the first music from it before you knew how to turn goat's milk sour
on the dungheap where you were whelped! By what
right do you demand a service of me?"

The bald little man raised his chin and said firmly,
"All the world knows that Lythande is a servant of
L-L-Law and not of Chaos, and no ma-ma-magician
bound to the L-Law would demean hi-hi-himself to
cheat an honest ma-ma-man. And what is more, noble
Ly-Lythande, this instru—tru-tru—this lute has been
cha-changed since it dwelt in your ha-ha-hands. Behold!"

Rastafyre struck a soft chord on the lute and began to
play a soft, melancholy tune. Lythande scowled and
demanded, "What do you—?"

Rastafyre gestured imperatively for silence. As the
notes quivered in the air, there was a little stirring in

the dark hallway, and suddenly, in the heavy air, a woman stood before them.

She was small and slender, with flowing fair hair, clad in the thinnest gown of spider-silk from the forests of Noidhan. Her eyes were blue, set deep under dark lashes in a lovely face; but the face was sorrowful and full of pain. She said in a lovely singing voice "Who thus disturbs the sleep of the enchanted?"

"Koira!" cried Lythande, and the neutral voice for once was high, athrob with agony. "Koira, how—what—?"

The fair-haired woman moved her hands in a spell-bound gesture. She murmured, "I know not—" and then, as if waking from deep sleep, she rubbed her eyes and cried out, "Ah, I thought I heard a voice that once I knew—Lythande, is it you? Was it you who enchanted me here, because I turned from you to the love of another? What would you? I was a woman—"

"Silence," said Lythande in a stifled voice, and Rastafyre saw the magician's mouth move as if in pain.

"As you see," said Rastafyre, "it is no longer the lute you knew." The woman's face was fading into air, and Lythande's taut voice whispered, "Where did she go? Summon her back for me!"

"She is now the slave of the enchanted lute," said Rastafyre, chuckling with what seemed obscene enthusiasm, "I could have had her for any service—but to ease your fastidious soul, magician, I will confess that I prefer my women more—" his hands sketched robust curves in the air, "So I have asked of her, only, that now and again she sing to the lute—knew you not this, Lythande? Was it not you who enchanted the woman thither, as she said?"

Within the hood Lythande's head moved in a negative shake, side to side. The face could not be seen, and Rastafyre wondered if he would, after all, be the first to see the mysterious Lythande weep. None had ever seen Lythande show the slightest emotion; never had

Lythande been known to eat or to drink wine in company—perhaps, it was believed, the mage *could* not, though most people guessed that it was simply one of the strange vows which bound a Pilgrim Adept.

But from within the hood, Lythande said slowly, "And you offer me this lute, in return for my services in the recovery of your wand?"

"I do, O noble Lythande. For I can see that the enchanted la-la-lady of the lute is known to you from old, and that you would have her as slave, concubine— what have you. And it is this, not the mu-mu-music of the lute alone, that I offer you—when my wa-wa-wand is my own again."

The blaze of the blue star brightened for a moment, then dimmed to a passive glow, and Lythande's voice was flat and neutral again.

"Be it so. For this lute I would undertake to recover the scattered pearls of the necklace of the Fish-goddess should she lose them in the sea; but are you certain that your wand is in the hands of Roygan the Proud, O Rastafyre?"

"I ha-ha-have no other en-en-enem—there is no one else who hates me," said Rastafyre, and again the restrained mirth gleamed for a moment.

"Fortunate are you, O Incom—" the hesitation, and the faint smile, "Incomparable. Well, I shall recover your wand—and the lute shall be mine."

"The lute—and the woman," said Rastafyre, "but only wh-wh-when my wand is again in my own ha-ha-hands."

"If Roygan has it," Lythande said, "it should present no very great difficulties for any *competent* magician."

Rastafyre wrapped the lute into the thick protective covering and fumbled it again into Ca-Ca-Carrier's capacious folds. Rastafyre gestured fussily with another spell.

"In the name of—" He mumbled something, then frowned. "It will not obey me so well without my wa-wa-wand," he mumbled. Again his hands twisted in the simple spell. "G-g-go, confound you, in the name of Indo-do-do—in the name of Indo-do—"

The bag flopped just a little and a corner of it disappeared, but the rest remained, hovering uneasily in the air. Lythande managed somehow not to shriek with laughter, but remarked:

"Allow me, O Incomp—O Incomparable," and made the spell with swift narrow fingers. "In the name of Indovici the Silent, I command you, Carrier—"

"Ca-Ca-Carrier," corrected Rastafyre, and Lythande, lips twitching, repeated the spell.

"In the name of Indovici the Silent, Ca-Ca-Carrier, I command you, go!"

The bag began slowly to fade, winked in and out for a moment, rose heavily into the air, and by the time it reached eye level, was gone.

"Indeed, bargain or no," Lythande said, "I must recover your wand, O Incompetent, lest the profession of magician become a jest for small boys from the Salt Desert to the Cold Hills!"

Rastafyre glared, but thought better of answering; he turned and fussed away, trailed by a small, lumpy brown shadow where Ca-Ca-Carrier stubbornly refused to stay either visible or invisible. Lythande watched him out of sight, then drew from the mage-robe a small pouch, shook out a small quantity of herbs and thoughtfully rolled them into a narrow tube; snapped narrow fingers to make a light, and slowly inhaled the fragrant smoke, letting it trickle out narrow nostrils into the heavy air of the hallway.

Roygan the Proud should present no very great challenge. Lythande knew Roygan of old; when that thief among magicians had first appeared in Lythande's life, Lythande had been young in sorcery and not yet tried in vigilance, and several precious items had vanished without trace from the house where Lythande then dwelt. Rastafyre would have been so easy a target that Lythande marveled that Roygan had not stolen Ca-Ca-Carrier, the hood and mage-robe Rastafyre wore, and perhaps his back teeth as well; there was an old saying in Gandrin, *if Roygan the Proud shakes your hand, count your fingers before he is out of sight*.

But Lythande had pursued Roygan through three cities and across the Great Salt Desert; and when Roygan had been trailed to his lair, Lythande had recovered wand, rings and magical dagger; and then had affixed one of the rings to Roygan's nose with a permanent binding-spell.

Wear this, Lythande had said, *in memory of your treachery, and that honest folk may know you and avoid you*. Now Lythande wondered idly if Roygan had ever found anyone to take the ring off his nose.

Roygan bears me a grudge, thought Lythande, and wondered if Rastafyre the Incompetent, lute and all, were a trap set for Lythande, to surprise the secret of the Pilgrim Adept's magic. For the strength of any Adept of the Blue Star lies in a certain concealed secret which must never be known; and the one who surprises the secret of a Pilgrim Adept can master all the magic of the Blue Star. And Roygan, with his grudge. . . .

Roygan was not worth worrying about. *But*, Lythande thought, *I have enemies among the Pilgrim Adepts themselves. Roygan might well be a tool of one of these. And so might Rastafyre*.

No, Roygan had not the strength for that; he was a thief, not a true magician or an adept. As for Rastafyre—soundlessly, Lythande laughed. If anyone sought to use that incompetent, the very incompetence of the fat, fussy little magician would recoil upon the accomplice. *I wish no worse for my enemies than Rastafyre for their friend*.

And when I have succeeded—it never occurred to Lythande to say *if*—*I shall have Koira; and the lute*.

She would not love me; but now, whether or no, she shall be mine, to sing for me whenever I will.

If it should become known to Lythande's enemies—and the magician knew that there were many of them, even here in Gandrin—that Roygan had somehow incurred the wrath of a Pilgrim Adept, they would be quick to sell the story to any other Pilgrim Adept they could find. Lythande, too, knew how to use that tactic; the knowledge of another Pilgrim Adept's Secret was the greatest protection known under the Twin Suns.

Speaking of Suns—Lythande cast a glance into the sky—it was near to First-sunset; Keth, red and somber, glowed on the horizon, with Reth like a bloody burning eye, an hour or two behind. Curse it, it was one of those nights where there would be long darkness. Lythande frowned, considering; but the darkness, too, could serve.

First Lythande must determine where in Old Gandrin, what corner or alley of that city of rogues and imposters, Roygan might be hiding.

Was there any Adept of the Blue Star who knew of the quarrel with Roygan? Lythande thought not. They had been alone when the deed was done; and Roygan would hardly boast of it; no doubt, that wretch had declared the ring in his nose to be a new fashion in jewelry! Therefore, by the Great Law of Magic, the law of Resonance, Lythande still possessed a tie to Roygan; the ring which once had been Lythande's own, if it was still on Roygan's nose, would lead to Roygan just as inescapably as a homing pigeon flies to its own croft.

There was no time to lose; Lythande would rather not brave the hiding place of Roygan the thief in full darkness, and already red Keth had slipped below the edge of the world. Two measures, perhaps, on a time-candle; no more time than that, or darkness would help to hide Roygan beneath its cloak, in the somber moonless streets of Old Gandrin.

The Pilgrim Adept needs no wand to make magic. Lythande raised one narrow, fine hand, drew it down in a curious, covering movement. Darkness flowed down from the slender fingers behind that movement, covering the magician with its veil; but inside the spelled circle, Lythande sat cross-legged on the stones, flooded with a neutral shadowless light.

Holding one hand toward the circle, Lythande whispered: "Ring of Lythande, ring which once caressed my finger, be joined to your sister."

Slowly the ring remaining on Lythande's finger began to gleam with an inner radiance. Beside it in the curious light, a second ring appeared, hanging formless and weightless in midair. And around this second ghost-ring, a pallid face took outline, first the beaky and aquiline nose, then the mouthful of broken teeth which had been tipped like fangs with shining metal, then the close-set dark-lashed eyes of Roygan the Proud.

He was not here within the spelled light-circle. Lythande knew that. Rather, the circle, like a mirror, reflected Roygan's face, and at a commanding gesture, the focus of the vision moved out, to encompass a room piled high with treasure, where Roygan had come to hide the fruits of his theft. Magpie Roygan! He did not use his treasure to enrich himself—like Lythande, he could have manufactured jewels at will—but to gain power over other magicians! And so, the links retaining their hold on their owners, Roygan was vulnerable to Lythande's magic as well.

If Rastafyre had been even a halfway competent magician—even the thought of that tubby little bungler curved Lythande's thin lips in a mocking smile—Rastafyre would have known of that bond, and tracked Roygan the proud himself. For the wand of a magician is a curious thing; in a very real sense it *is* the magician, for he must put into it one of his very real powers and senses. As the Blue Star, in a way, was Lythande's emotion—

for it glowed with blue flame when Lythande was angry or excited—so a wand, in those magicians who must use them, often reflects the most cherished power of a male magician. Again Lythande smiled mockingly; no bedroom athletics, no seduction of magicians' wives or daughters, till Rastafyre's wand was in his hand again!

Perhaps I should become a public benefactor, and never restore what Rastafyre considers so important, that the women of my fellow mages may be safe from his wiles! Yet Lythande knew, even as the image lingered, and the amusement, that Rastafyre must have back his wand and with it his power to do good or evil. For Law strives ever against Chaos, and every human soul must be free to take the part of one or another; this was the basic law that the Gods of Gandrin had established, and that all Gods everywhere stood as representative; that life itself, on the world of the Twin Suns as everywhere till the last star of Eternity is burnt out, is forever embodying that one Great Strife. And Lythande was sworn, through the Blue Star, servant to the Law. To deprive Rastafyre of one jot of his power to choose good or evil, was to set that basic truth at naught, setting Lythande's oath to Law in the place of Rastafyre's own choices, and that in itself was to let in Chaos.

And the karma of Lythande should stand forever responsible for the choice of Rastafyre. Guardians of the Blue Star, stand witness I want no such power, I carry enough karma of my own! I have set enough causes in motion and must see all their effects . . . abiding even to the Last Battle!

The image of Roygan, ring in nose, still hung in the air, and around it the pattern of Roygan's treasure room. But try as Lythande would, the Pilgrim Adept could not focus the image sufficiently to see if the wand of Rastafyre was among his treasure. So Lythande, with a commanding gesture, expanded the circle of vision still further, to include a street outside whatever cellar

or storeroom held Roygan and his treasures. The circle
expanded farther and farther, till at last the magician
saw a known landmark; the Fountain of Mermaids, in
the Street of the Seven Sailmakers. From there, apparently, the treasure room of Roygan the Thief must be
situated.

And Rastafyre had risked his wand for an affair with
Roygan's wife. Truly, Lythande thought, my maxim is
well-chosen, that a mage should have neither sweetheart nor wife. . . . and bitterness flooded Lythande,
making the Blue Star glimmer; *Look what I do, for
Koira's mere image or shadow! But how did Rastafyre
know?*

For in the days when Koira and Lythande played the
lute in the courts of their faraway home, both were
young, and no shadow of the Blue Star or Lythande's
quest after magic, even into the hidden Place which Is
Not of the Pilgrim Adepts, had cast its shadow between
them. And Lythande had borne another name.

*Yet Koira, or her shade, knew me, and called me by
the name Lythande bears now. Why called she not . . .*
and then, by an enormous effort, almost physical, which
brought sweat bursting from the brow beneath the Blue
Star, Lythande cut off that memory; with the trained
discipline of an Adept, even the memory of the old
name vanished.

*I am Lythande. The one I was before I bore that name
is dead, or wanders in the limbo of the forgotten.* With
another gesture, Lythande dissolved the spelled circle
of light, and stood again in the streets of Old Gandrin,
where Reth, too, had begun dangerously to approach
the horizon.

Lythande set off toward the Street of the Seven Sailmakers. Keeping ever to the shadows which hid the
dark mage-robe, and moving as noiselessly as a breath
of wind or a cat's ghost, the Pilgrim Adept traversed a
dozen streets, paying little heed to all that inhabited

them. Men brawled in taverns, and on the cobbled streets; merchants sold everything from knives to women; children, grubby and half-naked, played their own obscure games, vaulting over barrels and carts, screaming with the joys and tantrums of innocence. Lythande, intent on the magical mission, hardly saw or heard them.

At the Fountain of Mermaids, half a dozen women, draped in the loose robes which made even an ugly woman mysterious and alluring, drew water from the bubbling spring, chirping and twittering like birds; Lythande watched them with a curious, aching sadness. It would have been better to await their going, for the comings and goings of a Pilgrim Adept are better not gossiped about; but Reth was perilously near the horizon and Lythande sensed, in the way a magician will always know a danger, that even a Pilgrim Adept should not attempt to invade the quarters of Roygan the Proud under cover of total night.

They dissolved away, clutching with murmurs at their children, as Lythande appeared noiselessly, as if from thin air, at the edge of the fountain square. One child clung, giggling, to one of the sculptured mermaids, and the mother, who seemed to Lythande little more than a child herself, came and snatched it up, covertly making the sign against the Evil Eye—but not covertly enough. Lythande stood directly barring her path back to the other women, and said "Do you believe, woman, that I would curse you or your child?"

The woman looked at the ground, scuffing her sandaled foot on the cobbles, but her hands, clutching the child to her breast, were white at the knuckles with fear, and Lythande sighed. *Why did I do that?* At the sound of the sigh, the woman looked up, a quick darting glance like a bird's, as quickly averted.

"The blinded eye of Keth witness that I mean no harm to you or your child, and I would bless you if I

knew any blessings," Lythande said at last, and faded
into shadow so that the woman could gather the courage to scamper away across the street, her child's grubby
head clutched against her breast. The encounter had
left a taste of bitterness in Lythande's mouth, but with
iron discipline, the magician let it slide away into limbo,
to be taken out and examined, perhaps, when the bitterness had been attenuated by Time.

"Ring, sister of Roygan's ring, show me where, in the
nose of Roygan the thief, I must seek you!"

One of the shadowed buildings edging the square
seemed to fade somewhat in the dying sunset; through
the walls of the building, Lythande could see rooms,
walls, shadows, the moving shadow of a woman un-
veiled, a saucy round-bodied little creature with ring-
lets tumbled over a low brow, and the mark of a dimple
in her chin, and great dark-lashed eyes. So this was the
woman for whom Rastafyre the Incompetent had risked
wand and magic and the vengeance of Roygan?

*Do I scorn his choice because that path is barred to
me?*

*Still; madness, between the choice of love and power,
to choose such counterfeit of love as such a woman
could give.* For, silently approaching the walls which
were all but transparent to Lythande's spelled Sight,
the Pilgrim Adept could see beneath the outer surface
of artless coquetry, down to the very core of selfishness
and greed within the woman, her grasping at treasures,
not for their beauty but for the power they gave her.
Rastafyre had not seen so deep within. Was he blinded
by lust, then, or was it only further evidence of the
name Lythande had given him, *Incompetent?*

With a gesture, Lythande banished the spelled Sight;
there was no need of it now, but there was need of
haste, for Reth's orange rim actually caressed the west-
ern rim of the world. *Yet I can be in, and out, unseen,
before the light is wholly gone,* Lythande thought, and,

gesturing darkness to rise like a more enveloping mage-robe, stepped through the stone wall. It felt grainy, like walking through maize-dough, but nothing worse. Nevertheless Lythande hastened, pulling against the resistance of the stone; there were tales, horror tales told in the outer courts of the Pilgrim Adepts where this art was taught, of an Adept of the Blue Star who had lost his courage halfway through the wall, and stuck there, half of his body still trapped within the stone, shrieking with pain until he died. . . . Lythande hated to risk this walking through walls, and usually relied on silence, stealth and spells applied to locks. But there was no time even to find the locks, far less to sound them out by magic and press by magic upon the sensitive tumblers of the bolts. When all the magician's body was within the shadowy room, Lythande drew a breath of relief; even the smell of mold and cobwebs was preferable to the grainy feel of the wall, and now, whatever came, Lythande resolved to go out by the door.

And now, in the heavy darkness of Roygan's treasure room, the light of the Blue Star alone would serve; Lythande felt the curious prickling, half pain, as the Blue Star began to glow. . . . a blue light stole through the darkness, and by that subtle illumination, the Pilgrim Adept made out the contours of great chests, carelessly heaped jewels, bolted boxes . . . where, in all this hodgepodge of stolen treasure, laid up magpie fashion by Roygan's greed, was Rastafyre's wand to be found? Lythande paused, thoughtful, by one great heap of jewels, rubies blazing like Keth's rays at sunrise, sapphires flung like dazzling reflections of the light of the Blue Star, a superb diamond necklace loosely flung like a constellation blazing beneath the pole-star of a single great gem. Lythande had spoken truly to Rastefyre, jewels were no temptation, yet for a moment the magician thought almost sadly of the women whose throats and slender arms and fingers had once been adorned with these jewels; why should Roygan profit by their great losses, if they felt the need of these toys and trinkets to enhance their beauty? And Lythande hesitated, considering. There was a spell which, once spoken, would disperse all these jewels back to their rightful owners, by the Law of Resonances.

Yet why should Lythande take on the karma of these unknown women, women Lythande would never see or know? If it had not been their just fate to lose the jewels to the clever hands of a thief, no doubt Roygan would have sought in vain for the keys to their treasure chests.

By that same token, why should I interfere with my magic in the just karma of Rastafyre, who lost his wand because he could not contain his lust for the wife of Roygan? Would not the loss of wand and virility teach him a just respect for the discipline of continence? It would not be for long, only till he could take the trouble to fashion and consecrate another wand of Power . . .

But Lythande had given the word of a Pilgrim Adept; for the honor of the Blue Star, what was promised must be performed. Sworn to the Law, it was Lythande's sworn duty to punish a thief, and all the more because Roygan preyed, not on Lythande whose defenses were sufficient for revenge, but upon the harmless Rastafyre . . . and if Roygan's wife found him not sufficient, then that was Roygan's karma too. Shivering somewhat in the darkness of the storeroom, Lythande whispered the spell that would make the treasure boxes transparent to the Sight. By the witchlight, Lythande scanned box after box, seeing nothing which might, by the remotest chance, be the wand of Rastafyre.

And outside the light was fading fast, and in the darkness, all the things of magic would be loosed. . . .

And as if the thought had summoned it, suddenly it was there, though Lythande had not seen any door by which it could have entered the treasure chamber, a great grey shape, leaping high at the mage's throat. Lythande whirled, whipping out the dagger on the right, and thrust, hard, at the bane-wolf's throat.

It went through the throat as if through air. Not a true beast, then, but a magical one. . . . Lythande dropped the right-hand dagger, and snatched, left-handed, at the other, the dagger intended for fighting the powers and beasts of magic; but the delay had been nearly fatal; the teeth of the bane-wolf met, like fiery needles, in Lythande's right arm, forcing a cry from the magician's lips. It went unheard; the magical beast fought in silence, without a snarl or a sound even of breathing; Lythande thrust with the left-hand dagger, but could not reach the heart; then the bane-wolf's uncanny weight bore Lythande, writhing, to the ground. Again the needle-teeth of the enchanted creature met like flame in Lythande's shoulder, then in the knee thrust up to ward the beast from the throat. Lythande knew; if the fiery teeth met but once in the throat, it would cut off breath and life. Slowly, painfully, fighting upward, thrusting again and again, Lythande managed to wrestle the beast back, at the cost of bite after bite from the cruel flame-teeth; the bane-wolf's blazing eyes flashed against the light of the Blue Star, which grew fainter and feebler as Lythande's struggles weakened.

Have I come this far to die in a dark cellar in the maw of a wolf, and not even a true wolf, but a thing created by the filthy misuse of sorcery at the hands of a thief?

The thought maddened the magician; with a fierce effort, Lythande thrust the magical dagger deeper into the shoulder of the were-beast, seeking for the heart. With the ; ; thrust of the spell, backed by all Lythande's agony, the magician's very arm thrust through un-natural flesh and bone, striking inward to the lungs, into the very heart of the creature. . . . the blazing breath of the wolf smoked and failed; Lythande withdrew arm and dagger, slimed with the magical blood, as the beast, in eerie silence, writhed and died on the floor, slowly curling and melting into wisps of smoke, until only a little heap of ember, like burnt blood, remained on the floor of the treasure room.

Lythande's breath came loud in the silence as the Pilgrim Adept wiped the slime from the magical dagger, thrust it back into one sheath, then sought on the floor for where the right-hand dagger had fallen. There was slime on the magician's left hand, too, and the Adept wiped it, viciously, on a bolt of precious velvet; Roygan's things to Roygan, then! When the right-hand dagger was safe again in the other sheath, Lythande turned to the frantic search again for Rastafyre's wand. It was not to be thought of, that there would be much more time. Even if Roygan toyed with the wife who was all his now Rastafyre's power was gone, he could not stay with her forever, and if his magical power had created the bane-wolf, surely the death of the creature, drawing as it did on Roygan's own vitality, would alert him to the intrusion into his treasure room.

Through the lid of one of the boxes, Lythande could see, in the magical witchlight which responded only to the things of magical Power, a long narrow shape, wrapped in silks but still glowing with the light that singled out the things of magic. Surely that must be Rastafyre's wand, unless Roygan the Thief had a collection of such things—and the kind of incompetence which had allowed Roygan to get the wand, was uncommon among magicians . . . praise to Keth's all-seeing eye!

Lythande fumbled with the lock. Now that the excitement of the fight with the bane-wolf had subsided, shoulder and arm were aching like half-healed burns where the enchanted teeth had met in Lythande's flesh. Worse than burns, perhaps, Lythande thought, for they might not yield to ordinary burn remedies! The magician wanted to tear off the tattered tunic where the bane-wolf had torn, but there were reasons not to do this within an enemy's stronghold! Lythande drew the mage-robe's folds closer, bitten hands wrenching at the bolts. The Pilgrim Adept was very strong; unlike those magicians who relied always on magic and avoided exertion, Lythande had traveled afoot and alone over all the highroads and by-roads lighted by the Twin Suns, and the wiry arms, the elegant-looking hands, had the strength of the daggers they wielded. After a moment the first hinge of the chest yielded, with a sound as loud, in the darkening cellar, as the explosion of fireworks; Lythande flinched at the sound . . . surely even Roygan must hear that in his wife's very chamber! Now for the other hinge. The bitten hands were growing more painful by the moment; Lythande took the right-hand dagger, the one intended for objects which were natural and not magic, and tried to wedge it under the hinge, prying in grim silence without success. Was the damned thing spelled shut? No; for then Lythande's hands alone could not have budged the first bolt. Blood was dripping from the blistered hand before the second lock gave way, and Lythande reached into the chest, and recoiled as if from the very teeth of the bane-wolf. Howling with rage and pain and frustration, Lythande swept into the chest with the left-hand dagger; there was a small ghastly shrilling and something ugly, horrible and only half visible, writhed and died. But now Lythande held the wand of Rastafyre, triumphant.

Wincing at the pain, Lythande stripped the concealing cloths from the wand. A grimace of distaste came over the magician's narrow face as the phallic carvings and shape of the wand were revealed, but after all, this had been fairly obvious—that Rastafyre would arm his wand with his manhood. It was, after all, his own problem; it was not Lythande's karma to teach other magicians either discretion or manners. A bargain had been made and a service should be performed.

Hastily wadding the protective silks around the wand—it was easier to handle that way, and Lythande had no wish even to look upon the gross thing—Lythande turned to the business of getting out again. Not through the walls. Darkness had surely fallen by now; though in the windowless treasure-room it was hard to tell, but there must be a door somewhere.

Lythande had heard nothing; but abruptly, as the witch-light flared, Roygan the Proud stood directly in the center of the room.

"So, Lythande the Magician is Lythande the Thief! How like you the business of thievery, then, Magician?"

A trap, then. But Lythande's mellow, neutral voice was calm.

"It is written; from the thief all shall be stolen at last. By the ring in your nose, Roygan; you know the truth of what I say."

With an inarticulate howl of rage, Roygan hurled himself at Lythande. The magician stepped aside, and Roygan hurtled against a chest, giving a furious yelp of pain as his knees collided with the metalled edge of the chest. He whirled, but Lythande, dagger in hand, stood facing him.

"Ring of Lythande, ring of Roygan's shame, be welded to this," Lythande murmured, and the dagger flung itself against Roygan's face. Roygan grunted with pain as Lythande's dagger molded itself against the ring, curling around his face.

"Ai! Ai! Take it off, damn you by every god and godlet of Gandrin, or I—"

"You will *what*?" demanded Lythande, looking with an aloof grin at Roygan's face, the dagger curled around the end of his nose, and gripping, as if by a powerful magnet, at the metal tips of Roygan's teeth. Furious, howling, Roygan flung himself again at Lythande, his yell wordless now as the metal of the dagger fastened itself tighter to his teeth. Lythande laughed, stepping free easily from Roygan's clutching hands; but the thief's face was alight with sudden triumphant glee.

"Hoy," he mumbled through the edges of the dagger. "Now I have touched Lythande and I know your secret. . . . Lythande, Pilgrim Adept, wearer of the Blue Star, you are—ai! *Ai-ya!*" With a fearful screech of pain, Roygan fell to the floor, wordless as the dagger curled deeper into his mouth; blood burst from his lip, and in the next moment, Lythande's other dagger thrust through his heart, in the merciful release from agony.

Lythande bent, retrieved the dagger which had thrust into Roygan's heart. Then, Blue Star blazing magic, Lythande reached for the other dagger, which had bitten through Roygan's lips, tongue, throat. A murmured spell restored it to the shape of a dagger, the metal slowly uncurling under the stroking hands of the owner's sorcery. Slowly, sighing, Lythande sheathed both daggers.

I meant not to kill him. But I knew too well what his next words would be; and the magic of a Pilgrim Adept is void if the Secret is spoken aloud. And, knowing, I could not let him live. Why was she so regretful? Roygan was not the first Lythande had killed to keep that Secret, the words actually on Roygan's mutilated tongue; *Lythande, you are a woman.*

A woman. A woman, who in her pride had penetrated the courts of the Pilgrim Adepts in disguise; and when the Blue Star was already between her brows, had been punished and rewarded with the Secret she had kept well enough to deceive even the Great Adept in the Temple of the Blue Star.

Your Secret, then, shall be forever; for on the day when any man save myself shall speak your secret aloud, your power is void. Be then forever doomed with the

Secret you yourself have chosen, and be forever in the eyes of all men what you made us think you.

Bitterly, Lythande thrust the wand of Rastafyre under the folds of the mage-robe. Now she had leisure to find a way out by the doors. The locks yielded to the touch of magic; but before leaving the cellar, Lythande spoke the spell which would return Roygan's stolen jewels to their owners.

A small victory for the cause of Law. And Roygan the thief had met his just fate.

Stepping out into the fading sunlight, Lythande blinked. It had seemed to take hours, that silent struggle in the darkness of the Treasure-room. Yet the sun still lingered, and a little child played noiselessly, splashing her feet in the fountain, until a chubby young woman came to scold her merrily and tug her withindoors. Listening to the laughter, Lythande sighed. A thousand years, a thousand memories, cut her away from the woman and the child.

To love no man lest my Secret be known. To love no woman lest she be a target for my enemies in quest of the Secret.

And she risked exposure and powerlessness, again and again, for such as Rastafyre. *Why?*

Because I must. There was no answer other than that, a Pilgrim Adept's vow to Law against Chaos. Rastafyre should have his wand back. There was no law that all magicians should be competent.

She laid a narrow hand along the wand, trying not to flinch at the shape, and murmured, "Bring me to your master."

Lythande found Rastafyre in a tavern; and, having no wish for any public display of power, beckoned him outside. The tubby little magician stared up in awe at the blazing Blue Star.

"You have it? Already?"

Silently, Lythande held out the wrapped wand to Rastafyre. As he touched it, he seemed to grow taller, handsomer, less tubby; even his face fell into lines of strength, and virility.

"And now my fee," Lythande reminded him.

He said sullenly "How know I that Roygan the Proud will not come after me?"

"I knew not," said Lythande calmly, "that your magic had power to raise the dead, oh Rastafyre the Incomparable."

"You—you—k-k-k-he's dead?"

"He lies where his ill-gotten treasures rest, with the ring of Lythande still through his nose," Lythande said calmly. "Try, now, to keep your magic wand out of the power of other men's wives."

Rastafyre chuckled. He said "But wha-wha—what else would I do w-w-with my p-p-power?"

Lythande grimaced. "Koira's lute," she said, "or you will lie where Roygan lies."

Rastafyre the Incomparable raised his hand. "Ca-ca-Carrier," he intoned, and, flickering in and off in the dullness of the room, the velvet bag winked in, out again, came back, vanished again even as Rastafyre had his hand within it.

"Damn you, Ca-ca-Carrier! Come or go, but don't *flicker* like that! Stay! Stay, I said!" He sounded, Lythande thought, as if he were talking to a reluctant puppy dog.

Finally, when he got it entirely materialized, he drew forth the lute. With a grave bow, Lythande accepted it, tucking it out of sight under the mage-robe.

"Health and prosperity to you, O Lythande," he said—for once without stuttering; perhaps the wand did that for him too?

"Health and prosperity to you, O Rastafyre the incom—" Lythande hesitated, laughed aloud and said, "Incomparable."

He took himself off then and Lythande added silently, "And more luck in your adventures," as she watched Ca-ca-Carrier dimly lumping along like a small surly shadow at his heels, until at last it vanished entirely.

Alone, Lythande stepped into the dark street, under the cold and moonless sky. With a single gesture the magical circle blotted away all surroundings; there was neither time nor space. Then Lythande began to play the lute softly. There was a little stirring in the silence, and the figure of Koira, slender, delicate, her pale hair shimmering about her face and her body gleaming through wispy veils, appeared before her.

"Lythande—" she whispered. "It is you!"

"It is I, Koira. Sing to me," Lythande commanded. "Sing to me the song you sang when we sat together in the gardens of Hilarion."

Lythande's fingers moved on the lute, and Koira's soft contralto swelled out into an ancient song from a country half a world away and so many years Lythande feared to remember how many.

> "The years shall fall upon you, and the light
> That dwelled in you, go into endless night;
> As wine, poured out and sunk into the ground,
> Even your song shall leave no breath of sound,
> And as the leaves within the forest fall,
> Your memory will not remain at all,
> As a word said, a song sung, and be
> Forever with the memories—"

"Stop," Lythande said, strangled. Koira fell silent, at last whispering, "I sang at your command and now I am still at your command."

When Lythande could look up without the agony of despair, Koira too was silent. Lythande said at last, "What binds you to the lute, Koira whom once I loved?"

"I know not," Koira said, and it seemed that the

ghost of her voice was bitter, "I know only that while this lute survives, I am enslaved to it."

"And to my will?"

"Even so, Lythande."

Lythande set her mouth hard. She said, "You would not love me when you might; now shall I have you whether you will or no."

"Love—" Koira was silent. "We were maidens then and we loved after the fashion of young maidens; and then you went into a far country where I would not follow, for my heart was a woman's heart, and you—"

"What do you know of my heart?" Lythande cried out in despair.

"I knew that my heart was a woman's heart and longed for a love other than yours," Koira said. "What would you, Lythande? You too are a woman; I call that no love . . ."

Lythande's eyes were closed. But at last the voice was stubborn. "Yet you are here and you shall sing forever at my will, and be forever silent about your desire for a man's love . . . for you there is none other than I, now!"

Koira bowed deeply, but it seemed to Lythande that there was mockery in the bow.

She said sharply "What enslaves you to the lute? Are you bound for a space, or forever?"

"I know not," Koira said, "Or if I know I cannot speak it."

So it was often with enchantments; Lythande knew. . . . and now she would have all of time before her, and sooner or later, sooner or later, Koira would love her. . . . Koira was her slave, she could bid her come and go with her hands on the lute as once they had sought for more than a shared song and a maiden's kiss . . .

But a slave's counterfeit of love is not love. Lythande raised the lute in her hands, poising her fingers on the

strings; Koira's form began to waver a little, and then,
acting swiftly before she could think better of it, Lythande
raised the lute, brought it crashing down and broke it
over her knee.

Koira's face wavered, between astonishment and sudden delirious happiness. "Free!" she cried, "Free at
last—O, Lythande, now do I know you truly loved
me. . . ." and a whisper swirled and faded and was still,
and there was only the empty bubble of magic, void,
silent, without light or sound.

Lythande stood still, the broken lute in her hands. If
Rastafyre could only see. She had risked life, sanity,
magic, Secret itself and the Blue Star's power, for this
lute, and within moments she had broken it and set
free the one who could, over the years, been drawn to
her, captive . . . unable to refuse, unable to break
Lythande's pride further. . . .

He would think me, too, an incompetent magician.

I wonder which two of us would be right?

With a long sigh, Lythande drew the mage-robe about
her thin shoulders, made sure the two daggers were
secure in their sheaths—for at this hour, in the moonless
streets of Old Gandrin there were many dangers, real
and magical—and went on her solitary way, stepping
over the fragments of the broken lute.

Introduction to
Somebody Else's Magic

*About the time I started writing Lythande stories I was
engaged in a series of feminist arguments with people
who thought I wasn't sufficiently feminist, or didn't
understand what feminism was all about, or something
like that. No doubt they are right. Someone criticized
Lythande and my other characters for lack of true
feminism, and I thought, Yes, perhaps Lythande should
have identified herself with woman's magic instead of
disguising herself as a male.* But had she ever had that
option?

*I was convinced that she had not. Lythande's basic
decency might guide her to intervene in another person's karma—as in this story, where she attempts (too
late) to save a woman from rape, but in a world where
the prime directive is not to mind anyone else's business, the penalty for such a thing might be to become
entangled in someone else's magic.*

And Lythande's resentment of woman's magic is simple:
where was this woman's magic when I needed it? *No
doubt, Lythande would have preferred it to magic where
she must compete with men at their own carefully
guarded game. But such women as the first few to enter
medical colleges (where they were preached against in
church, ignored, and finally forced to fight through by
being* at least twice as good *as men)—women who have*

proved themselves competing against men are not very sympathetic to the protected women's spaces and quotas. "Of course," we say, "you can do it under those conditions—but we suspect you couldn't have done it at all in the days when you had to prove yourself. Do you want everyone saying that you only got into medical school, not because you were good enough, but because they had to give so many places to women, qualified or not?"

No doubt women and other minorities will tell me again that I just don't understand . . . sure that if I only understood I would certainly agree with them. Wrong. I understand, all right, I just don't agree. Like Lythande, I won my credentials when it had to be done the hard way . . . not protected by special consideration for minorities.Women who had to be at least twice as good as men don't take kindly to such comments as, "When will women be allowed to be mediocre, as men are allowed to be mediocre?"

I think no one should be allowed to be mediocre, or ask it, or think of it. Lythande—and I—are content to be judged simply by what we are.

But I find I am writing something almost like feminist rhetoric here. Forgive me. Lythande can speak for herself, but I must editorialize.

SOMEBODY ELSE'S MAGIC

In a place like the Thieves' Quarter of Old Gandrin, there is no survival skill more important than the ability to mind your own business. Come robbery, rape, arson, blood feud, or the strange doings of wizards, a carefully cultivated deaf ear for other people's problems— not to mention a blind eye, or better, two, for anything that is not your affair—is the best way, maybe the only way, to keep out of trouble.

It is no accident that everywhere in Old Gandrin, and everywhere else under the Twin Suns, they speak of the blinded eye of Keth-Ketha. A god knows better than to watch the doings of his creatures too carefully.

Lythande, the mercenary-magician, knew this perfectly well. When the first scream rang down the quarter, despite an involuntary shoulder twitch, Lythande knew that the proper thing was to look straight ahead and keep right on walking in the same direction. It was one of the reasons why Lythande had survived this long; through cultivating superb skill at own-business-minding in a place where there were a variety of strange businesses to be minded.

Yet there was a certain note to the screams—

Ordinary robbery or even rape might not have penetrated that carefully cultivated shell of blindness, deafness, looking straight into the thick of it. Lythande's hand gripped almost without thought at the hilt of the right-hand knife, the black-handled one that hung from the red girdle knotted over the mage-robe, flipped it out, and ran straight into trouble.

The woman was lying on the ground now, and there had been at least a dozen of them, long odds even for the Thieves Quarter. Somehow, before they had gotten her down, she had managed to kill at least four of them, but there were others, standing around and cheering the survivors on. The Blue Star between Lythande's brows, the mark of a Pilgrim Adept, had begun to glow and flicker with blue lightnings, in time with the in-and-out flicker of the blade. Two, then three went down before they knew what had hit them, and a fourth was spitted in the middle of his foul work, ejaculating and dying with a single cry. Two more fell, spouting blood, one from a headless neck, the other falling sidewise, unbalanced by an arm lopped away at the shoulder, bled out before he hit the ground. The rest took to their heels, shrieking. Lythande wiped the blade on the cloak of one of the dead men and bent over the dying woman.

She was small and frail to have done so much damage to her assailants; and they had made her pay for it. She wore the leather garments of a swordsman; they had been ripped off her, and she was bleeding everywhere, but she was not defeated—even now she made a feeble gesture toward her sword and snarled, her bitten lips drawn back over bared teeth, "Wait ten minutes, animal, and I will be beyond caring; then you may take your pleasure from my corpse and be damned to you!"

A swift look round showed Lythande that nothing human was alive within hearing. It was nowhere within the bounds of possibility that this woman could live and betray her. Lythande knelt, crushing the woman's head gently against her breast.

"Hush, hush, my sister. I will not harm you."

The woman looked up at her in wonder, and a smile spread over the dying face. She whispered, "I thought I had betrayed my last trust—I was sworn to die first; but there were too many for me. The Goddess does not forgive—those who submit—"

She was slipping away. Lythande whispered, "Be at peace, child. The Goddess does not condemn. . . ." And thought: *I would not give a fart in sulphurous hell for a goddess who would*.

"My sword—" the woman groped; already she found it hard to see. Lythande put the hilt into her fingers.

"My sword—dishonored—" she whispered. "I am Larith. The sword must go—back to her shrine. Take it. Swear—"

Larithae! Lythande knew of the shrine of that hidden goddess and of the vow her women made. She could now understand, though never excuse, the thugs who had attacked and killed the woman. Larithae were fair game everywhere from the Southern Waste to Falthot in the Ice Hills. The shrine of the Goddess as Larith lay at the end of the longest and most dangerous road in the Forbidden Country, and it was a road Lythande had no reason nor wish to tread. A road, moreover, that by her own oath she was forbidden, for she might never reveal herself as a woman, at the cost of the Power that had set the Blue Star between her brows. And only women sought, or could come to, the shrine of Larith.

Firmly, denying, Lythande shook her head.

"My poor girl, I cannot; I am sworn elsewhere, and serve not your Goddess. Let her sword remain honorably in your hand. No," she repeated, putting away the woman's pleading hand, "I cannot, Sister. Let me bind up your wounds, and you shall take that road yourself another day."

She knew the woman was dying; but it would give her something, Lythande thought, to occupy her thoughts in death. And if, in secret and in her own heart, she cursed the impetus that had prompted her to ignore that old survival law of minding her own business, no hint of it came into the hard but compassionate face she bent on the dying swordswoman.

The Laritha was silent, smiling faintly beneath Lythande's gentle ministrations; she let Lythande straighten her twisted limbs, try to stanch the blood that now had slowed to a trickle. But already her eyes were dulling and glazing. She caught at Lythande's fingers and whispered, in a voice so thready that only by Lythande's skill at magic could the words be distinguished, "Take the sword, Sister. Larith witness I give it to you freely without oath. . . ."

With a mental shrug, Lythande whispered, "So be it, without oath . . . bear witness for me in that dark country, Sister, and hold me free of it."

Pain flitted over the dulled eyes for the last time.

"Go free—if you can—" the woman whispered, and with her last movement thrust the hilt of the *larith* sword into Lythande's palm. Lythande, startled, by pure reflex closed her hand on the hilt, then abruptly realized what she was doing—rumor had many tales of *larith* magic, and Lythande wanted none of their swords! She let it go and tried to push it back into the woman's hand. But the fingers had locked in death and would not receive it.

Lythande sighed and laid the woman gently down. Now what was to be done? She had made it clear that she would not take the sword; one of the few things that was really known about the Larithae was that their shrine was a shrine of women swordpriestesses, and that no man might touch their magic, on pain of penalties too dreadful to be imagined. Lythande, Pilgrim Adept, who had paid more highly for the Blue Star than any other Adept in the history of the Order, dared not be found anywhere in the light of Keth or her sister

Reth with a sword of Larith in her possession. For the very life of Lythande's magic depended on this: that she never be known as a woman.

The doom had been just, of course. The shrine of the Blue Star had been forbidden to women for more centuries than can be counted upon the fingers of both hands. In all the history of the Pilgrim Adepts, no woman before Lythande had penetrated their secrets in disguise; and when at last she was exposed and discovered, she was so far into the secrets of the Order that she was covered by the dreadful oath that forbids one Pilgrim Adept to slay another—for all are sworn to fight, on the Last Day of All, for Law against Chaos. They could not kill her; and since already she bore all the secrets of their Order, she could not be bidden to depart.

But the doom laid on her had been what she had, unknowing, chosen when she came into the Temple of the Blue Star under concealment.

"As you have chosen to conceal your womanhood, so shall you forever conceal it," thus had fallen the doom, "for on that secret shall hang your power; on the day that any other Adept of the Blue Star shall proclaim forth your true sex, on that day is your power fallen, and ended with it the sanctity that protects you against vengeance upon one who stole our secrets. Be, then, what you have chosen to be, and be so throughout the eternity until the Last Battle of Law against Chaos."

And so, fenced about with all the other vows of a Pilgrim Adept, Lythande bore that doom of eternal concealment. Never might she reveal herself to any man; nor to any woman save one she could trust with power and life. Only three times had she dared confide in any, and of those three, two were dead. One had died by torture when a rival Adept of the Blue Star had sought to wring Lythande's secret from her; had died still faithful. And the other had died in her arms, minutes ago. Lythande smothered a curse; her weak admission to a dying woman might have saddled her with a curse, even though she had sworn nothing. If she were seen with a *larith* sword, she might as well proclaim her true sex aloud from the High Temple steps at midday in Old Gandrin!

Well, she would not be seen with it. The sword should lie in the grave of the Laritha who had honorably defended it.

Lythande stood up, drawing down the hood of the mage-robe over her face so that the Blue Star was in shadow. Nothing about her—tall, lean, angular—betrayed that she was other than any Pilgrim Adept; her smooth, hairless face might have been the hairlessness of a freak or an effeminate had there been any to question it—which there was not—and the pale hair, square-cut after an ancient fashion, the narrow hawk-features, were strong and sexless, the jawline too hard for most women. Never, for an instant, by action, word, mannerism, or inattention, had she ever betrayed that she was other than magician, mercenary. Under the mage-robe was the ordinary dress of a north-countryman—leather breeches; high, laceless boots; sleeveless leather jerkin—and the laced and ruffled under-tunic of a dandy. The ringless hands were calloused and square, ready to either of the swords that were girded at the narrow waist; the right-hand blade for material enemies, the left-hand blade against things of magic.

Lythande picked up the *larith* blade and held it distastefully at arm's length. Somehow she must see to having the woman buried, and the heap of corpses they had made between them. By fantastic luck, no one had entered the street till now, but a drunken snatch of song raised raucous echoes between the old buildings, and a drunken man reeled down the street, with two or three companions to hold him upright, and seeing

Lythande standing over the heap of bodies, got the obvious impression.

"Murder!" he howled. "Here's murder and death! Ho, the watch, the guards—help, murder!"

"Stop howling," Lythande said, "the victim is dead, and all the rest of her assailants fled."

The man came to stare drunkenly down at the body.

"Pretty one, too," said the first man. "Did you get your turn before she died?"

"She was too far gone," Lythande said truthfully. "But she is a countrywoman of mine, and I promised her I would see her decently buried." A hand went into the mage-robe and came out with a glint of gold. "Where do I arrange for it?"

"I hear the watchmen," said one man, less drunk than his companions, and Lythande, too, could hear the ringing of boots on stone, the clash of pikes. "For that kind of gold, you could have half the city buried, and if there weren't enough corpses, I'd make you a few more myself."

Lythande flung the drunk some coins. "Get her buried, then, and that carrion with her."

"I'll see to it," said the least drunk, "and not even toss you a coin for that fine sword of hers; you can take it to her kinfolk."

Lythande stared at the sword in her hand. She would have sworn she had laid it properly across the dead woman's breast. Well, it had been a confusing half hour. She bent and laid it on the lifeless breast. "Touch it not; it is a *larith* sword; I dare not think what the Larithae would do to you, should they find you with *that* in your hand."

The drunken men shrank back. "May I defile virgin goats if I touch it," said one of them, with a superstitious gesture. "But do you not fear the curse?"

And now she was confused enough that she had picked up the *larith* blade again. This time she put it carefully down across the Laritha's body and spoke the words of an unbinding-spell in case the dying woman's gesture had somehow sought to bind that sword to her. Then she moved into the shadows of the street in that noiseless and unseen way that often caused people to swear, truthfully, that they had seen Lythande appearing or disappearing into thin air. She looked on from the shadows until the watchmen had come, cursing, and dragged away the bodies for burial. In this city, they knew little of the Goddess Larith and her worship, and Lythande thought, conscience-stricken, that she should have seen to it that the woman and her ravishers were not buried in the same grave. Well, and what if they were? They were all dead, and might await the Last Battle against Chaos together; they could have no further care for what befell their corpses, or if they did, they could tell it to whatever judges awaited them on the far side of death's gate.

This story is not concerned with the business that had brought Lythande to Old Gandrin, but when it was completed the next day, and the mercenary-magician emerged from a certain house in the Merchants' Quarter, stowing more coins into the convenient folds of the mage-robe, and ruefully remembering the depleted stocks of magical herbs and stones in the pouches and pockets stowed in odd places about that mage-robe, Lythande, with a most unpleasant start, found her fingers entangled with a strange object of metal tied about her waist. It was the *larith* sword; and it was, moreover, tied there with a strange knot that gave her fingers some little trouble to untie, and was certainly not her own work!

"Chaos and hellfire!" swore Lythande. "There is more to *larith* magic than I ever thought!"

That damnable impulse that had prompted her to meddle in somebody else's business had now, it seemed, saddled her with someone else's magic. Furthermore, her unbinding-spell had not worked. Now she must make strong magic that would not fail; and first she must find herself a safe place to do it.

In Old Gandrin she had no safe-house established, and the business that had brought her here, though important and well paid, was not of the kind that makes many friends or incurs much gratitude. She had been gifted past what she had asked for her services; but should Lythande present herself at that same door where she had worked spells to thrust out ghosts and haunts, she did not deceive herself that she would receive much welcome. What, then, to do? A Pilgrim Adept did not make magic in the street like a wandering juggler!

A common tavern? Some shelter, indeed, she must find before the burning eye of Reth sank below the horizon; she was carrying much gold, and had no wish to defend it in the night-streets of the Thieves' Quarter. She must also replenish her stocks of magical herbs, and also find a place to rest, and eat, and drink, before she set off northward to the shrine of the Goddess as Larith. . . .

Lythande cursed aloud, so angrily that a passerby in the street turned and stared in protest. Northward to Larith? Was that forever-be-damned sorcerous sword beginning to work on her very thoughts? This was strong magic; but she would not go to Larith, no, by the Final Battle, she would *not* go northward, but south, and nowhere near that accursed shrine of the Larithae! *Not while there is magic left in the arsenal of a Pilgrim Adept, I will not!*

In the market, moving noiselessly in the concealment of the mage-robe, she found a stall where magical herbs were for sale, and bartered briefly for them; briefly, because the law of magic states that whatever is wanted for the making of magic must be bought without haggling, gold being no more than dross at the service of magical arts. Yet, Lythande mused darkly, that knowledge had evidently become common among herb-sellers and spell-candlers of the Gandrin market, and as a result their prices had gone from the merely outrageous to the unthinkable. Lythande remonstrated briefly with a woman at one of these stalls.

"Come, come, four Thirds for a handful of darkleaf?"

"And how am I to know that when ye give me gold, ye havena' spelled it from copper or worse?" demanded the herb-seller. "Last moon I sold one of your Order a full quartern of dreamroot and bloodleaf, full cured by a fire o' hazel and spellroot, and that defiler of virgin goats paid me wi' two rounds of gold—he said. But when the moon changed, I looked at 'em, and it was no more than a handful of barley stuck together wi' spellroot and smelling worse than the devil's farts! I take that risk into account when I set my prices, magician!"

"Such folk bring disrepute on the name of the magician," Lythande agreed gravely, but secretly wished she knew that spell. There were dishonest innkeepers who would be better paid in barley grains; in fact, the grain would be worth more than their services! The spell-candler was looking at Lythande as if she had more to say, and Lythande raised inquiring eyebrows.

"I'd give you the stuff for half if you'd show me a spell to tell true gold from false, magician."

Lythande looked round, and on a nearby stall saw the crystals she wanted. She picked up one of them.

"The crystal called *blue zeth* is a touchstone of magic," Lythande said. "False gold will not have a true gold shimmer; and other things spelled to look like gold will show what they are, but only if you blink thrice and look between the second and third blink. That bracelet on your arm, good woman—"

The woman slid the bracelet down over her plump

hand; Lythande took it up and looked through the *blue zeth* crystal.

"As you can clearly see," she said, "this bracelet is—" and to her surprise, concluded—"false gold; pot-metal gilded."

The woman squinted, blinked at the bracelet. "Why, that defiler of virgin goats," she howled. "I will kick his arse from here to the river! Him and his tales of his uncle the goldsmith—"

Lythande restrained a smile, though the corners of her lips twitched. "Have I created trouble with husband or lover, O good woman?"

"Only that he'd like to be, I make no doubt," muttered the woman, throwing the cheap bracelet down with contempt.

"Look at something I know to be true gold, then," Lythande said, and picked up one of the coins she had given the woman. "True gold will look like *this*—" And at her wave, the woman bent to look at the golden shimmer of the coin. "What is *not* gold will take on the blue color of the *zeth* crystal, or"—she took up a copper, gestured, and the copper shone with a deceptive gold luster; she thrust it under the crystal—"if you blink three times and look between the second and third blink, you can tell what it is really made of."

Delighted, the stallkeeper bought a handful of *blue zeth* crystals at the neighboring stall. "Take the herbs, then, gift for gift," she said, then asked suspiciously, "What else will you ask me for this spell? For it is truly priceless—"

"Priceless, indeed," Lythande agreed. "I ask only that you tell the spell to three other persons, and exact a promise that each person to whom it is told tell three others. Dishonest magicians bring evil repute—and then it is hard for an honest one to make a living."

And, of course, what nine market women knew would

soon be known everywhere in the city. The sellers of *blue zeth* would profit, but not beyond their merits.

"Yet the magicians of the Blue Star are honest, so far as I've had dealings with 'em," the woman said, putting away the *blue zeth* crystals into a capacious and not-very-clean pocket. "I got decent gold from the one who bought spellroot from me last New Moon."

Lythande froze and went very still, but the Blue Star on the browless forehead began to sparkle slightly and glow. "Know you his name? I knew not that a brother of my Order had been within Old Gandrin this season."

It meant nothing, of course. But, like all Pilgrim Adepts, Lythande was a solitary, and would have preferred that what she did in Old Gandrin should not be spied on by another. And it lent urgency to her errand; above all, she must not be seen with the *larith* sword, lest the secret of her sex become known; it was not well known within Gandrin—for the Larithae seldom came so far south—but in the North it was known that only a woman might touch, handle, or wield a *larith* sword.

"Upon reflection," she said, "I have done you, as you say, a priceless service; do you one for me in return."

The woman hesitated for a moment, and Lythande for one did not blame her. It is not, as a general rule, wise to entangle oneself in the private affairs of wizards, and certainly not when that wizard glows with lightning flash of the Blue Star. The woman glowered at the false gold bracelet and muttered, "What is your need?"

"Direct me to a safe lodging place this night—one where I may make magic, and see to it that I do so unobserved."

The woman said at last, grudgingly, "I am no tavern, and have no public-room and no great kitchens for roasting meat. Yet now and again I let out my upper chamber, if the tenant is sober and respectable. And my son—he's nineteen and like a bull about the shoulders—he'll stand below wi' a cudgel and keep away anyone who would spy. I'll gi' you that room for a half o' gold."

A half? That was more outrageous than the price she had set on her baggin of spellroot. But now, of all times, Lythande dared not haggle.

"Done, but I must have a decent meal served me in privacy."

The woman considered adding to the charge, but under the glare of the Blue Star, she said quickly, "I'll send out to the cookshop round the corner and get ye roast fowl and a honey-cake."

Lythande nodded, thinking of the sword of Larith tied under the mage-robe. In privacy, then, she could work her best unbinding-spell, then bury the sword by the riverbank and hasten southward.

"I shall be here at sunset," she said.

As the crimson face of Reth faded below the horizon, Lythande locked herself within the upper chamber. She was fiercely hungry and thirsty—among the dozen or more vows that fenced about the power of a Pilgrim Adept, it was forbidden to eat or drink within the sight of any man. The prohibition did not apply to women, but, ever conscious of the possibility of disguise like her own, she had fenced it with unending vigilance and discipline; she could not, now, have forced herself to swallow a morsel of food or drink except in the presence of one or two of her trusted confidantes, and only one of these knew Lythande to be a woman. But that woman was far away, in a city beyond the world's end, and Lythande had no trusted associate nearer than that.

She had managed, hours ago, a sip of water at a public fountain in a deserted square. She had eaten nothing for several days save for a few bites of dried fruit, taken under cover of darkness, from a small store she kept in pockets of the mage-robe. The rare luxury of a hot meal in assured privacy was almost enough to break her control, but before touching anything, she checked the locks and searched the walls for unseen spy-holes where she might be overlooked; unlikely, she knew, but Lythande's survival all these years had rested on just such unsparing vigilance.

Then she drank from the ewer of water, washed herself carefully, and setting a little water to heat by the good fire in the room, carefully shaved her eyebrows, a pretense she had kept up ever since she began to look too old to pass for a beardless boy. She left the razor and soap carefully by the hearth where they could be seen. She could, if she must, briefly create an illusion of beard, and sometimes smeared her face with dirt to add to it, but it was difficult and demanded close concentration, and she dared not rely on it; so she shaved her eyebrows close, with the thought that a man known to shave his eyebrows would probably have to shave his beard as well.

Hearing steps on the stair, she drew the mage-robe about her, and the herb-seller puffed up the last steps and into the opened door. She set the smoking tray on the table, murmured, "I'll empty that for ye," and took up the bowl of soapy water and the slop jar. "My son's at the stairway wi' his cudgel; none will disturb you here, magician."

Nevertheless, Lythande, alone again, made very sure the bolt was well-drawn and the room still free of spy-eyes or spells; who knew what the herb-seller might have brought with her? Some spell-candlers had pretensions to the arts of sorcery. Moreover, the woman had mentioned that she had seen another Adept of the Blue Star; and Lythande had enemies among them. Suppose the herb-seller were in the pay of Rabben the Half-handed, or Beccolo, or . . . Lythande dismissed this unprofitable speculation. The room appeared empty and harmless. The smell of roast fowl and the freshly baked loaf was dizzying in her famished condition, but magic could not be made on a full stomach, so she packed away the smell into a remote corner of her consciousness and drew out the Larith's sword.

It felt warm to the touch, and there was the small tingling that reminded Lythande that powerful magic resided in it.

She cast a pinch of a certain herb into the fire and, breathing the powerful scent, focused all her powers into one spell. Under her feet, the floor rocked as the Word of Power died, and there was a faint, faraway rumble as of falling walls and towers—or was it only distant summer thunder?

She passed her hand lightly above the sword, careful not to touch it. She was not really familiar with the magic of the Larithae; as Lythande the Pilgrim Adept, she could not be, and while she still lived as a woman, she had never come closer than to know what every passorby knew. But it seemed to her that whatever magic dwelt in the sword was gone; perhaps not banished, but sleeping.

From her pack she sacrificed one of the spare tunics she carried, and carefully wrapped the sword. The tunic was a good one, heavy white silk from the walled and ancient city of Jumathe, where the silkworms were tended by a special caste of women, blinded in childhood so that their fingers would have more sensitivity when the time came to strip the silk from the cocoons. Their songs were legendary, and Lythande had once gone there, dressed as a woman, a cloak hiding the Blue Star, grateful for the women's blindness so that she could speak in her own voice; she had sung them songs of her own north-country, and heard their songs in return, while they thought her only a wandering minstrel girl. The sighted overseer, however, had been suspicious, and had finally accused her of being a man in disguise—for a man to approach the blind women was a crime punishable by death in a particularly unpleasant fashion—and it had taken all of Lythande's magic to extricate herself. But that is another story.

Lythande wrapped the sword in the tunic. She regretted the necessity of giving it up—she had had it for a long time; she shrank from thinking how many years ago she had sung her songs within the house of the blind silkworm-tenders in Jumathe! But for such magic a real sacrifice was necessary, and she had nothing else to sacrifice that meant the least thing to her; so she wrapped the sword in it, and bound it with the cord she had passed through the herb-smoke, tying it with the magical ninefold knot.

Then she set it aside and sat down to eat up the roast fowl and the freshly baked bread with the sense of a task well done.

When the house was quiet, and the herb-seller's son had put his cudgel away and retired to rest, Lythande slipped down the stairs noiselessly as a shadow. She had to spell the lock so that it would not creak, and a somewhat smaller spell would make any passerby think that the drawn-back bolt, open padlock, and open door were firmly shut and bolted. Silken bundle under her arm, she slipped silently to the riverbank and, working by the dim light of the smaller moon, dug a hole and buried the bundle; then, speaking a final spell, strode away without looking back.

Returning to the herb-seller's house, she thought she saw something following in the street, and turned to look. No, it was only a shadow. She slipped in through the open door—which still looked charmed and locked—locked it tight from within, and regained her room with less sound than a mouse in the walls.

The fire had burned to coals. Lythande sat by the fire and took from her pack a small supply of sweet herbs with no magical properties whatever, rolled them into a narrow tube, and sparked it alight. So relaxed was she that she did not even use her fire-ring, but stooped to

light the tube from the last coals of the fire. She leaned
back, inhaling the fragrant smoke and letting it trickle
out slowly from her nostrils. When she had smoked it
down to a small stub, she took off her heavy boots,
wrapped herself tightly in the mage-robe and then in
the herb-seller's blanket, and lay down to sleep.

Before dawn she would arise and vanish as if by
magic, leaving the door bolted behind her on the inside—
there was no special reason for this, but a magician
must preserve some mystery, and if she left by the
stairs in the ordinary way, perhaps the innkeeper would
be left with the impression that perhaps magicians were
not so extraordinary after all, since they ate good dinners and washed and shaved and filled slop jars like any
ordinary mortal. So when Lythande had gone, the room
would be set to rights without a wrinkle in the bed-
clothes or an ash in the fireplace, the door still bolted
on the inside as if no one had left the room at all.

And besides, it was more amusing that way.

But for now, she would sleep for a few hours in
peace, grateful that the clumsiness that had entangled
her in somebody else's magic had come to a good end.
No whisper disturbed her sleep to the effect that it
hadn't really even started yet.

The last of the prowling thieves had slipped away to
their holes and corners, and the red eye of Keth was
still blinded by night when Lythande slipped out of Old
Gandrin by the southern gate. She took the road south
for two reasons: there was always work for mercenary or
magician in the prosperous seaport of Gwennane, and
also she wished to be certain in her own mind that after
her drastic unbinding-spell, nothing called her northward to the Larith shrine.

The least of the moons had waned and set, and it was
that black-dark hour when dawn is not even a promise
in the sky. The gate was locked and barred, and the

sleepy watchman, when Lythande asked quietly for the gate to be opened, growled that he wouldn't open the gate at that hour for the High Autarch of Gandrin himself, far less for some ne'er-do-well prowling when honest folk and dishonest folk were all sleeping, or ought to be. He remembered afterward that the star between the ridges where Lythande's brows ought to have been had begun to sparkle and flare blue lightning, and he could never explain why he found himself meekly opening the gate and then doing it up again afterward. "Because," he said earnestly, "I never saw that fellow in the mage-robe go *through* the gate, not at all; he turned hisself invisible!" And because Lythande was not all that well known in Old Gandrin, no one ever told him it was merely Lythande's way.

Lythande breathed a sigh of relief when the gate was shut behind her, and began to walk swiftly in the dark, striding long and full and silent. At that pace, the Pilgrim Adept covered several leagues before a faint flush in the sky told where the eye of Keth would stare through the dawn clouds. Reth would follow some hours later. Lythande continued, covering ground at a rate, then was vaguely troubled by something she could not quite identify. Yes, something was wrong. . . .

. . . It certainly was. Keth was rising, which was as it should be, but Keth was rising on her *right* hand, which was *not* as it should be; she had taken the southward road out of Old Gandrin, yet here she was, striding northward at a fast pace. To the north. Toward the shrine of Larith.

Yet she could not remember turning round for long enough to become confused and take the wrong direction in the darkness. She must have done so somehow. She stopped in mid-stride, whirled about, and put the sun where it should be, on her left, and began pacing steadily south.

But after a time she felt the prickle in her shins and

buttocks and the cold-flame glow of the Blue Star between her brows, which told her that magic was being made somewhere about her. And the sun was shining on her right hand, and she was standing directly outside the gates of Old Gandrin.

Lythande said aloud, "No. Damnation and Chaos!" disturbing a little knot of milkwomen who were driving their cows to market. They stared at the tall, sexless figure and whispered, but Lythande cared nothing for their gossip. She started to turn round again and found herself actually walking through the gates of Old Gandrin again.

Through the south gate. Traveling north.

Now this is ridiculous, Lythande thought. I buried the sword myself, locked there with my strongest unbinding spell! Yet her pack bulged strangely; ripping out a gutter obscenity, Lythande unslung the pack and discovered what she had known she would discover the moment she felt that strange prickling cramp that told her there was magic in use—somebody else's magic! At the very top of the pack, wedged in awkwardly, was the white silk tunic, draggled with the soil of the riverbank, and thrusting through it—as if, Lythande thought with a shudder, it were trying to get out—was the *larith* sword.

Lythande had not survived this long under the Twin Suns without becoming oblivious to hysteria. The Adepts of the Blue Star held powerful magic; but every mage knew that sooner or later, everyone would encounter magic stronger yet. Now she felt rage rather than fear. Heartily, Lythande damned the momentary impulse of compassion for a dying woman that led her to reveal herself. Well, done was done. She had the *larith* sword and seemed likely—Lythande thought with a flicker of irony—to have it until she could devise a strong enough magic to get rid of it again.

Was she fit for a really prolonged magical duel? It

would attract attention; and somewhere within the walls of Old Gandrin—or so the herb-seller had told her—there was another Adept of the Blue Star. If she began making really powerful magic—and the unbinding-spell itself had been a risk—sooner or later she would attract the attention of whichever Pilgrim Adept had come here. With the kind of luck that seemed to be dogging her, it would be one of her worst enemies within the Order: Rabben the Half-handed, or Beccolo, or. . . .

Lythande grimaced. Bitter as it was to concede defeat, the safest course seemed to be to go north as the *Larith* sword wanted. If, then, when she arrived there, she could somehow contrive to return the sword to larith's own shrine. She had resolved to leave Old Gandrin anyway, and one direction was no better than another.

So be it. She would take the damned thing north to the Forbidden Shrine, and there she would leave it. Somehow she would manage to plant it on someone who could enter the shrine where she could not enter . . . rather, the worst was that she *could* enter but dared not be known to do so. Northward, then, to Larith's shrine—

But within the hour, though Lythande had been in Old Gandrin for a score of sunrises and should have known her way, the Adept was hopelessly lost. Whatever path Lythande found through marketplace or square, thieves' market or red-lamp quarter, however she tried to keep the sun on her right hand, within minutes she was hopelessly turned round. Four separate times she inquired for the north gate, and once it was actually within sight, when it seemed as if the cobbled street would shake itself and give itself a little twist, and Lythande would discover she was lost in the labyrinthine old streets again. Finally, exhausted, furiously hungry and thirsty, and without a chance of finding a moment to eat or drink in privacy now that the sun was high and the streets thronged, she dropped grimly on the edge of a fountain in a public square, maddened by the splashing of the water she dared not drink, and sat there to think it over.

What did the damned thing want, anyway? She was bound north to the Forbidden Shrine as she thought she was commanded to go, yet she was prevented by the sword, or by the magic in the sword, from finding the northern gate, as she had been prevented from taking the road south. Was she to stay in Old Gandrin indefinitely? That did not seem reasonable, but then, there was nothing reasonable about this business.

At least this will teach me to mind my own business in the future!

Grimly, Lythande considered what alternatives were open. To try and find the burial place of the ravished Laritha and bury the sword with a binding-spell stronger yet? Even if she could find the place, she had no assurance that the sword would stay buried, and all kinds of assurances that it would not. The chances now seemed that all the power of the Blue Star would be expended in vain, unless Lythande wished to expend that kind of power that would in turn leave her powerless for days.

To seek safety in the Place Which Is Not, outside the boundaries of the world, and there attempt to find out what the sword really wanted and why it would not allow her to leave the city? For that, the cover of darkness was needful; was she to spend this day aimlessly wandering the streets of Old Gandrin? The smell of food from a nearby cookshop tantalized her, but she was accustomed to that and resolutely ignored it. Later, in some deserted street or alley, some of the dried fruit in the pockets of the mage-robe might find their way into her mouth, but not now.

At least she could enjoy a moment's rest here on the fountain. But even as that thought crossed her mind, she discovered she was on her feet and moving restlessly across the square, thrusting the little packet of smoking-herbs back into the pocket.

She wondered angrily where in the hells she was going now. Her hand was lightly on the hilt of the *larith* sword, and she could only hope that none of the bystanders in the street could see it or would know what it meant if they did. She bashed into someone who snarled at her and accused her in a surly tone of some perversion involving being a rapist of immature nanny goats. The profanity of Old Gandrin, she concluded, was no more imaginative, and just as repetitive, as it was anywhere beneath the blinded eye of Keth-Ketha.

Across the fountain square, then, and into a narrow, winding street that emerged, a good half hour's walk later, into another square, this one facing a long, narrow barracks. Lythande was in a curiously dreamy state that she recognized, later, as almost hypnotic; she watched herself from inside, walking purposefully across the square, quite as if she knew where she was going and why, feeling that at any time, if she wished, she *could* resist this eerie compulsion—but that was simply too much trouble; why not go along and see what the *larith* wanted?

Four men were sloshing their faces in the great water trough before the barracks, their riding animals snorting in the water beside them. The Larith's sword was in her hand, and one man's head was bobbing like an apple in the water trough before Lythande knew what she—or rather, the sword—was doing. A second went down, spitted, before the other two had their swords out. The *larith* sword had lost its compulsion and was slack in her hand as she heard their outraged shouts, thinking ironically that she was as bewildered by the whole thing as they were, or maybe more so. She scrambled to get control of the sword, for now she was

fighting for her life. There was no way these men were
going to let her escape, now that she had slain two of
their companions unprovoked. She managed to disarm
one man, but the second drove her back and back,
holding her ground as best she could; thrust, parry,
recover, lunge—her foot slipped in something slick on
the ground, and she went down, staggering for the
support of the wall; somehow got the sword up and saw
it go into the man's breast; he groaned and fell across
the bodies of his companions, two dead and one sorely
wounded.

Lythande started to turn away, sickened and outraged—at least the fifth man need not be murdered in
cold blood—then realized she had no choice. That survi-
vor could testify to a magician with the Blue Star
blazing between hairless brows, bearing the *larith* sword,
and any Pilgrim Adept who might ever hear the story
would know that Lythande had borne the *larith* unscathed. As only a woman could do. She whipped out
the sword again. The man shouted, "Help! Murder!
Don't kill me, I have no quarrel with you—" and took
to his heels, but Lythande strode swiftly after him, like
a relentless avenging angel, and ran him through, gri-
macing in sick self-disgust. Then she ran, seeing other
men flooding out of the barracks at their comrades'
death cries, losing herself in the tangle of streets again.

Eventually, she had to stop to recover her breath.
Why had the sword demanded those deaths? Immediately the answer came, imprinting the faces of the first
two men she had killed—or the sword had killed almost
without her help or knowledge—on her mind; they had
been in the jeering circle of men who had ravished the
dying priestess-swordswoman. So among other powers,
the *larith* sword was spelled to vengeance on its own.

But she, Lythande, had not even stopped with killing
the men the sword wished to kill. She had killed the

other two men in cold blood to protect the secret of her
sex and her magic.

Now the damned thing has entangled me not only in
someone else's magic but in someone else's revenge!

Had the sword drunk its fill, or was it one of those
that would go on killing and killing until it was somehow, unthinkably, sated? But now it seemed quiet
enough in her scabbard. And after all, when she had
killed the two who had either witnessed or shared in
the rape of the Laritha, the compulsion had departed;
the others she had killed more or less of her own free
will.

A picture flashed behind her eyes: a burly man with a
hook nose and ginger whiskers. He had been in the
crowd around the dying Laritha and had escaped. He
was not in the barracks behind the fountain, or no doubt
the sword would have dragged her inside to kill him,
probably killing everyone that lay between them.

Now, perhaps, she could depart the city—she was
not sure how far to the north lay the Forbidden Shrine,
but she grudged every hour now before the *larith* sword
was out of her hands.

*And I swear, from this day forth, I will never
interfere—come battle, arson, murder, rape, or death—
in any of the 9,090 forms the blinded eye of Keth has
seen. I have had enough of somebody else's magic!*

Lythande turned and took a path toward the northern gate, striding with a long, competent pace that
fairly ate up the distance, and that compelled young
children playing in the streets or idlers lounging there
to get out of the way, sometimes with most undignified
haste. Still, it was late in the day and one of the pallid
moons had appeared, like a shadowy corpse-face in the
sky, before she sighted the northern gate. But she was
no longer heading in its direction.

Damnation! Had the thing spotted another prey? Now
it took all Lythande's concentration to keep from snatch-

ing out the *larith* and holding it in her hand. She tried,
deliberately, to slow her pace. She *could* do it, when
she concentrated, which relieved her a little; at least
she was not completely helpless before the magic of the
Larithae. But it took fierce effort, and whenever her
concentration slipped even a little, she was hurrying,
pushed on by the infernal thing that nagged at her. If
only it would let her know where it was going!

No doubt the dead and ravished Laritha, the priestess who owned the sword or was owned by it, *she* was
in the sword's confidence. Would Lythande really want
that, to be symbiote, sharing consciousness and purpose with some damned enchanted sword? Or was the
sword enchanted only by the death of its owner, and
did the Larithae normally carry it only for the purposes
of an ordinary weapon?

She wished the wretched sword would make up its
mind. Again the face renewed itself in her mind, a man
with ginger whiskers and a hook nose, but the chin of a
rabbit with protruding buck teeth. Of course. Most
men who would stoop to rape were ugly and near to
impotence, anyhow; anything recognizably male could
get a woman without resorting to force.

Damn it, must she track down and kill everyone even
in the crowd who had seen? If all who had witnessed
the violation were dead, was the disgrace then can-
celed, or did it run so in the philosophy of the Larithae
and their swords? She didn't want to know any more
about it than she knew already. She wanted only to be
rid of the thing.

"Have a care where you step, ravisher of virgin goats,"
snarled a passerby, and Lythande realized she had stumbled again in her haste. She forced herself to stammer
an apology, glad that the mage-robe was drawn about
her face so that the Blue Star was invisible. Damn it,
this had gone far enough. It was beginning to infringe
on her very personality—she was Lythande, the core of

whose reputation was for appearing and disappearing as if made of shadow. Her best spells could not rid her of it. She must now contrive to give it what it wanted, and be done with it, and swiftly. It would be just as bad if the marketplace gossiped about an Adept of the Blue Star bearing Larith magic, as if she should encounter her worst enemy so; only less swift.

It would be easier if she knew where she was going. There was the continual temptation to fall into the dreamy hypnotic state, dragged on by the *larith* sword; but Lythande fought to remain alert. Once again she was lost in the tangled streets of a quarter in the city where she had never been. And then, crossing the square in front of a wineshop, one of those where the customs and drinkers all came spilling out into the street, she saw him: Ginger Whiskers.

She wanted to stop and get a good look at the man she was fated to kill. It was against her principles to kill, for unknown reasons, men whose names she did not know.

Yet she knew enough about him; he had violated, or attempted to violate, or witnessed the violation of a Laritha. In general, if rape were a capital crime in Old Gandrin, the city would be depopulated, thought Lythande; or inhabited only by women and those virgin goats who formed such a part in the profanity of that city. She supposed that was why there were not many unaccompanied women walking the streets in Old Gandrin.

The Laritha and I. And she did not escape; and I only because my womanhood is unknown. The women of Old Gandrin seem to submit to that unwritten law, that the woman who walks alone can expect no more than ravishment. The Laritha sought to challenge it, and died.

But she will be avenged. . . . And Lythande swore under her breath. She was acting as if it mattered a damn to her if every woman who had not the sense of

wisdom to stay out of a ravisher's hands paid the penalty of that foolishness or incaution. She had had her fill
of taking upon herself someone else's curse and someone else's magic.

Was the sword of *larith*, then, which might never be
borne by a man, beginning to work its accursed magic
upon her? Lythande stopped dead in the middle of the
square, trying not to stare across the intervening space
at Ginger Whiskers. If she fought the sword's magic,
could she let him live and turn and go on her way? Let
someone else right the wrongs of the Larithae!

*What, after all, have I to do with women? If they do
not wish for the common fate of women, let them do as
I have done, renounce skirts and silks and the arts of
the women's quarters, and put on sword and breeches
or a mage-robe and dare the risks I have dared to leave
all that behind me. I paid dear for my immunity.*

She suspected the Laritha had paid no less a price.
But that was, after all, none of her concern. She took a
deep breath, summoned her strongest spell, and by a
great effort turned her back on Ginger Whiskers, walking in the opposite direction.

Just in time, too. The hood of Lythande's mage-robe
was drawn over her head, concealing the Blue Star; but
beneath the heavy folds she could feel the small sting-
ing that meant the star was flaming, sparkling, and
could see the blue lightnings above her eyes. *Magic.* . . .

It was not the *larith* sword. That was quiet in her
belt . . . no, somehow she had it in her hands. Lythande
stood quietly, trying to fight back, and dared a peep
beneath the mage-robe.

It was not the flare of the Blue Star between her
brows. Somehow she had seen, had seen . . . where
was it, what had she seen? The man's back was turned
to her, she could see the brown folds of a mage-robe
not too unlike her own; but though she could not see

forehead or star, she felt the Blue Star resonate in time
with her own.

*He would feel it, too. I had better get out of here as
fast as I can.* Which settled it. Ginger Whiskers would
not pay for his part in the ravishment of the Laritha.
She, Lythande, had had enough of someone else's magic;
she would take the *larith* sword northward to its shrine,
but she was not, by Chaos and the Last Battle, going to
be seen here in the presence of another of her Order,
doing battle—or call it by its right name, murder—
with a *larith* sword.

The sword was quiet in her hand and made no apparent struggle when she slid it back into the scabbard,
though at the last moment it seemed to Lythande that
it squirmed a little, reluctant to be forced into the
sheath. Too bad, she would give it no choice. Lythande
muttered the words of a bonding-spell to keep it there,
carefully slipped behind a pillar in the square, and
cautiously, moving like a breath of wind or a northland
ghost, circled about until she could see, unseen, the
man in the mage-robe. On her forehead, the Blue Star
throbbed, and she could see by tiny movements of the
man's hood that he, too, was trying to look about him
unseen to know if another Pilgrim Adept was truly
within the crowd in the square. Well, that was her
greatest skill, to see without being seen.

The man's hands, long-fingered and muscular, swordsman's hands, were clasped over the staff he bore. Not
Rabben the Half-handed, then. He was tall and burly; if
it was Ruhaven, he was one of her few friends in the
Order, and he was not a north-country man, he would
not know the technicalities of a Larith curse, would
not, probably, know that a larith could be borne only
by a woman. Lythande toyed briefly with the notion, if
it *was* Ruhaven, of making some part of her predicament known to him. No more than she must, only that
she had become saddled with an enchanted sword,

perhaps ask his help in formulating a stronger unbinding-spell.

The Pilgrim Adept turned with a slight twitch of his shoulders, and Lythande caught a glimpse of dark hair under the hood. Not Ruhaven, then—Ruhaven's gray hair was already turning white—and he was the only one in the Order to whom she felt she might have turned, at least before the Last Battle between Law and Chaos.

And then the Pilgrim Adept made a gesture she recognized, and Lythande ducked her head further within the mage-robe's folds and tried to slither into the crowd, to reach its edge and drift unseen into the alley beyond the square and the tavern. Beccolo! It could hardly be worse. Yes, he thought Lythande a man. But they had once been pitted, within the Temple of the Star, in a magical duel, and it had not been Lythande who had lost face that day.

Beccolo might not know the details of Larith magic. He probably did not. But if he once recognized her, and especially if he should guess that she was hagridden by a curse, he would be in a hurry to have his revenge.

And then with horror Lythande realized that while she was thinking about Beccolo and her consternation that it should be one of her worst enemies within the Pilgrim Adepts, she had lost her fierce concentration, by which alone she had kept control of the *larith* sword; it was out of the scabbard, naked now in her hand, and she was striking straight through the crowd, men and women shrinking back from her purposeful stride. Ginger Whiskers saw her and shrank back in consternation. Yesterday he had stood and cheered on the violation of a Larith—at least, of a woman rendered helpless by fearful odds. And he had been among those who took to their heels as a tall, lean fighter in a mage-robe with a

Blue Star blazing lightning had cut down four men within as many seconds.

His bench went over and he kicked away the man who went down with it, making for the far end of the square. Lythande thought, wrathfully: Go on, get the hell out of here; I don't want to kill you any more than you want to be killed. And she knew Beccolo's eyes were on her, and on the Blue Star now blazing between her brows. And Beccolo would have known her without that Known her for the fellow Pilgrim Adept who had humiliated him in the outer courts of the Temple of the Star, when they were both novices and before the blazing star was set between either of their brows.

She almost thought for a moment that he would get away. Then she kicked the fallen bench aside and leaped on him, the sword out to run him through. This one was not so easy; he had jerked out his own sword and warded her off with no small skill. Men and women and children surged back to leave them a clear space for fighting, and Lythande, angry because she did not really want to kill him at all, nevertheless knew it was a fight for life, a fight she dared not lose. She crashed down backward, stumbling as she backed away; and then the world went into slow motion. It seemed a minute, an hour that Ginger Whiskers bent over her, sword in hand, coming at her naked throat slowly, slowly. And then Lythande's foot was in his belly, he grunted in pain, and then she had scrambled to her feet and her sword went through his throat. She backed away from the jetting blood. Her only feeling was rage, not against Ginger Whiskers, but against the *larith*. She slammed it back into the scabbard and strode away without stopping to look back. Fortunately, the *larith* did not resist this time, and she made off toward the northern gate. Maybe she could make it there before Beccolo could get through the crowd to trail her. Within mere minutes, Lythande was out of the city and strid-

ing north, and behind her—as yet—there was no sign
of Beccolo. Of course not. How could he know to which
quarter of the compass she was making her course?

All that day, and into much of the night that followed, Lythande strode northward at a steady pace that
ate up the leagues. She was weary and would have
welcomed rest, but the nagging compulsion of the *larith*
at her belt allowed her no halt. At least this way—she
thought dimly—there was less likelihood that Beccolo
would trail her out of the city and northward.

Shortly after Keth sank into the darkness, in the dim
half-twilight of Reth's darkened eye, she paused for a
time on the bank of a river, but she could not rest; she
only cleaned, with meticulous care, the blade of the
larith and secured it in the scabbard. Dim humps and
hillocks on the riverbank showed where travelers slept,
and she surveyed them with vague envy, but soon she
strode on, walking swiftly with apparent purpose. But
in reality she moved within a dark dream, hardly aware
when the last dim light of Reth's setting beams died
away altogether. After a time, the blotched and leprous
face of the larger moon cast a little light on the pathway, but it made no difference to Lythande's pace.

She did not know where she was going. The sword
knew, and that seemed to be enough.

Some hidden part of Lythande knew what was happening to her and was infuriated. It was her work as
magician to act, not to remain passive and be acted
upon. That was for women, and again she felt the revulsion to this kind of women's sorcery where the priestess
became passive tool in the hands of her sword . . . that
was no better than being slave to a man! But perhaps
the Larithae themselves were not so bound; she had
been put under compulsion by the ravished Laritha and
had no choice.

The Laritha requited the impulse that caused me to

*stop, in the vain hope of saving her life or delivering
her from her ravishers—by binding me with this curse!*
And when that came to her mind, Lythande would
curse softly and vow revenge on the Larithae. But most
of that night she walked in that same waking dream,
her mind empty of thought.

Under cover of the darkness, on her solitary road,
she munched dried fruit, her mind as empty as a cow
chewing its cud. Toward morning she slept for a little,
in the shelter of a thicket of trees, careful to set a
watch-spell that would waken her if anyone came within
thirty paces. She wondered at herself; in man's garb,
she had wandered everywhere beneath the Twin Suns,
and now she was behaving like a fearful woman afraid of
ravishment; was it the *larith,* accustomed to being borne
by women who did not conceal their sex, but walked
abroad defending it as they must, that had put this
woman's watchfulness again on her? How many years
had it been since Lythande had even considered the
possibility that she might be surprised alone, stripped,
discovered as a woman?

She felt rage—and worse, revulsion—at herself that
she could still think in these woman's ways. As if *I were
a woman in truth, not a magician,* she thought furiously, and for a moment the rage she felt congested in
her forehead and brought tears to her eyes, and she
forced them back with an effort that sent pain lancing
through her head.

But *I am a woman,* she thought, and then in a furious
backlash: *No! I am a magician, not a woman!* the wizard
is neither male nor female, but a being apart! She
resolved to take off the watch-spell and sleep in her
customary uncaring peace, but when she tried it, her
heart pounded, and finally she set the watch-spell again
to guard her and fell asleep. Was it the sword itself that
was fearful, guarding the slumbers of the woman who
bore it?

When she woke, Keth was divided in half at the
eastern horizon, and she moved on, her jaw grim and
set as she covered the ground with the long, even-
striding paces that ate up the distance under her feet.
She was growing accustomed to the weight of the *larith*
at her waist; absently, now and again, her hand caressed it. A light sword, an admirable sword for the
hand of a woman.

Children were playing at the second river; they scattered back to their mothers as Lythande approached
the ferry, flinging coins at the ferryman in a silent rage.
*Children. I might have had children, had my life gone
otherwise, and that is a deeper magic than my own.*
She could not tell whence that alien thought had come.
Even as a young maiden, she had never felt anything
but revulsion at the thought of subjecting herself to the
desire of a man, and when her maiden companions
giggled and whispered together about that eventuality,
Lythande had stood apart, scornful, shrugging with contempt. Her name had not been Lythande then. She had
been called . . . and Lythande started with horror,
knowing that in the ripples of the lapping water she had
almost heard the sound of her old name, a name she
had sworn never again to speak when once she put on
men's garb, a name she had vowed to forget, no, *a
name she had forgotten . . . altogether forgotten.*

"Are you fearful, traveler?" asked a gentle voice beside her. "The ferry rocks about, it is true, but never in
human memory has it capsized nor has a passenger
fallen into the water, and this ferry has run here since
before the Goddess came northward to establish her
shrine as Larith. You are quite safe."

Lythande muttered ungracious thanks, refusing to
look round. She could sense the form of the young girl
at her shoulder, smiling up expectantly at her. It would
be noted if she did not speak, if she simply moved

northward like the accursed, hell-driven thing she was. She cast about for some innocuous thing to say.

"Have you traveled this road often?" she asked.

"Often, yes, but never so far," said the gentle girlish voice. "Now I travel north to the Forbidden Shrine, where the Goddess reigns as Larith. Know you the shrine?"

Lythande mumbled that she had heard of it. She thought the words would choke her.

"If I am accepted," the young voice went on, "I shall serve the Goddess as one of her priestesses, a Laritha."

Lythande turned slowly to look at the speaker. She was very young, with that boyish look some young girls keep until they are in their twenties or more. The magician asked quietly, "Why, child? Know you not that every man's hand will be against you?" and stopped herself. She had been on the point of telling the story of the woman who had been ravished and killed in the streets of Old Gandrin.

The young girl's smile was luminous: "But if every man's hand is against me, still, I shall have all those who serve the Goddess at my side."

Lythande found herself opening her lips for something cynical. That had not been her experience, that women could stand together. Yet why should she spoil this girl's illusion? Let her find it out herself, in bitterness. This girl still cherished a dream that women could be sisters. Why should Lythande foul and embitter that dream before she must? She turned pointedly away and stared at the muddy water under the prow of the ferry.

The girl did not move away from her side. From under the mage-hood, Lythande surveyed her without seeming to do so: the ripples of sunny hair, the unlined forehead, the small snub nose still indefinite, the lips and earlobes so soft that they looked babyish, the soft little fingers, the boyish freckles she did not trouble to paint.

If she goes to the Larith shrine, perhaps then I might prevail upon her to take the sword of Larith thither. Yet if she knows that I, an apparent male, bear such a sword—if she goes to petition the shrine—surely she must know that no man may lay a hand upon one of the *larith* swords without such penalty as were better imagined than spoken.

And since I bear that sword unscathed, then am I either accused of blasphemy—or revealed as a woman, naked to my enemies. And now, close to her destination, Lythande realized her dilemma. Neither as a man nor as a woman could she step inside the shrine of the Goddess as Larith. What, then, could she do with the sword?

The sword didn't care. So long as the damned thing got home in one piece, she supposed, it mattered not what the carrier was—swordswoman, a girl like that one, or one of those virgin goats who played such a part in the profanity of Gandrin. If she simply asked the girl to take it to the shrine, she revealed either her blasphemy or her true sex.

She might plant the sword upon her, spelled or enchanted into something else; a loaf of bread, perhaps, as the herb-seller had been given barley grains spelled to look like gold. It was not, after all, as if she were sending anything into the Larith shrine to do them harm, only something of its own, and something, moreover, that had played hell with Lythande's life and given her four—no, five; no, there were all the ones she had killed over the body of the Laritha—had given her eleven or a dozen lives to fight among the legions of the dead at the Last Battle where Law shall fight at last against Chaos and conquer or die once and for all. And something that had dragged Lythande all this weary way to get back where it was going.

She seriously considered that. Give the girl the sword,

enchanted to look like something other than what it was. A gift for the shrine of the Goddess as Larith.

The girl was still standing at her side. Lythande knew her voice was abrupt and harsh. "Well, will you take a gift to the shrine, then, from me?"

The girl's guileless smile seemed to mock her. "I cannot. This Goddess accepts no gifts save from her own."

Lythande said with a cynical smile, "You say so? The key to every shrine is forged of gold, and the more gold, the nearer the heart of the shrine, or the god."

The girl looked as if Lythande had slapped her. But after a moment, she said quietly, "Then I am sorry you have known such shrines and such gods, traveler. No man may know our Goddess, or I would try to show you better," and looked down at the deck. Rebuked, Lythande stood silent at the ferry bumped gently against the land. The passengers on the ferry began to stream onto the shore. Lythande awaited the subsidence of the crowd, the *larith* sword for once quiet inside the mage-robe.

The town was small, a straggle of houses, farms outside the gates, and high on the hill above a sprawling market, the shrine of Larith. One thing, at least, the girl spoke true: there was nothing of gold about this shrine, at least where the passerby could see; it was a massive fortress of unpretentious gray stone.

Lythande noticed that the girl was still at her side as she stepped onshore. "One gift at least your Goddess has accepted from the sex she affects to despise," Lythande said. "No women's hands built that keep, which is more fortress than shrine to my eyes!"

"No, you are mistaken," the girl said. "Do you not believe, stranger, that a woman could be as strong as you yourself?"

"No," Lythande said, "I do not. One woman in a hundred—a thousand, perhaps. The others are weak."

"But if we are weak," said the girl, "still our hands

are many." She spoke a formal farewell, and Lythande, repeating it, jaws clenched, stood and watched her walk away.

Why am I so angry? Why did I wish to hurt her?

And the answer rushed over her in a flood. *Because she goes where I can never go, goes freely. There was a time when I would willingly have pawned my soul, had there been a place where a woman might go to learn the arts of sorcery and the skills of the sword. Yet there was no place, no place. I pawned my soul and my sex to seek the secrets of the Blue Star, and this, this soft-handed child, with her patter of sisterhood . . . where were my sisters on that day when I knew despair and renounced the truth of my self? I stood alone; it was not enough that every man's hand was against me on that day, every woman's hand was against me as well!*

Pain beat furiously in her head, pain that made her clench her teeth and scowl and tighten her fists on the hilts of her own twin swords. One would think, she said to herself, deliberately distancing herself from the pain, that I were about to weep. But I forgot how to weep more than a century ago, and no doubt there will be more cause than this for weeping before I stand at the Last Battle and fight against Chaos. But I shall not live to that battle unless somehow I can contrive to enter where no man may enter and return the cursed *larith* where it belongs!

For already she felt, streaming from the *larith*, the same intense, nagging compulsion, to plunge up the hill, walk into the shrine, and throw down the sword before the Goddess who had dragged it here and Lythande with it.

Within the shrine, all women are welcomed as sisters. . . . did the whisper come from the girl who had spoken of the shrine? Or did it come from the sword itself, eager to tempt her on with someone else's magic? *Not I. It is too late for me.* Through the pain in

her head, Lythande's old watchfulness suddenly as-
serted itself. The ferry had moved from the shore again,
and at the far shore, passengers again were streaming
on its deck. Among them, among them—no, it was too
far to see, but with the magical sight of the Blue Star
throbbing between her brows, Lythande knew a form
in a mage-robe not unlike her own. Somehow Beccolo
had trailed her here.

He did not necessarily know the laws of the shrine.
All of the north-country was scattered with shrines to
every god from the God of Smiths to the Goddess of
Light Love. And her shrine, too, is forbidden to me, as
all is forbidden save the magical arts for which I renounced all. Forbidden to men lest they know my
Secret; to women, lest some man attempt to wrest it
from them. . . . Beccolo probably did not know the
peculiarities of the Larithae. If she could lead him into
the shrine itself somehow, then would the priestesses
work on him the wrath they were reputed to work on
every man who found his way inside there, and then
would Lythande be free of his meddling. What, indeed,
would the Goddess as Larith do to any man who penetrated her shrine as Lythande had done to the Temple
of the Blue Star, in disguise, wearing the garb and the
guise of a sex that was not her own?

She fought to resist the magical compulsion in her
mind. The *larith* that had brought her all this way,
almost sleepwalking, was now awake and screaming to
be returned to its home, and Lythande could hear that
screaming in her mind, even as her own rage and
confusion fought to silence it. She could not enter the
Larith's shrine as Lythande, nor as the Adept of the
Blue Star, though at least if she did, Beccolo could not
follow her there—or if he tried, would meet swift
vengeance.

She saw the ferry approaching the shore, and now
could see with her own tired eyes, not with the magical ,

sight, the narrow form of the Pilgrim Adept who had trailed her all this long way. The Twin Suns stood high in the sky, Keth racing Reth for the zenith, dazzling the water into brilliant swords of light that blinded Lythande's eyes with painful flame. She stepped into the market, trying to summon around herself the magical stillness, so that everywhere beneath the Twin Suns those who knew Lythande spoke of the magician's ability to appear or disappear before their very eyes.

Most women seek to attract all men's eyes. Even before I came to the Temple of the Blue Star, I sought to turn their eyes away. Magic cannot give to any magician the thing not desired.

And as that thought came within her mind, Lythande stood perfectly still. All the long road here, she had cursed the mischance that had led her into somebody else's magic. Yet nothing bad forced her to turn aside from her path to save the Laritha from violation; she could never have been entangled in the magic of the *larith* sword had something within her not consented to it. Had she turned aside from a woman's ravishment, then would Lythande have been supporting Chaos in the place of Law.

Nonsense. What is a stranger woman to me? And, pain splitting her head asunder, Lythande fought the answer that came, without her consent and against her will.

She is myself. She walks where I dare not, a woman for all to see.

In a rage, Lythande turned aside and sought darkness between the stalls of a market. Early as it was in the day, men brawled in the shadow of a wineshop. Market women milked their goats and sold the fresh milk. A caravan master loaded protesting pack animals. In Lythande's mind, the *larith* sword nagged, knowing its home was not far.

Could she send it now by some unwitting traveler

bound for the shrine? She could not enter. She need not. Perhaps now she could seek a binding-spell that would return it home, or an unbinding-spell, now that the *larith* was in its own country, to free her of its curse, as she had freed herself of the curse of being no more than woman when the Blue Star was set between her brows. She had performed the most massive unbinding-spell of all, culminating in that day when she had been doom-set to live forever as what she had pretended to be. This lesser unbinding-spell should be simple by comparison with that.

From here she could survey, unseen, the upward road to the shrine of the Larithae. Women went upward, seeking whatever mysterious comfort they could have from that Goddess; they led goats to the shrine, whether for sacrifice or to sell milk Lythande neither knew or cared. She fancied that among them she could see the young girl of the ferry, who had come to offer herself to the Goddess, and Lythande found herself following, in her mind, that young girl whose name she would never know.

Never could I have been entangled in the magic of the Larithae, or in anyone else's magic, unless something within me claimed it as mine, Lythande thought. It was not a comfortable thought. Was I perhaps secretly longing for the womanhood I had renounced and for which the Laritha died?

Was it a will to death that brought me here?

Rage and the pain in her head, flaring like the lightnings of the Blue Star, burst in revulsion. What folly is it that dragged me here, questioning all that I am and all that I have done? I am Lythande! Who dares challenge me, man or woman or goddess?

One would think I had come here to die as a woman among my own kind! And what would these sworn priestesses, sworn to the sword and to magic, think then of a woman who had renounced her self—?

But I did not renounce my self! Only my vulnerability to the hazards of being woman and bearing sword and magic. . . .

Which they bear with such courage as they can, her mind reminded her, and again the dying eyes of the ravished Laritha, smiling as she pressed the sword into Lythande's fingers, haunted her. Well. So she died for walking abroad as a woman. That was *her* choice. This is mine, Lythande said to herself, and clutched the mage-robe about her, setting her hand on her two swords— the right-handed knife for the enemies of this world, the knife on the left for the evils and terrors of magic. And the *larith* sword, tucked uncomfortably between them. *Still, I am Lythande!*

The shrine is forbidden to me, as the silk-woman of Jumathe were forbidden to me. And into that shrine I went, among the blind silk-weavers. But the Larithae are not so conveniently devoid of sight. If I walk among them as an Adept of the Blue Star, they will believe—as the overseer of the blind silk-women believed—that I am a man come among them to despoil or conquer. The very best that could befall is that I should be stripped and revealed a woman. And soon or late, the ripples stirred by that stone would reach my enemies, and Lythande be proclaimed abroad what no man may know.

She was walking now between two stalls where articles of women's clothing were displayed in brilliant folds, colorfully woven skirts of the thick cotton of the Salt Deserts, long scarves and shawls, all the soft and colored things women doted on and for which they pawned their lives and their souls, pretty trash! Lythande curled her lip with scorn and contempt, then stood completely motionless.

It is forbidden that any man may know me for a woman. For on that day when any man shall speak it aloud or hear that I am a woman, then is my Power forfeit to him and I may be slain like a beast. Yet within the walls of the Larith shrine, no man may come, so no man may see. The idea flamed in her mind with the brilliance of Keth-Ketha at zenith; she would penetrate the shrine of the Larithae *disguised as a woman!*

It is truly a disguise, she thought with a curl of her lip. She had no idea how many years it had been since she had worn women's garb, and by now it would be pure pretense to put it on. It was no longer her self.

Nor could she, a man, purchase such things openly. If an apparent man should vanish after purchasing women's garments, and a strange woman, suddenly appear at the shrine—well, one could not conveniently hope that all the Larithae would be so conveniently stupid, nor all who kept their gates and brought them gifts.

She must, then, manage to steal the garments unseen. No very great trick, after all, for one whose teasing nickname in the outer courts of the Blue Star had been "Lythande, the Shadow." To appear and disappear unseen was her special gift. She had begun to move stealthily, a shadow against the darkness of the tents of the sellers, out of sight of Keth and Reth. Later that day, a skirt-seller would discover that only six skirts hung in their colorful bands where seven had hung before; a seller of fards and cosmetics discovered that three little pots of paint had vanished before his very eyes, and although he remembered a lanky stranger in a mage-robe lounging nearby, he would swear he had not taken his eyes for a minute from the stranger's hands; and a woolen shawl and a veil likewise found their way out of a tangled pile of castoffs and were never missed at all.

Keth was declining again when a lean and angular woman, with an awkward bundle on her back, striding like a man, made her way up the hill toward the shrine. Her forehead appeared strangely scarred, and her eyebrows and cheeks were painted, her eyes deeply underlined with kohl. She stumbled against a woman leading

pack animals, who cursed her as a despoiler of virgin
goats. So they had that oath here, too. Lythande was
ready to assure the woman, in that mellow and cynical
voice, that her maiden beasts were perfectly safe, but it
seemed not worth the trouble. Wearing the unfamiliar
garments of a woman was penance enough. At least she
could bear the *larith* opening, tied awkwardly about
her waist as a woman not accustomed to the handling of
a sword would do. And she knew she moved so clumsily in the skirts she had not had about her knees in a
century, that at any moment she might be accused of
being a man in disguise. Which would, she thought
grimly, be the ultimate irony.

*I have worn a mask for more years than most of this
crowd has been alive.* Against her will, she remembered an old horror tale that a nurse, decades since
dust and ashes, had told to frighten a girl whose name
Lythande now honestly could not remember, of a mask
worn so long that it had frozen to the face and *become*
the face. *I have become what I pretended. And that is
all my reward or my punishment.*

There is no woman, now, under these skirts, and it
would be just, she thought, if I were exposed as a man.
Yet she had considered and refused a glamouring-spell
that might make her more visibly a woman. She would
go into the Larith shrine with such resources as were
her own, without magic. Yet the Blue Star beneath the
paint throbbed as if with unshed tears.

Between a woman leading goats and a woman bearing a
sick child, Lythande stepped between the pillars of the
shrine of the Goddess as Larith, built at some time by
the hands of women. She did not know or care when
she had begun to believe that. But obscurely it com-
forted her that women could build such an edifice.

Against her will, a curious question nagged at her,

like the voice of the *larith* tied clumsily with a rope at her waist:

If I had not forsaken or forsworn myself for the Blue Star, if I had joined my hands to the weak and despised hands of my sisters, would this temple have risen the sooner? She dismissed the thought with an effort that made her eyes throb, asking herself in scornful wrath, *If the stone lions of Khoumari had kittened, would the Khoumari shepards guard their lambs more safely of nights?*

She stood on a great floor, mosaiced in black and white stone in a pentagram pattern. Above her rose a great blue dome, and before her stood the great figure of the Goddess as Larith, fashioned of stone and without any trace of gold. The girl had spoken truth, then. And at the far end, where a little band of priestesses stood, accepting the gifts of the pilgrims in that outer court, she fancied she could see the slender and boyish form of the girl among them. It was only fancy! No doubt they had whisked her away into their inner courts, there to await that mysterious transition into a Laritha, under the eyes of their stone Goddess. A pregnant warrior! Lythande heard herself make a small inner sound of contempt, but she was in their territory and she knew she dared not draw attention to herself. She must behave like a woman and be meek and silent here. Well, she was skilled at disguise; it was no more than a challenge to her.

I would like to take the girl with me, rather than letting her go to these women-sorceresses and their flimsy magic! (Not so flimsy, after all; it had dragged her here!) *I would teach her the arts of the sword and the laws of magic. I would be alone no longer. . . .*

Daydream. Fantasy. Yet it persisted. Outsiders might think her no more than a mercenary-magician who traveled with an apprentice, as many did; and even if any of them suspected her apprentice to be a maiden, they would think her only the more manly. And the girl would know her secret, but it would not matter, for Lythande would be teacher, master, lover. . . .

The woman ahead of her, bearing a sick child, was standing now before the priestess of the Larith who accepted gifts for the shrine. The woman tried to hand her a golden bracelet, but the priestess shook her head.

"The Goddess accepts gifts only from her own, my sister. Larith the Compassionate bestows gifts upon the children of men, but does not accept them. You would have healing for your son? Go through yonder door into the outer court, and one of the healers there shall give you a brew for his fever; the Goddess is merciful."

The woman murmured thanks and knelt for a blessing, and Lythande was looking into the eyes of the priestess.

"I bring you—your own," said Lythande, and fumbled at the strings that bore the *larith* sword. For the first time, she looked at it clearly and found she was cradling it in her fingers as if reluctant to let it go. The priestess said, in her gentle voice, "How have you come by this?"

"One of your own lay violated and dying; she spelled this sword to me that I should return it here."

The priestess—she was old, Lythande thought; not as old as Lythande, but no magical immunity gave her the appearance of youth—said gently, "Then you have our thanks, my sister." Her eyes rested on the reluctance with which Lythande's fingers released the blade. Her voice was even more gentle.

"You may remain here if you will, my sister. You may be trained in the ways of the sword and of magic, and will wander the world no more alone."

Here? Within walls? Among women? Lythande felt her lip curling again with scorn, and yet her eyes ached. *If I had not forgotten how, I would think I were about to weep.*

"I thank you," she forced herself to say thickly, "but I cannot. I am pledged elsewhere."

"Then I honor what oath keeps you, Sister," the priestess said, and Lythande knew she should turn from the shrine. Yet she made no move to go, and the priestess asked her softly, "What would you have from the Goddess in return for this great gift?"

"It is no gift," said Lythande bluntly. "I had no choice, or I would not have come; surely you must know that your *larith* swords do not await a freely given pilgrimage. I came at the *larith*'s will, not my own. And you have no gifts I seek."

"Gifts are not always asked," said the priestess, almost inaudibly, and laid her hands in blessing on Lythande's brow. "May you be healed of the pain you cannot speak, my sister."

I am no sister of yours! But Lythande did not speak the words aloud; she pressed her lips tight against them, and saw blue lights glare against the priestess's fingers. Would the woman expose her, recognizing the Blue Star? But the woman only made a gesture of blessing, and Lythande turned away.

At least it was over. Her venture into the Larith shrine was ended, and now she must get out safely. She held her breath as she recrossed the great mosaic floor with the pattern of stars. She passed beneath the doorway and out of the shrine. Now, standing again in the free light of Keth, trailed down the sky by the eye of Reth, she had come safe and free from this adventure of someone else's magic.

And then a cynical voice cut through her sense of sudden peace.

"By all the gods, Lythande! So the Shadow is at his old trick of thievery and silence? And you have forced yourself into this alien shrine? How much of their gold did you cozen from their shrine, O Lythande?"

The voice of Beccolo! So even in women's garments,

he had recognized her! But of course he would think it
only the most clever and subtle of disguises.

"There is no gold in the shrine of the Larithae," she
said in her most mellow tones. "But if you doubt me,
Beccolo, seek for yourself within that shrine; freely I
grant you my share of any Larith gold."

"Generous Lythande!" Beccolo taunted, while Lythande stood silent, angry because in this alien guise,
skirts about her body, Blue Star hidden behind paint,
she knew herself at his mercy. She longed for the
comfort of her knives at her waist, the familiar breeches
and mage-robe. Even the *larith* sword would have been
comforting at this moment.

"And you make a pretty woman indeed," Beccolo
taunted. "Perhaps the gold within the shrine is only the
bodies of her priestesses; did you find, then, that gold?"

She turned a little, her hands fumbling swiftly within
her pack. The sword was in her hand. But she could tell
by the feel that it was the wrong sword, the one that
killed only the creatures of magic, the bane-wolf or
werewolf, the ghoul and the ghost would fall before it;
but against Beccolo she was helpless, and that sword of
no avail. Her hands buried in her pack, she fumbled in
the folds of the bundled-up mage-robe and the hard
leather of her own breeches to find the hilt of the sword
that was effective against an enemy as unpleasantly
corporeal as Beccolo. The Blue Star between his brows
mocked her with its flare; she swept one hand over her
forehead and wiped the cosmetic from her own.

"Ah, don't do that," Beccolo mocked. "Shame to
spoil a pretty woman with your scrawny hawk-face. And
here you are where perhaps I can make Lythande as
much of a fool as you made me in yonder courts of the
Temple of the Star! Suppose, now, I shouted to all men
to come and see Lythande the Magician, Lythande the
Shadow, here disguised as a woman, primed for some
mischief in their shrine—what then, Lythande?"

It is only his malice. He does not know the law of Larith. Yet if he should carry out his threat, there were those in this town who would know—or believe—that Lythande, a man, an Adept of the Blue Star, had cheated her way into the shrine where no man might set his foot. There was no safety here for Lythande either as a man or a woman; and now she had her hand on the hilt of her right-hand blade but could not extricate it from the tangled belongings of her pack.

It would serve her right, she thought, if for this womanish folly she was entrapped here in a duel with Beccolo cumbered with skirts and disarmed by her own precautions. She had hidden her swords too well, thinking she would have leisure and the cover of night to shed the disguise!

"Yet before Lythande is Lythande again," Beccolo's hateful, mocking voice snarled, "perhaps I should try whether or not it is not more fitting to Lythande to put skirts about his knees . . . how good a woman do you make, then, O fellow Pilgrim?" His hand dragged Lythande to him; his free hand sought to ruffle the fair hair. Lythande wrenched away, snarling a gutter obscenity of Old Gandrin, and Beccolo, snatching back a blackened hand that smoked with fire, howled in anguish.

I should have stood still and let him have his fun until I could get my sword in my hand. . . .

Lightning flared from the Blue Star, and Lythande brought her own hand up in a warding-spell, furiously rummaging for her right-hand sword. The smell of magic crackled in the air, but Beccolo plunged at Lythande, yelling in fury.

If he touches me, he will know I am a woman. And if the secret of any Adept is spoken aloud, then is his Power forfeit. He has only to say, *Lythande, you are a woman*, and he is revenged for all time for that foolishness in the outer court of the Blue Star.

"Damn you, Lythande, no one makes a fool of Beccolo twice—"

"No," said Lythande, with calm contempt, "you do so admirably yourself." Desperately she wrenched at the trapped sword. He yelled again, and a spell sizzled in the air between them.

"Thief! Hedgerow-sorcerer," Lythande shouted at him, delaying as the sword sawed at the leather holding it in the pack, "Defiler of virgin goats!"

Only for a moment Beccolo paused; but she caught the flash of despair in his eyes. Somehow, in the careless profanity of Old Gandrin, had Beccolo delivered himself into her hands? Had the spirit of the *larith* prompted her to a curse Lythande had never used before and would never use again?

What, after all, had she now to lose, without even a sword in her hand? "Beccolo," she repeated, slowly and deliberately, "you are a despoiler of virgin goats!"

He stood motionless as the words echoed in the square around them. She could feel the voiding of Power from the Blue Star. Truly she had stumbled upon his Secret; he stood silent, unmoving, as she got the sword in her hand and ran him through with it.

A crowd was gathering; Lythande picked up her skirts without dignity, the sword in her hand along with the fold of her skirt, and ran, disappearing around a market-stall and there enfolding herself in a magical sphere of silence. The shouts and yells of the crowd were cut off in a thick, quenched, *clogged* silence, as the utter stillness of the Place Which Is Not enfolded her, a sphere of nothingness, like colorless water or dazzling fire. Lythande drew a long breath and began to shuck her borrowed skirts. Now for the unbinding-spell that would return these things to the stalls of their owners, somewhat the worse of wear. As she spoke the spell, she began to chuckle at the picture of Beccolo engaged in the Secret on which he had gambled his life—for the secret spoken in careless abuse, hidden out in the open, was harmless; only when Lythande spoke it openly to his face did it acquire the magical Power of an Adept's Secret.

But not even in secret may I be a woman. . . .

Setting her lips tight, she waved her hand and dispelled the sorcerous sphere. Once again Lythande had appeared in a strange street from thin air, and that would do her reputation no harm either, nor the reputation of the Pilgrim Adepts.

Glancing at the sky, she noticed that the time-annihilating magical sphere had cost her a day and more; Keth again stood at the zenith. She wondered what they had done with Beccolo's body. She did not care. A stream of pilgrims was winding its way upward still to the shrine of the Goddess as Larith, and Lythande stood watching for a moment, remembering the face of the young girl and the soft-spoken blessing of a priestess. Her hand felt empty without the *larith* sword.

Then she turned her back on the shrine and strode toward the ferry.

"Watch where you step, you swaggering defiler of virgin goats," a man snarled as the Adept passed in the swirling mage-robe.

Lythande laughed. She said, "Not I," and stepped on board the ferry, turning her back on the shrine of women's magic.

Introduction to Sea Wrack

The antecedent of this story—though I did not know it until long after it had been written and printed in The Magazine of Fantasy and Science Fiction*—is the old story of the Siren Song. I remember one story—probably by the late great Theodore Sturgeon—in which a mermaid appeared to men as a desirable woman, but to women as a man. This too is the siren-song story, where to every comer the siren—or the lorelei, or the harpy—appears to the wanderer, as she appeared to the homeless Ulysses, and, as in the old folksong,*

> *"Sings, in sad sweet undertone,*
> *The song of heart's desire."*

But Lythande, who professed to have no loves and no heart's desire, would she be vulnerable to such an apparition? I had intended this story to be wry and ironic—no use appealing to the heart of the heartless—and discovered it was sentimental and bittersweet.

As I have said before, I never know what my stories are about until after I've written them. I often find myself toying with an idea then write it to find out what it's about.

SEA WRACK

The crimson eye of Keth hovered near the horizon, with the smaller sun of Reth less than an hour behind. At this hour the fishing fleet should have been sailing into the harbor. But there was no sign of any fleet; only a single boat, far out, struggling against the tide.

Lythande had walked far that day along the shore, enjoying the solitude and singing old, soft sea-songs to the sounds of the surf. Tonight, surely, the Pilgrim-Adept thought, supper must be earned by singing to the lute, for in a simple place like this there would be none to need the services of a mercenary magician, no need for spells or magics, only simple folk, living simply to the rhythms of sea and tides.

Perhaps it was a holiday; all the boats lay drawn up along the shore. But there was no holiday feel in the single street: angry knots of men sat clumped together scowling and talking in low voices, while a little group of women were staring out to sea, watching the single boat struggling against the tide.

"Women! By the blinded eyes of Keth-Ketha, how are women to handle a boat?" one of the men snarled. "How are they to handle fishing nets? Curse that—"

"Keep your voice down," admonished a second, "That—that thing might hear, and wake!"

Lythande looked out into the bay and saw what had

117

not been apparent before; the approaching boat was crewed, not by men, but by four hearty half-grown girls in their teens. Their muscular arms were bare to the shoulder, skirts tucked up to the knee, their feet clumsy in sea-boots. They seemed to be handling the nets competently enough; and were evidently enormously strong, the kind of women who, if they had been milking a cow, could sling the beast over their shoulder and fetch it home out of a bog. But the men were watching with a jealous fury poorly concealed.

"Tomorrow I take my own boat out, and the lasses stay home and bake bread where they belong!"

"That's what Leukas did, and you know what happened to him—his whole crew wrecked on the rocks, and—and something, some *thing* out there ate boat and all! All they ever found was his hat, and his fishing net chewed half-through! An' seven sons for the village to feed till they're big enough to go out to the fishing— that's supposing we ever have any more fishing around here, and that whatever-it-is out there ever goes away again!"

Lythande raised a questioning eyebrow. Some menace, to the mercenary magician. Though Lythande bore two swords, girdled at the narrow waist of the magerobe, the right-hand sword for the everyday menace of threatening humankind or natural beast, the left-hand sword to slay ghost or ghast or ghoul or any manner of supernatural menace, the Adept had no intention of here joining battle against some sea-monster. For that the village must await some hero or fighting man. Lythande was magician and minstrel, and though the sword was for hire where there was need, the Adept had no love for ordinary warfare, and less for fighting some menacing thing needing only brute strength and not craft.

There was but one inn in the village; Lythande made for it, ordered a pot of ale, and sat in the corner, not touching it—one of the vows fencing the power of an

Adept of the Blue Star was that they might never be
seen to eat or drink before men—but the price of a
drink gave the mage a seat at the center of the action,
where all the news of the village could be heard. They
were still grousing about the fear that kept them out of
the water. One man complained that already the ribs of
his boat were cracking and drying and would need
mending before he could put it back into the water.

"If there's ever to be any fishing here again . . ."

"Ye could send the wife and daughters out in the
boat like Lubert—"

"Better we all starve or eat porridge for all our lives!"

"If we ha' no fish to trade for bread or porridge, what
then?"

"Forgive my curiosity," Lythande said in the mellow,
neutral voice that marked a trained minstrel, "but if a
sea-monster is threatening the shore, why should women
be safe in a boat when men are not?"

It was the wife of the innkeeper who answered her.
"If it was a sea monster, we could go out there, all of us,
even with fish-spears, and kill it, like the plainsmen do
with the tusk-beasts. It's a mermaid, an' she sits and
sings and lures our menfolk to the rocks—look yonder
at my goodman," she said in a lowered voice, pointing
to a man who sat apart before the fire, back turned to
the company, clothing all unkempt, shirt half-buttoned,
staring into the fire. His fingers fiddled nervously with
the lacings of his clothing, snarling them into loops.

"He heard her," she said in a tone of such horror that
hearing, the little hairs rose and tingled on Lythande's
arms and the Blue Star between the magician's brows
began to crackle and send forth lightnings. "He *heard*
her, and his men dragged him away from the rocks.
And there he sits from that day to this—him that was
the jolliest man in all this town, staring and weeping
and I have to feed him like a little child, and never take
my eyes off him for half a minute or he'll walk out into

the sea and drown, and there are times"—her voice
sank in despair—"I'm minded to let him go, for he'll
never have his wits again—I even have to guide him
out to the privy, for he's forgotten even that!" And
indeed, Lythande could see a moist spreading stain on
the man's trousers, while the woman hastened, embarrassed, to lead her husband outside.

Lythande had seen the man's eyes; empty, lost, not
seeing his wife, staring at something beyond the room.

Far from the sea, Lythande had heard tales of mermaids, of their enchantments and their songs. The minstrel in Lythande had half-desired to hear those songs,
to walk on the rocks and listen to the singing that could,
it was said, make the hearer forget all the troubles and
joys of the world. But after seeing the man's empty
eyes, Lythande decided to forgo the experience.

"And that is why some of the women have gone in
the boats?"

"Not women," said the innkeeper's potboy, stopping
with a tray of tankards to speak to the stranger, "girls
too young for men. For they say that to women, it calls
in the voice of their lover—Natzer's wife went out last
full moon, swearing she'd bring in fish for her children
at least, and no one ever saw her again; but a hank of
her hair, all torn and bloody, came in on the tide."

"I never heard that a mermaid was a flesh-eater,"
Lythande observed.

"Nor I. But I think she sings, and lures 'im on the
rocks, where the fishes eat them. . . ."

"There is the old stratagem," Lythande suggested.
"Put cotton or wax plugs in your ears—"

"Say, stranger," said a man belligerently, "you think
we're all fools out here? We tried that; but she sits on
the rocks and she's so beautiful . . . the men went mad,
just seeing her, threw me overboard—you can't blind-
fold yourself, not on the sea with the rocks and all—
there's never been a blind fisherman and never will. I

swam ashore, and they drove the boat on the rocks, and
only the blinded eyes of Keth-Ketha know where they've
gone, but no doubt somewhere in the Sea-God's lockup."
Lythande turned to face the man, he saw the Blue Star
shining out from under the mage-robe and demanded,
"Are you a spell-speaker?"

"I am a Pilgrim-Adept of the Blue Star," Lythande
said gravely, "and while mankind awaits the Final Battle of Law and Chaos, I wander the world seeking what
may come."

"I heard of the Temple of the Blue Star," said one
woman fearfully. "Could you free us of this mermaid wi'
your magic?"

"I do not know. I have never seen a mermaid," said
Lythande, "and I have no great desire for the experience."

Yet why not? Under the world of the Twin Suns, in a
life lasting more than most people's imaginations could
believe, the Pilgrim-Adept had seen most things, and
the mermaid was new. Lythande pondered how one
would attack a creature whose only harm seemed to be
that it gave forth with beautiful music—so beautiful that
the hearer forgot home and family, loved ones, wife or
child; and if the hearer escaped—Lythande shuddered.
It was not a fate to be desired—sitting day after day
staring into the fire, longing only to hear again that
song.

Yet whatever magic could make, could be unmade
again by magic. And Lythande held all the magic of
the Temple of the Blue Star, having paid a price more
terrifying than any other Adept in the history of the
Pilgrim-Adepts. Should that magic now be tried against
the unfamiliar magic of a mermaid?

"We are dying and hungering," said the woman.
"Isn't that enough? I believed wizards were sworn to
free the world from evil—"

"How many wizards have you known?" asked Lythande.

"None, though my mother said her granny told her,

once a wizard came and done away wi' a sea-monster on them same rocks."

"Time is a great artificer," said Lythande, "for even wizards must live, my good woman; the pride of magic, while a suitable diversion while we all await the burning out of the Twin Suns and the Final Battle between Law and Chaos, puts no beans on the table. I have no great desire to test my powers against your mermaid, and I'll wager you anything you like that yonder old wizard charged your town a pretty penny for ridding the world of that sea-monster."

"We have nothing to give," said the innkeeper's wife, "but if you can restore my man, I'll give you my gold ring that he gave me when we were wedded. And since he's been enchanted, what kind of man are you if you can't take away one magic with another?" She tugged at her fat finger, and held out the ring, thin and worn, in the palm of her hand. Her fingers clung to it, and there were tears in her eyes, but she held it out valiantly.

"What kind of man am I?" Lythande asked with an ironic smile. "Like none you will ever see. I have no need of gold, but give me tonight's lodging, and I will do what I can."

The woman slid the ring back on her hand with shaking fingers. "My best chamber. But, oh, restore him! Or would ye have some supper first?"

"Work first, then pay," said Lythande. The man was sitting again in the corner by the fire, staring into the flames, and from his lips came a small, tuneless humming. Lythande unslung the lute in its bag, and took it out, bending over the strings. Long, thin fingers strayed over the keys, head bent close as Lythande listened for the sound, tuning and twisting the pegs that held the strings.

At last, touching the strings, Lythande began to play. As the sound of the lute stole through the big common room, it was as if the chinks letting in the late sun had widened, and the light spread in the room; Lythande played sunlight and the happy breeze on the shore. Softly, on tiptoe, not wanting to let any random sound interrupt the music, the people in the inn stole nearer to listen to the soft notes. Sunlight, the shore winds, the sounds of the soft, splashing waves. Then Lythande began to sing.

Afterward—and for years, all those who heard often spoke of it—no one could remember what song was sung, though to everyone it sounded familiar, so that every hearer was sure it was a song they had heard at their mother's knee. To everyone it called, in the voice of husband or lover or child or wife, the voice of the one most loved. One old man said, with tears in his eyes, that he had heard his mother singing him to sleep with an old lullaby he had not heard in more than half a century. And at last, even the man who sat by the fire, clothes unkempt and stinking, hair rough and tangled, and his eyes lost in another world, slowly raised his head and turned to listen to the voice of Lythande, soft contralto or tenor; neutral, sexless, yet holding all the sweetness of either sex. Lythande sang of the simple things of the world, of sunlight and rain and wind, of the voices of children, of grass and wind and harvest and the silences of dawn and twilight. Then, the tempo quickening a little, she sang of home and fireside, where the children gathered in the evening, calling to their fathers to come home from the sea. And at last, the soft voice deepening and growing quieter so that the listeners had to lean forward to hear it, yet every whispered note clearly audible even to the rafters of the inn, Lythande sang of love.

And the eyes of every man widened, and the cheek of every woman reddened to a blush, yet to the innocent children there, every word was innocent as a mother's kiss on their cheek.

And when the song fell silent, the man by the fireside raised his head and brushed the tears from his eyes.

"Mhari, lass," he said hoarsely, "where are ye—ye and the babes—why, ha' I been sitting here the day-long and not out to the fishing? Why, lass, ye're crying, what ails the girl?" And he drew her to his knee and kissed her, and his face changed, and he shook his head, bewildered.

"Why, I dreamed—I dreamed—" His face contorted, but the woman drew his head down on her breast, and she, too, was weeping.

"Don't think of it, goodman, ye' were enchanted, but by the mercy of the gods and this good wizard here, ye're safe home and yourself again. . . ."

He rose, his hands straying to his uncombed hair and unshaven chin. "How long? Aye, what devil's magic kept me here? And"—he looked around, seeing Lythande laying the lute in the case—"what brought me back? I owe ye gratitude, Lord Wizard," he said. "All my poor house may offer is at your command." His voice held the dignity of a poor workingman, and Lythande bent graciously to acknowledge it.

"I will take a lodging for the night, and a meal served in private in my room, no more." And though both the fisherman and his wife pressed Lythande to accept the ring and other gifts, even to the profits of a year's fishing, the wizard would accept nothing more.

But the others in the room crowded near, clamoring.

"No such magic has ever been seen in these parts! Surely you can free us, with your magic, from this evil wizardry! We beg you, we are at your mercy—we have nothing worthy of you, but such as we can, we will give. . . ."

Lythande listened, impassive, to the pleading. It was to be expected; magic had been demonstrated, and knowing what it could do, they were greedy for more. Yet it was not greed alone. Their lives and their livelihood were at stake. These poor folk could not continue to live by the fishing if the mermaid continued to lure them onto the rocks, to be wrecked or eaten by sea-monsters, or, if they came safe and alive to their homes, to live on rapt away by the memory.

Yet what reason could this mermaid have for her evildoing? Lythande was well acquainted with the laws of magic, and magical things did not exercise their powers only out of a desire to make mischief among men. Why, after all, had this mermaid come to sing and enchant these simple shore folk? What could her purpose be?

"I will have a meal served in private, that I may consider this," the magician said, "and tomorrow I will speak with everyone in the village who has heard this creature's song or looked upon her. And then I will decide whether my magic can do anything for you. Further than that I will not go."

When the woman had departed, leaving the tray of food, Lythande locked and double-locked the door of the room behind her. A fine baked fish lay on a clean white napkin—Lythande suspected it was the best of the meager catch brought in by the young girls, which alone kept the village from starving. The fish was seasoned with fragrant herbs, and there was a hot, coarse loaf of maize-bread, with butter and cream, and a dish of sweet boiled seaweed on the tray.

First Lythande cast about the room, the Blue Star blazing between the narrow brows, seeking hidden spy-holes or magical traps. Eternal vigilance was the price of safety for any Adept of the Blue Star, even in a village as isolated as this one. It was not likely that some enemy had trailed Lythande here, nor prear-ranged a trap, but stranger things had happened in the Adept's long life.

But the room was nowhere overlooked and seemed

impregnable, so that at last Lythande was free to take off the voluminous mage-robe and even to ungird the belt with the two swords, and draw off the soft dyed-leather boots. So revealed, Lythande presented still the outward appearance of a slender, beardless man, tall and strongly framed and sexless; yet, free of observation, Lythande was revealed as what she was; a woman. Yet a woman who might never be known to be so in the sight of any living man.

A masquerade that had become truth; for into the Temple of the Pilgrim-Adepts, Lythande alone in all their long history had successfully penetrated in male disguise. Not till the Blue Star already shone between her brows, symbol and sign of Adepthood, had she been discovered and exposed; and by then she was sacrosanct, bearing their innermost secrets. And then the Master of the Pilgrim-Adepts had laid on her the doom she still bore.

"So be it; be then in truth what you have chosen to seem. Till Law and Chaos meet in that Final Battle where all things must die, be what you have pretended; for on that day when any Pilgrim-Adept save myself shall proclaim your true sex, on that day is your power forfeit and you may be slain."

So together with all the vows that fenced about the power of a Pilgrim-Adept, Lythande bore this burden as well; that of concealing her true sex to the end of the world.

She was not, of course, the only Adept heavily burdened with a *geas;* every Adept of the Blue Star bore some such Secret in whose concealment, even from other Adepts of the Order, lay all his magic and all his strength. Lythande might even have a woman confidante, if she could find one she could trust with her life and her powers.

The minstrel-Adept ate the fish, and nibbled at the boiled seaweed, which was not to her taste. The maize bread, well wrapped against grease, found its way into the pockets of the mage-robe, against some time when she might not be able to manage privacy for a meal and must snatch a concealed bite as she traveled.

This done, she drew from a small pouch at her waist a quantity of herbs that had no magical properties whatever (unless the property of bringing relaxation and peace to the weary can be counted magical), rolled them into a narrow tube, and set them alight with a spark blazing from the ring she bore. She inhaled deeply, leaned back with her narrow feet stretched out to the fire, for the sea-wind was damp and cold, and considered.

Did she wish, for the prestige of the Order, and the pride of a Pilgrim-Adept, to go out against a mermaid?

Powerful as was the magic of the Blue Star, Lythande knew that somewhere beneath the world of the Twin Suns, a magic might lie next to which a Pilgrim-Adept's powers were mere hearth-magic and trumperies. There were moments when she wearied, indeed, of her long life of concealment and felt she would welcome death, more especially if it came in honorable battle. But these were brief moods of the night, and always when day came, she wakened with renewed curiosity about all the new adventures that might lie around the next bend in the road. She had no wish to cut it short in futile striving against an unknown enemy.

Her music had indeed recalled the enchanted man to himself. Did this mean her magic was stronger than that of the mermaid? Probably not; she had needed only to break through the magical focus of the man's attention, to remind him of the beauty of the world he had forgotten. Then, hearing again, his mind had chosen that real beauty over the false beauty of the enchantment, for beneath the magic that held him entranced, the mind of the man must have been already in despair, struggling to break free. A simple magic and nothing to give overconfidence in her strength against the unknown magic of mermaids.

She wrapped herself in the mage-robe and laid herself down to sleep, halfway inclined to rise before dawn and be far away before anyone in the village was astir. What were the troubles of a fishing village to her? Already she had given them a gift of magic, restoring the innkeeper's husband to himself; what else did she owe them?

Yet, a few minutes before the rising of the pale face of Keth, she woke knowing she would remain. Was it only the challenge of testing an unknown magic against her own? Or had the helplessness of these people touched her heart?

Most likely, Lythande thought with a cynical smile, it was her own wish to see a new magic. In the years she had wandered under the eyes of Keth and Reth, she had seen many magics, and most were simple and almost mechanical, set once in motion and kept going by something not much better than inertia.

Once, she remembered, she had encountered a haunted oak grove, with a legend of a dryad spirit who seduced all male passersby. It had proved to be no more than an echo of a dryad's wrath when spurned by a man she had tried and failed to seduce; her rage and counterspell had persisted more than forty seasons, even when the dryad's tree had fallen, lightning-struck, and withered. The remnants of the spell had lingered till it was no more than an empty grove where women took their reluctant lovers, that the leftover powers of the angry dryad might arouse at least a little lust. Lythande, despite the pleas of the women fearing to lose their husbands to the power of the spell, had not chosen to meddle; the last she heard, the place had acquired a pleasant reputation for restoring potency, at least for a night, to any man who slept there.

The village was already astir. Lythande went out into the reddening sunrise, where the fishermen gathered from habit, though they were not dragging down their boats to the edge of the tide. Seeing Lythande, they left the boats and crowded around.

"Say, wizard, will you help us or no?"

"I have not yet decided," said Lythande. "First I must speak with everyone in the village who has encountered the creature."

"Ye can't do that," said one old man with a fierce grin, " 'less ye can walk down into the Sea-God's lockup an' question them down there! Or maybe wizards can do that, too?"

Rebuked, Lythande wondered if she were taking their predicament too lightly. To her, perhaps, it was challenge and curiosity; to these folk it was their lives and their livelihood, their very survival at stake.

"I am sorry; I should have said, of course, those who have encountered the creature and lived." There were not, she supposed, too many of those.

She spoke first to the fisherman she had recalled with her magic. He spoke with a certain self-consciousness, his eyes fixed on the ground away from her.

"I heard her singing, that's all I can remember, and it seemed there was nothing in the world but only that song. Mad, it is, I don't care all that much for music— savin' your presence, minstrel," he added sheepishly. "Only I heard that song, somehow it was different, I wanted no more than just to listen to it forever. . . ." He stood silent, thoughtful. "For all that, I wish I could remember. . . ." And his eyes sought the distant horizon.

"Be grateful you cannot," Lythande said crisply, "or you would still be sitting by your fire without wit to feed or clean yourself. If you wish my advice, never let yourself think of it again for more than a moment."

"Oh, ye're right, I know that, but still an' all, it was beautiful—" He sighed, shook himself like a great dog, and looked up at Lythande. "I suppose my mates must ha' dragged me away an' back to the shore; next I knew I was sitting by my fireplace listening to your music, minstrel, an' Mhari cryin' and all."

She turned away; from him she had learned no more than she had known before. "Is there anyone else who met the beast, the mermaid, and survived the meeting?"

It seemed there were none; for the young girls who had taken out the boat either had not encountered the mermaid or it had not chosen to show itself to them. At last one of the women of the village said hesitantly, "When first it came, and the men were hearin' it and never coming back, there was Lulie—she went out with some of the women—she didna' hear anything, they say; she can't hear anything, she's been deaf these thirty years. And she says she saw it, but she wouldna' talk about it. Maybe, knowin' what you're intending to do, she'll tell you, magician."

A deaf woman. Surely there was logic to this, as there was logic to all the things of magic if you could only find out the underlying pattern to it. The deaf woman had survived the mermaid because she could not hear the song. Then why had the men of the village been unable to conquer it by the old ruse of plugging their ears with wax?

It attacked the eyes, too, apparently, for one of the men had spoken of it as "so beautiful." This man said he had leaped from the boat and tried to swim ashore. Ashore—or on the rocks toward the creature? She should try to speak with him, too, if she could find him. Why was he not here among the men? Well, first, Lythande decided, she would speak with the deaf woman.

She found her in the village bake shop, supervising a single crooked-bodied apprentice in unloading two or three limp-looking sacks of poor-quality flour, mixed with husks and straw. The village's business, then, was so much with the fishing that only those who were physically unable to go into the boats found it permissible to follow any other trade.

The deaf woman glowered at Lythande, set her lips tight, and gestured to the cripple to go on with what he was doing, bustling about her ovens. The doings of a magician, said her every truculent look, were no business of hers and she wanted nothing to do with them.

She went to the apprentice and stood over him. Lythande was a very tall woman, and he was a wee small withered fellow; as he looked up, he had to tilt his head back. The deaf woman scowled, but Lythande deliberately ignored her.

"I will talk with you," she said deliberately, "since your mistress is too deaf and perhaps too stupid to hear what I have to say."

The little apprentice was shaking in his shoes.

"Oh, no, Lord Magician . . . I can't. . . . She knows every word we say, she reads lips, and I swear she knows what I say even before I say it. . . ."

"Does she indeed?" Lythande said. "So now I know." She went and stood over the deaf woman until she raised her sullen face. "You are Lulie, and they tell me that you met the seabeast, the mermaid, whatever it is, and that it did not kill you. Why?"

"How should I know?" The woman's voice was rusty as if from long disuse; it grated on Lythande's musical ear.

It was unfair to think ill of a woman because of her misfortune; yet Lythande found herself disliking this woman very much. Distaste made her voice harsh.

"You have heard that I have committed myself to rid the village of this creature that is preying on it." Lythande did not realize that she had, in fact, committed herself until she heard herself say so. "In order to do this, I must know what it is that I face. Tell me all you know of this thing, whatever it may be."

"Why do you think I know anything at all?"

"You survived." And, thought Lythande, I would like to know why, for when I know why it spared this very unprepossessing woman, perhaps I will know what I must do to kill it—if it must be killed, after all. Or would it be enough to drive it away from here?"

Lulie stared at the floor. Lythande knew she was at an impasse; the woman could not hear, and she, Lythande, could not command her with her eyes and presence, or even with her magic, as long as the woman would not meet her eyes. Anger flared in her; she could feel, between her brows, the crackling blaze of the Blue Star; her anger and the blaze of magic reached the baker woman and she looked up.

Lythande said angrily, "Tell me what you know of this creature! How did you survive the mermaid?"

"How am I to know that? I survived. Why? You are the magician, not I; let you tell me that, wizard."

With an effort Lythande moderated her anger. "Yet I implore you, for the safety of all these people, tell me what you know, however little."

"What do I care for the folk of this village?" Lythande wondered what her grudge was that her voice should be so filled with wrath and contempt. It was probably useless to try and find out. Grudges were often quite irrational; perhaps she blamed them for her loss of hearing, perhaps for the isolation that had descended on her when, as with many deaf people, she had withdrawn into a world of her own, cut off from friends and kin.

"Nevertheless, you are the only one who has survived a meeting with this thing," Lythande said, "and if you will tell me your secret, I will not tell them."

After a long time the woman said, "It—called to me. It called in the last voice I heard; my child, him that died o' the same fever that lost me my hearing; crying and calling out to me. And so for a time I thought they'd lied to me when they said my boy was dead of the fever, that somehow he lived, out there on the wild shores. I spent the night seeking him. And when the morning came, I came to my senses, and knew if he had lived, he wouldna' call me in that baby voice—he died thirty years ago, by now he'd be a man grown, and how could he have lived all this time alone?" She stared at the floor again, stubbornly.

There was nothing Lythande could say. She could hardly thank the woman for a story Lythande had wrenched from her, if not by force, so near it as not to matter.

So I was on the wrong track, Lythande thought. The deaf woman had not been keeping from Lythande some secret that could have helped to deal with the menace to this village. She was only concealing what would have made her feel a fool.

And who am I to judge her, I who hold a secret deeper and darker than hers?

She had been wrong and must begin again. But the time had not been wasted, not quite, for now she knew that whereas it called to men in the voices of the ones they loved, it was not wholly a sexual enticement, as she had heard some mermaids were. It called to men in the voice of a loved woman; to at least one woman, it had called in the voice of her dead child. Was it, then, that it called to everyone in the voice of what they loved best?

This, then, would explain why the young girls were at least partly immune. Before the power of love came into a life, a young boy or girl loved his parents, yes, but because of the lack of experience, the parents were still seen as someone who could protect and care for the child, not to be selflessly cared for.

Love alone could create that selflessness.

Then— thought Lythande—it will be safe for me to go out against the monster. For there is, now, no one and nothing I love. Never have I loved any man. Such women as I have loved are separated from me by more than a lifetime, and I know enough to be wary if any should call to me in the voice of the heart's desire, then I am safe from it. For I love no one, and my heart, if indeed I still have a heart, desires nothing.

I will go and tell them that I am ready to rid the village of their curse.

They gave her their best boat, and would have given her one of the half-grown girls to row it out for her, but Lythande declined. How could she be sure the girl was too young to have loved, and thus become vulnerable to the call of the sea-creature? Also, for safety, Lythande left her lute on the shore, partly because she wished to show them that she trusted them with it, but mostly because she feared what the damp in the boat might do to the fragile and cherished instrument. More, if it came to a fight, she might step on it or break it in the boat's crowded conditions.

It was a clear and brilliant day, and Lythande, who was physically stronger than most men, sculled the boat briskly into the strong offshore wind. Small clouds scudded along the edge of the horizon, and each breaking wave folded over and collapsed with a soft, musical splashing. The noise of the breakers was strong in her ear, and it seemed to Lythande that under the sound of the waves, there was a faraway song; like the song of a shell held to the ear. For a few minutes she sang to herself in an undertone, listening to the sound of her own voice against the voice of the sea's breaking; an illusion, she knew, but one she found pleasurable. She thought, if only she had her lute, she would enjoy improvising harmonies to this curious blending. The words she sang against the waves were nonsense syllables, but they seemed to take on an obscure and magical meaning as she sang.

She was never sure, afterward, how long this lasted.

After a time, though she believed at first that it was simply another pleasant illusion like the shell held to the ear, she heard a soft voice inserting itself into the harmonies she was creating with the wave-song and her own voice; somewhere there was a third voice, wordless and incredibly sweet. Lythande went on singing, but something inside her pricked up its ears—or was it the tingling of the Blue Star that sensed the working of magic somewhere close to her?

The song, then, of the mermaid. Sweet as it was, there were no words. *As I thought, then. the creature works upon the heart's desire. I am desireless, therefore immune to the call. It cannot harm me.*

She raised her eyes. For a moment she saw only the great mass of rocks of which they had warned her, and against its mass a dark and featureless shadow. As she looked at the shadow, the Blue Star on her brow tingling, she willed to see more clearly. Then she saw—

What was it? Mermaid, they had said. Creature. Could they possibly call it evil?

In form, it was no more than a young girl, naked but for a necklace of small, rare, glimmering shells; the shells that had a crease running down the center, so that they looked like a woman's private parts. Her hair was dark, with the glisten of water on the smooth globes of bladder wrack lying on the sand at high tide. The face was smooth and young, with regular features. And the eyes. . . .

Lythande could never remember anything about the eyes, though at the time she must have had some impression about the color. Perhaps they were that same color of the sea where it rolled and rippled smooth beyond the white breakers. She had no attention to spare for the eyes, for she was listening to the voice. Yet she knew she must be cautious; if she were vulnerable at all to this thing, it would be through the voice, she to whom music had been friend and lover and solace for more than a lifetime.

Now she was close enough to see. How like a young girl the mermaid looked, young and vulnerable, with a soft, childish mouth. One of the small teeth, teeth like irregular pearls, was chipped out of line, and it made her look very childish. A soft mouth. *A mouth too young for kissing*, Lythande thought, and wondered what she had meant by it.

Once I, even I was as young as that, Lythande thought, her mind straying among perilous ways of memory; a time—how many lifetimes ago?—when she had been a young girl already restless at the life of the women's quarters, dreaming of magic and adventure; a time when she had borne another name, a name she had vowed never to remember. But already, though she had not yet glimpsed the steep road that was to lead her at last to the Temple of the Blue Star and to the great renunciations that lay ahead of her as a Pilgrim-Adept, she knew her path did not lie among young girls like these—with soft, vulnerable mouths and soft, vulnerable dreams, lovers and husbands and babies clinging around their necks as the necklace of little female shells clung to the neck of the mermaid. Her world was already too wide to be narrowed so far.

Never vulnerable like that, so that this creature should call to me in the voice of a dead and beloved child. . . .

And as if in answer, suddenly there were words in the mermaid's song, and a voice Lythande had not remembered for a lifetime. She had forgotten his face and his name; but her memory was the memory of a trained minstrel, a musician's memory. A man, a name, a life might be forgotten; a song or a voice—no, never.

My princess and my beloved, forget these dreams of magic and adventure; together we will sing such songs of love that life need hold no more for either of us.

A swift glance at the rocks told her he sat there, the

face she had forgotten, in another moment she would remember his name. . . . *No! this was illusion; he was dead, he had been dead for more years than she could imagine.* . . . *Go away,* she said to the illusion. *You are dead, and I am not to be deceived that way, not yet.*

They had told her the vision could call in the voice of the dead. But it could not trick her, not that way; as the illusion vanished, Lythande sensed a little ripple of laughter, like the breaking of a tiny wave against the rocks where the mermaid sat. Her laugh was delicious. Was that illusion, too?

To a woman, then, it calls in the voice of a lover. But never had Lythande been vulnerable to that call. He had not been the only one; only the one to whom Lythande had come the closest to yielding. She had almost remembered his name; for a moment her mind lingered, floating, seeking a name, a name . . . then, deliberately, but almost with merriment turned her mind willfully away from the tensed fascination of the search.

She need not try to remember. That had been long, long ago, in a country so far from here that no living man within a ten-day's journey knew so much as the name of that country. So why remember? She knew the answer to that; this sea-creature, this mermaid, defended itself this way, reaching into her mind and memory, as it had reached into the mind and memory of the fishermen who sought to pass by it, losing them in a labyrinth of the past, of old loves, heart's desires. Lythande repressed a shudder, remembering the man seated by the fire, lost in his endless dream. How narrowly had she escaped that? And there would have been none to rescue her.

But a Pilgrim-Adept was not to be caught so simply. The creature was simple, using on her its only defense, forcing the mind and memory: and she had escaped. Desireless, Lythande was immune to that call of desire.

Young girl as she looked, that at least must be illusion, the mermaid was an ageless creature . . . like herself, Lythande thought.

For the creature had tried for a moment to show herself to Lythande in that illusory form of a past lover—no, he had never been Lythande's lover, but in the form of an old memory to trap her in the illusory country of heart's desire. But Lythande had never been vulnerable in that way to the heart's desire.

Never?

Never, creature of dreams. Not even when I was younger than you appear now to be.

But was this the mermaid's true form, or something like it? The momentary illusion vanished, the mermaid had returned to the semblance of the young girl, touchingly young; there must then be some truth to the appearance of the childish mouth, the eyes that were full of dreams, the vulnerable smile. The mermaiden was protecting itself in the best way it could, for certainly a sea-maiden so frail and defenseless, seeming so young and fair, would be at the mercy of the men of the fisherfolk, men who would see only a maiden to be preyed upon.

There were many such tales along these shores, still told around the hearthfires, of mermaids and of men who had loved them. Men who had taken them home as wives, bringing a free sea-maiden to live in the smoke of the hearthfire, to cook and spin, servant to man, a mockery of the free creature she should be. Often the story ended when the imprisoned sea-maiden found her dress of fish scales and seaweed and plunged into the sea again to find her freedom, leaving the fisherman to mourn his lost love.

Or the loss of his prisoner . . . ? In this case, Lythande's sympathy was with the mermaid.

Yet she had pledged herself to free the village of this danger. And surely it was a danger, if only of a beauty more terrible than they dared to know and understand, a fragile and fleeting beauty like the echo of a song, or like the sea wrack in the ebb and flow of the tide. For with illusion gone, the mermaid was only this frail-looking creature, ageless but with the eternal illusion of youth. *We are alike*, thought Lythande; *in that sense, we are sisters, but I am freer than she is.*

She was beginning to be aware of the mermaid's song again, and knew it was dangerous to listen. She sang to herself to try and block it away from her awareness. But she felt an enormous sympathy for the creature, here at the mercy of a crude fishing village, protecting herself as best she could, and cursed for her beauty.

She looked so like one of the young girls Lythande had known in that faraway country. They had made music together on the harp and the lute and the bamboo flute. Her name had been . . . Lythande found the name in her mind without a search . . . her name had been Riella, and it seemed to her that the mermaid sang in Riella's voice.

Not of love, for already at that time Lythande had known that such love as the other young girls dreamed of was not for her, but there had been an awareness between them. Never acknowledged; but Lythande had begun to know that even for a woman who cared nothing for man's desire, life need not be altogether empty. There were dreams and desires that had nothing to do with those simpler dreams of the other women, dreams of husband or lover or child.

And then Lythande heard the first syllable of a name, a name she had vowed to forget, a name once her own, a name she would not—no. No. A name she *could* not remember. Sweating, the Blue Star blazing with her anger, she looked at the rocks. Riella's form there wavered and was gone.

Again the creature had attempted to call to her in the

voice of the dead. There was no longer the least trace of amusement in Lythande's mind. Once again she had almost fatally underestimated the sea-creature because it looked so young and childlike, because it reminded her of Riella and of the other young girls she had loved in a world, and a life, long lost to her. She would not be caught that way again. Lythande gripped the hilt of the left-hand dagger, warder against magic, as she felt the boat beneath her scrape on the rocks.

She stepped out onto the surface of the small, rocky holt, wrinkling her nose at the rankness of dead fish and sea wrack left by the tide, a carrion smell—how could so young and fair a creature live in this stench?

The mermaid said in the small voice of a very young girl, "Did they send you to kill me, Lythande?"

Lythande gripped the handle of her left-hand dagger. She had no wish to engage in conversation with the creature; she had vowed to rid the village of this thing, and rid it she would. Yet even as she raised the dagger, she hesitated.

The mermaid, still in that timid little-girl voice, said, "I admit that I tried to ensnare you. You must be a great magician to escape from me so easily. My poor magic could not hold you at all!"

Lythande said, "I am an Adept of the Blue Star."

"I do not know of the Blue Star. Yet I can feel its power," said the sea-maiden. "Your magic is very great—"

"And yours is to flatter me," said Lythande carefully, and the mermaid gave a delicious, childish giggle.

"You see what I mean? I can't deceive you at all, can I, Lythande? But why did you come here to kill me, when I can't harm you in any way? And why are you holding that horrible dagger?"

Why, indeed? Lythande wondered, and slid it back into its sheath. This creature could not hurt her. Yet surely she had come here for some reason, and she groped for it. She said at last, "The folk of the village cannot fish for their livelihood and they will all starve. Why do you want to do this?"

"Why not?" asked the mermaid innocently.

That made Lythande think a little. She had listened to the villagers and their story; she had not stopped to consider the mermaid's side of the business. The sea did not belong, after all, to the fishermen; it belonged to the fish and to the creatures of the sea—birds and fish and waves, shellfish of the deep, eels and dolphins and great whales who had nothing to do with humankind at all—and, yes, to the mermaids and stranger sea creatures as well.

Yet Lythande was vowed to fight on the side of Law against Chaos till the Final Battle should come. And if humankind could not get its living as did the other creatures inhabiting the world, what would become of them?

"Why should they live by killing the fish in the sea?" the mermaid asked. "Have they any better right to survive than the fish?"

That was a question not all that easily answered. Yet as she glanced about the shore, smelling the rankness of the tide, Lythande knew what she should say next.

"You live upon the fish, do you not? There are enough fish in the sea for all the people of the shore, as well as for your kind. And if the fishermen do not kill the fish and eat them, the fish will only be eaten by other fish. Why not leave the fisherfolk in peace, to take what they need?"

"Well, perhaps I will," said the mermaid, giggling again, so that Lythande was again astonished; what a childish creature this was, after all. Did she even know what harm she had done?

"Perhaps I can find another place to go. Perhaps you could help me?" She raised her large and luminous eyes to Lythande. "I heard you singing. Do you know any new songs, magician? And will you sing them to me?"

Why, the poor creature is like a child; lonely, and even restless, all alone here on the rocks. How like a child she was when she said it. . . . Do you know any new songs? Lythande wished for a moment that she had not left her lute on the shore.

"Do you want me to sing to you?"

"I heard you singing, and it sounded so sweet across the water, my sister. I am sure we have songs and magics to teach one another."

Lythande said gently, "I will sing to you."

First she sang, letting her mind stray in the mists of time past, a song she had sung to the sound of the bamboo reed-flute, more than a lifetime ago. It seemed for a moment that Riella sat beside her on the rocks. Only an illusion created by the mermaid, of course. But surely a harmless one! Still, perhaps it was not wise to allow the illusion to continue; Lythande wrenched her mind from the past, and sang the sea-song that she had composed yesterday, as she walked along the shore to this village.

"Beautiful, my sister," murmured the mermaid, smiling so that the charming little gap in her pearly teeth showed. "Such a musician I have never heard. Do all the people who live on land sing so beautifully?"

"Very few of them," said Lythande. "Not for many years have I heard such sweet music as yours."

"Sing again, Sister," said the mermaid, smiling. "Come close to me and sing again. And then I shall sing to you."

"And you will come away and let the fisherfolk live in peace?" Lythande asked craftily.

"Of course I will, if you ask it, Sister," the mermaid said. It had been so many years since anyone had spoken to Lythande, woman to woman, without fear. It was death for her to allow any man to know that she was a woman; and the women in whom she dared confide were so few. It was soothing balm to her heart.

Why, after all, should she go back to the land again? Why not stay here in the quiet peace of the sea, sharing songs and magical spells with her sister, the mermaid? There were greater magics here than she had ever known, yes, and sweeter music, too.

She sang, hearing her voice ring out across the water. The mermaid sat quietly, her head a little turned to the side, listening as if in utter enchantment, and Lythande felt she had never sung so sweetly. For a moment she wondered if, hearing her song echoing from the ocean, any passerby would think that he heard the true song of a mermaid. For surely she, too, Lythande, could enchant with her song. Should she stay here, cease denying her true sex, where she could be at once woman and magician and minstrel? She, too, could sit on the rocks, enchanting with her music, letting time and sea roll over her, forgetting the struggle of her life as Pilgrim-Adept, being only what she was in herself. She was a great magician; she could feel the very tingle of her magic in the Blue Star on her brow, crackling lightings. . . .

"Come nearer to me, Sister, that I can hear the sweetness of your song," murmured the mermaid. "Truly, it is you who have enchanted me, magician—"

As if in a dream, Lythande took a step farther up the beach. A shell crunched hard under her foot. Or was it a bone? She never knew what made her look down, to see that her foot had turned on a skull.

Lythande felt ice run through her veins. This was no illusion. Quickly she gripped the left-hand dagger and whispered a spell that would clear the air of illusion and void all magic, including her own. She should have done it before.

The mermaid gave a despairing cry. "No, no, my sister, my sister musician, stay with me . . . now you will hate me too. . . ." But even as the words died out, like the fading sound of a lute's broken string, the mermaid was gone, and Lythande stared in horror at what sat on the rocks.

It was not remotely human in form. It was three or four times the size of the largest sea-beast she had ever seen, crouching huge and greenish, the color of sea-weed and sea wrack. All she could see of the head was rows and rows of teeth, huge teeth gaping before her. And the true horror was that one of the great fangs had a chip knocked from it.

Little pearly teeth with a little chip. . . .

Gods of Chaos! I almost walked down that thing's throat!"

Retching, Lythande swung the dagger; almost at once she whipped out the right-hand knife, which was effective against material menace; struck toward the heart of the thing. An eerie howl went up as blackish green blood, smelling of sea wrack and carrion, spurted over the Pilgrim-Adept. Lythande, shuddering, struck again and again until the cries were silent. She looked down at the dead thing, the rows of teeth, the tentacles and squirming suckers. Before her eyes was a childish face, a voice whose memory would never leave her.

And I called the thing "Sister". . . .

It had even been easy to kill. It had no weapons, no defenses except its song and its illusions. Lythande had been so proud of her ability to escape the illusions, proud that she was not vulnerable to the call of lover or of memory.

Yet it had called, after all, to the heart's desire . . . for music. For magic. For the illusion of a moment where something that never existed, never could exist, had called her "Sister," speaking to a womanhood re-nounced forever. She looked at the dead thing on the beach, and knew she was weeping as she had not wept for three ordinary lifetimes.

The mermaid had called her "Sister," and she had killed it.

She told herself, even as her body shook with sobs, that her tears were mad. If she had not killed it, she would have died in those great and dreadful rows of teeth, and it would not have been a pleasant death.

Yet for that illusion, I would have been ready to die. . . .

She was crying for something that had never existed.

She was crying *because* it had never existed, and because, for her, it would never exist, not even in memory. After a long time, she stooped down and, from the mass that was melting like decaying seaweed, she picked up a fang with a chip out of it. She stood looking at it for a long time. Then, her lips tightening grimly, she flung it out to sea, and clambered back into the boat. As she sculled back to shore, she found she was listening to the sound in the waves, like a shell held to the ear. And when she realized that she was listening again for another voice, she began to sing the rowdiest drinking song she knew.

Introduction to The
Wandering Lute

Once, not too many years ago, Robert Adams and Andre Norton got together to do an anthology about a magical world they called The Fair at Ithkar. *The theory seemed to me not unlike Thieves World, and so I created a Lythande story just for Ithkar—but Adams & Norton rejected the story because, forsooth, Lythande was "associated with Thieves World"—even though I had withdrawn from Thieves World after the first volume, and for all intents and purposes withdrawn Lythande too.*

The character—and her salamander—who introduces Lythande to this story is from the first Ithkar volume, in a story called "Cold Spell," by Elisabeth Waters, and her name and attributes are used by permission.

Lythande, as we learned in "Somebody Else's Magic," is not as good at unbinding-spells as she is at other kinds of magic. Maybe she needs more detachment?

THE WANDERING LUTE

In the glass bowl the salamander hissed blue fire. Lythande bent over the bowl, extending numbed white fingers; the morning chill at Old Gandrin nipped nose and fingers. At a warning hiss from the bowl, the magician stepped back, looking questioningly at the young candlemaker.

"Does he bite?"

"*Her* name is Alnath," Eirthe said. "She usually doesn't need to."

"Allow me to beg her pardon," Lythande said. "Essence of Fire, may I borrow your warmth?"

Fire streamed upward; Lythande bent gratefully over the bowl; Alnath coiled within, a miniature dragon, flames streaming upward from the fire elemental's substance.

"She likes you," said Eirthe. "When Prince Tashgan came here, she hissed at him and the silk covering of his lute began to smolder; he went out faster than he came in."

The hood of the mage-robe was thrown back, and by the light of the fire streaming upward, the Blue Star could be clearly seen on Lythande's high, narrow forehead.

"Tashgan? I know him only by reputation," Lythande said, "Will you enjoy living in a palace, Eirthe? Will

Her Brilliance adapt kindly to a bowl of jewels and diamonds?"

Eirthe giggled, for Prince Tashgan was known throughout Old Gandrin as a womanizer. "He was looking for *you*, Lythande. How do *you* feel about life in a palace?"

"For me? What need could the prince have of a mercenary-magician?

"Perhaps," Eirthe said, "he wishes to take music lessons." She nodded at the lute slung across the magician's shoulder. "I have heard Tashgan play at three summer-festivals, and he plays not half so well as you. The lute is not his best instrument." She giggled, with a suggestive roll of her eyes.

Lythande enjoyed a raunchy joke as well as anyone; the magician's mellow chuckle filled the room. "It is frequently so with those who take up the lute for pleasure. As for those who wear a crown, who can tell them their playing could be bettered, whatever the instrument? Flattery ruins much talent."

"Tashgan wears no crown, nor ever will," Eirthe said. "The High-lord of Tschardain had three sons— know you not the story?"

"Is he the third son of Tschardain? I had heard he was in exile," Lythande said, "but I have only passed briefly through Tschardain."

"The old King had a stroke, seven years ago; while he lingered, paralyzed and unable to speak, his older son assumed the power; his second son became his brother's adviser and marshal of his armies. Tashgan was, they said, weak, absentminded, and a womanizer; I daresay it was only that the young Lord wanted few claimants to challenge his position."

She bent to rummage briefly under her worktable and pulled out a silk-wrapped bundle. "Here are the candles you ordered. Remember that they're spelled not to burn unless they're in one of Cadmon's glasses—

though you can probably find a counter-spell easily enough."

"One of Cadmon's glasses I have already." Lythande took the candles, but lingered, close to the salamander's heat. Eirthe glanced at the lute on an embroidered leather band across Lythande's shoulder.

She asked, "Were you magician first or minstrel? It seems a strange combination."

"I was musician from childhood," Lythande said, "and when I took up magic I deserted my first love. But the lute is a forgiving mistress." The magician bestowed the packet of candles in one of the concealed pockets in the dark mage-robe, bowed in courtly fashion to Eirthe, and murmured to the salamander:

"Essence of Fire, my thanks for your warmth."

A streamer of cobalt fire surged upward out of the bowl; leaped to Lythande's outstretched hand. Lythande did not flinch as the salamander perched for a moment on the slender wrist, though it left a red mark. Eirthe whistled faintly in surprise.

"She *never* does that to strangers!" The girl glanced at the callus on her own wrist where the salamander habitually rested.

"She is like a were-dragon made small in appearance." Hearing that, Alnath hissed again, stretching out her long fiery neck, and as Eirthe watched in astonishment, Lythande stroked the flaming scales. "Perhaps she knows we are kindred spirits; she is not the first fire-elemental I have known," said the magician. "A good part of the business of an adept is playing with fire. There, fair Essence of the purest of all Elements, go to your true Mistress." Lythande raised an arm in a graceful gesture; streamers of fire seared the air as Alnath flashed toward Eirthe's wrist and came to rest there. "Should Tashgan seek me again, tell him I lodge at the Blue Dragon."

But Lythande saw Prince Tashgan before Eirthe did.

The Adept was seated in the common-room of the Blue Dragon, a pot of ale untouched on the table—for one of the many vows fencing the powers of an Adept of the Blue Star was that they might never be seen to eat or drink before strangers. Nevertheless, the pot of ale was the magician's unquestioned passport to sit among the townsfolk and listen to whatever might be happening among them.

"Will you favor us with a song, High-born?" asked the innkeeper. The Pilgrim Adept uncovered the lute and began to play a ballad of the countryside. As the soft notes stole into the room, the drinkers fell silent, listening to the mellow sound of Lythande's voice, soft, neutral, and sexless.

As the last note died away, a tall, richly clad man, standing at the back of the room, came forward.

"Master Minstrel, I salute you," he said. "I had heard from afar of your skill with the lute and came here a little before my proper season, to hear you play and—other things. You lodge here? Might I buy you a drink in privacy, Magician? I have heard that your services are for hire; I have need of them."

"I am a mercenary magician," Lythande said, "I give no instruction on the lute."

"Nevertheless let us discuss in private whether it would be worth your while to give me lessons," said the man. "I am Tashgan, son of Idriash of Tschardain."

Some of the watchers in the room had the uneasy sense that the Blue Star on Lythande's brow shrugged itself and focused to look at Tashgan. Lythande said, "So be it. Before the final battle of Law and Chaos many unusual things may come to pass, and for all I know this may well be one of them."

"Will it please you to speak in your chamber, or in mine?"

"Let it be in yours," said Lythande. The items with which any person chose to surround himself could often give the magician an important clue to character; if this prince was to be a client—for the services of magician or minstrel—such clues might prove valuable.

Tashgan had commanded the most luxurious chamber at the Blue Dragon; its original character had almost been obscured by silken hangings and cushions. Elegant small musical instruments—a tambour adorned with silk ribbons, a *borain*, a pair of serpent rattles, and a gilded sistrum—hung on the wall. As the door opened, a slight girl in a chemise, arms bare and hair loosened and falling in a disheveled cloud over her bared young breasts, rolled from the bed and scurried away behind the hangings. Lythande's face drew together into a frown of distaste.

"Charming, is she not?" asked Tashgan negligently. "A local maiden; I want no permanent ties in this town. Indeed, it is of ties of this sort—undesired ties, and involuntary—that I would speak. Lissini, bring wine from my private stock."

The girl poured wine; Lythande formally lifted the cup without, however, tasting it, and bowed to Tashgan.

"How may I serve your Excellency?"

"It is a long story." Tashgan unfastened the strap of the lute across his shoulder. "What think you of this lute?" His weak, watery blue eyes followed the instrument as he undid the case and displayed it.

Lythande studied the instrument briefly; smaller than Lythande's own lute, exquisitely crafted of fruitwood inlaid with mother-of-pearl.

"I remember not one so fairly crafted since I came into this country."

"Appearances are deceiving," said Tashgan. "This instrument, magician, is at once my curse and my blessing."

"May I?" Lythande put forth a slender hand and touched the delicately fretted neck. The blue star blazed suddenly, and Lythande frowned.

"This lute is under enchantment. This is the long story of which you spoke. The night is young; long live the night. Tell on."

Tashgan signaled to the girl to pour more of the fragrant wine. "Know you what it is to be a third son in a royal line, magician?"

Lythande only smiled enigmatically. Royal birth in a faraway country was a claim made by many rogues and wandering magicians; Lythande never made such a claim. "It is your story, Highness."

"A second son insures the succession and may serve as counselor to the first, but after my elder brothers were safely past childhood ailments, my royal parents knew not what to do with this inconvenient third prince. Had I been a daughter, they could have schooled me for a good marriage, but a third son? Only a possible pretender for factions or a rebel against his brethren. So they cast about to give my life some semblance of purpose, and had me instructed in music."

"There are worse fates," murmured Lythande. "In many lands a minstrel holds honor higher than a prince."

"It is not so in Tschardain," Tashgan gestured for more wine. Lythande lifted the glass and inhaled the delicate bouquet of the wine, without, however, touching or tasting it.

Tashgan went on: "It is not so in Tschardain; therefore I came to Old Gandrin where a minstrel has his own honor. For many years my life has assumed its regular character; guested in the spring on the borders of Tschardain, then northward into Old Gandrin for fair time, and northerly through the summer, to North-wander. Then at the summer's height I turn southward again, through Old Gandrin, retracing my steps, guested and welcomed as a minstrel in castle and manor and at last, for Yule-feast, to Tschardain. There I am welcomed for a hand-span of days by father and brothers. So it has been for twelve years, since I was only a little

154

lad; it changed nothing when my father the High-lord was laid low by a stroke and my brother Rasthan assumed his powers. It seemed that it would go on for a lifetime, till I grew too old to threaten my brother's throne or the throne of his sons."

"It sounds not too ill a life," Lythande observed neutrally.

"Not so indeed," said Tashgan, with a lascivious roll of his eyes. "Here in Old Gandrin, a musician is highly favored, as indeed you did say, and when I am guested in castle and manor—well, I suppose ladies tire of queendom, and a musician who can give them lessons on his instrument—" another suggestive wink and roll of his eyes—"Well, master magician and minstrel, you too bear a lute, I dare say you too could tell tales, if you would, of how women give hospitality to a minstrel."

The blue star on Lythande's brow furrowed again with hidden distaste; the magician said only, "Is there, then, some reason why it cannot go on as you willed it?"

"Say rather as my father and my brother Rasthan willed it," said Tashgan. "They took no chances that I would choose to stay more than my appointed hand of days every year in Tschardain. My father's court magician made for me this lute, and set it about with enchantments, so that my wanderings with the lute would bring me never, for instance, into the country of any noble who might be plotting against Tschardain's throne, or allow me to linger long enough anywhere to make alliances. Day by day, season by season and year by year, my rounds are as duly set as the rising of sun and moon or the procession of solstice following equinox and back again to solstice; a week here, ten days there, three days in this place and a fortnight in that. . . . I cannot tarry in any place beyond my allotted span, for the compulsion in the lute sets me to wandering again."

"And so?"

"And so for many years it was not unwelcome," said Tashgan, "among other things—well, it freed me from the fear that any of those women—" yet once more the suggestive roll of the watery eyes—"would entrap me for more than a little—dalliance. But three moons ago, a messenger from Tschardain reached me. A were-dragon came from the south, and both my brothers perished in his flame. So that I, with no training or inclination to rule, am suddenly the High-lord's only heir—and my father may die at any moment, or linger for another hand of years as a paralyzed figurehead. My father's vizier has bidden me return at once to Tschardain and claim my heritage."

Tashgan slammed his hand with rage on the table, making the lute rattle and the ribbons tremble.

"And I cannot! The enchantment of this accursed lute compels me northward, even to Northwander! If I set out southward to my kingdom, I am racked with queasiness and pain, I can stomach neither food nor wine, nor can I even look on a woman with pleasure till I have set off in the appointed direction for the time of year. I can go nowhere save upon my appointed rounds, for this damnable enchanted lute compels me!"

Lythande's tall narrow body shook with laughter, and Tashgan's ill-natured scowl fixed itself upon the Adept.

"You laugh at my curse, magician?"

"Everything under the sun has a funny side," Lythande said, and struggled to control unseemly laughter. "Bethink yourself, my prince; had this happened to another, would you not find it funny?"

Tashgan's eyes narrowed to slits, but finally he grinned weakly and said, "I fear so. But if it was your predicament, magician, would you laugh?"

Lythande laughed again. "I fear not, highness. And that says much about what folk call amusement. So now tell me; how can I serve you?"

"Is it not obvious from my tale? Take this enchantment off the lute!" Lythande was silent, and Tashgan leaned forward in his chair, demanding aggressively, "*Can* you take off such a binding-spell, magician?"

"Perhaps I can, if the price is right, highness," Lythande said slowly. "But why put yourself at the mercy of a stranger, a mercenary magician? Surely the court magician who obliged your father would be more than happy to ingratiate himself with his new monarch by freeing you from this singularly inconvenient spell."

"Surely," Tashgan said glumly, "but there is one great difficulty in that. The wizard whom I have to *thank*—" he weighted the word with another of his ill-natured scowls—"was Ellifanwy."

"Oh." Ellifanwy's messy end in the lair of a were-dragon was known from Northwander to the Southron Sea. Lythande said, "I knew Ellifanwy of old. I told Ellifanwy that she could not handle any were-dragon and proffered my services for a small fee, but she begrudged the gold. And now she lies charred in the caves of the dragonswamp."

"I am not surprised," said Tashgan, "I am sure you will agree with me that women have no business with the High Magic. Small magics, yes, like love charms— and I must say Ellifanwy's love charms were superb," he added, preening himself like a peacock. "But for dragons and such, I think you will agree with me, seeing Ellifanwy's fate, that female wizards should mind their cauldrons and spin love charms."

Lythande did not answer, leaning forward to take up the lute. Again the lightning from the Blue Star on the magician's brow glared in the room.

"So you would have me undo Ellifanwy's spell? That should present no trouble," Lythande said, caressing the lute; slender fingers strayed for a moment over the strings. "What fee will you give?"

"Ah, there lies the problem," said Tashgan, "I have but little gold; the messenger who brought news of the deaths of my brothers expected to be richly rewarded, and I have lived mostly as guest for these many years; given all I could desire, rich food and rich clothing, wine and women, but little in the way of ready money. But if you will unbind this spell, I shall reward you well when you come to Tschardain—"

Lythande smiled enigmatically. "I am well acquainted with the gratitude of kings, highness." Tashgan would hardly wish Lythande's presence in Tschardain, able to tell his future subjects of their new high-lord's former ridiculous plight. "Some other way must be found."

The magician's hands lingered for a moment on Tashgan's lute. "I have taken a fancy to your lute, highness, binding-spell and all. I have long desired to travel to Northwander. But I do not know the way. Do I assume correctly that this lute will keep its bearer on the direct path?"

Tashgan said sourly, "No native guide could do better. Should I ever stray from the path, as I have done once or twice after too much hospitality, the lute would bring me back within a few dozen paces. It is like being a child again, clinging to a nanny's hand!"

"It sounds intriguing," Lythande murmured. "I lost the only lute which meant anything to me in—shall we say, a magical encounter—and had little ready money with which to replace it; but the one I bear now has a fine tone. Exchange lutes with me, noble Tashgan, and I shall travel to Northwander, and deal with the unbinding-spell at my leisure."

Tashgan hesitated only a moment. "Done," he said, and picked up Lythande's plain lute, leaving the magician to put the elaborate inlaid one, with its interlaced designs of mother-of-pearl, into its leather case. "I leave for Tschardain at dawn. May I offer you another cup of wine, magician?"

Lythande politely declined, and bowed to Tashgan for leave to withdraw.

"So you will travel to Northwander on my circuit of castle and court? They will welcome you, magician. Good fortune." Tashgan chuckled, with a suggestive roll of his eyes. "There are many ladies bored with ladylike accomplishments. Give my love to Beauty."

"Beauty?"

"You will meet her—and many others—if you follow my lute very far," said Tashgan, licking his lips. "I almost envy you, Lythande; you have not had time to become wearied of their—friendly devices. But," he added, this time with a frank leer, "no doubt there are many new adventures awaiting me in my father's courts."

"I wish you joy of them," said Lythande, bowing gravely. On the stairs, the magician resolved that when the sun rose, Old Gandrin would be far behind. Tashgan might not wish anyone surviving who could tell this tale. True, he had seemed grateful; but Lythande had reason to distrust the gratitude of kings.

Northward from Old Gandrin the hills were steeper; on some of them snow was still lying. Lightly burdened only with pack and lute, Lythande traveled with a long athletic stride that ate up the miles.

Three days north of Old Gandrin, the road forked, and Lythande surveyed the paths ahead. One led down toward a city, dominated by a tall castle; the other led upward, farther into the hills. After a moment's thought, Lythande took the upward road.

For a time, nothing happened. The brilliant sunlight had given Lythande a headache; the magician's eyes narrowed against the sun. After a few more paces, the headache was joined with a roiling queasiness. Lythande scowled, wondering if the bread eaten for breakfast had become tainted. But under the hood of the mage-robe Lythande could feel the burning prickle of the Blue Star.

Magic. Strong magic. . . .

The lute. The enchantment. Of course. Experimentally, Lythande took a few more steps up the forest road. The sickness increased, and the pressure of the Blue Star was painful.

"So," Lythande said aloud, and turned back, retracing the path; then took the road leading down to city and castle. At once the headache diminished, the queasiness subsided, even the air seemed to smell fresher. The Blue Star was again quiescent on Lythande's brow.

"So." Tashgan had not exaggerated the enchantment of the lute. Shrugging slightly, Lythande took the road down into the city, feeling an enthusiasm and haste which was quite alien to the magician's own attitude. Magic. But Lythande was no stranger to magic.

Lythande could almost feel the lute's pleasure like a gigantic cat purring. Then the spell was silent and Lythande was standing in the courtyard of the castle.

A liveried servant bowed.

"I welcome you, stranger. May I serve you?"

With a mental shrug, Lythande resolved to test Tashgan's truth. "I bear the lute of Prince Tashgan of Tschardain, who has returned to his own country. I come in the peace of a minstrel."

The servant bowed, if possible, even lower. "In the name of my lady, I welcome you. All minstrels are welcome here, and my lady is a lover of music. Come with me, minstrel, rest and refresh yourself, and I will conduct you to my lady."

So Tashgan had not exaggerated the tales of hospitality. Lythande was conducted to a guest chamber, brought elegant food and wine and offered a luxurious bath in a marble bathroom with water spouting from golden spigots in the shape of dolphins. Guest-garments of silk and velvet were readied by servants.

Alone, unspied-upon (Adepts of the Blue Star have ways of knowing whether they are being watched), Lythande ate modestly of the fine foods, and drank a

little of the wine, but resumed the dark mage-robe.
Waiting in the elaborate guest quarters, Lythande took
the elegant lute from its case, tuned it carefully, and
awaited the summons.

It was not long in coming. A pair of deferential
servants led Lythande along paneled corridors and into a
great salon, where a handsome, richly dressed lady
awaited the musician. She extended a slender, per-
fumed hand.

"Any friend and colleague of Tashgan is my friend as
well, minstrel; I bid you a hundred thousand welcomes.
Come here." She patted the side of her elegant seat as
if—Lythande thought—she was inviting one of the little
lapdogs in the salon to jump up into her lap. Lythande
went closer and bowed, but an Adept of the Blue Star
knelt to no mortal.

"Lady, my lute and I are here to serve you."

"I am *so* fond of music," she murmured gushingly,
and patted Lythande's hand. "Play for me, my dear."

With a mental shrug, Lythande decided that rumor
had not exaggerated Tashgan's accomplishments. Lythande
unslung the lute and sang a number of simple ballads,
judging accurately the level of the lady's taste. She
listened with a faintly bored smile, tapping her fingers
restlessly and not even, Lythande noticed, in time to
the music. Well, it was shelter for the night.

"Tashgan, dear fellow, always gave me lessons on the
lute and on the clavier," the lady murmured. "I understand that you have come to—take over his lessons?
How kind of the dear man; I am so bored here, and so
alone, I spend all my time with my music. But now the
palace servants will be escorting us to dinner, and my
husband, the Count, is so jealous. Please do play for
dinner in the Great Hall? And you *will* stay for a few
days, will you not, to give me—private lessons?"

Lythande said, of course, that such talents as the
gods had given were all entirely at the lady's service.

At dinner in the great hall, the Count, a huge, bluff, and not unkindly man whom Lythande liked at once, called in all his servants, nobles, housefolk, and even allowed the waiters and cooks to come in from the kitchens that they might hear the minstrel's music. Lythande was glad to play a succession of ballads and songs, to give the news of Tashgan's succession to the High-lordship of Tschardain, and to tell whatever news had been making the rounds of the fair at Old Gandrin.

The pretty Countess listened to music and news with the same bored expression. But when the party was about to break up for the night, she murmured to Lythande, "Tomorrow the Count will hunt. Perhaps then we could meet for my—lessons?" Lythande noted that the Countess's hands were literally trembling with eagerness.

I should have known, Lythande thought. *With Tashgan's reputation as a womanizer, with all that he said about Ellifanwy's love charms. Now what am I to do?* Lythande stared morosely at the enchanted lute, cursing Tashgan and the curiosity which had impelled the exchange of instruments.

To attempt an unbinding-spell, even if it destroyed the lute? Lythande was not quite ready for that yet. It was a beautiful lute. And no matter how lascivious the Countess, however eager for illicit adventure, there would be, there always were, servants and witnesses.

Who ever thought I would think of a fat chamberlain and a couple of inept ladies-in-waiting as chaperones?

All the next morning, and all the three mornings after that, Lythande, under the eyes of the servants, deferentially placed and replaced the Countess's fingers on the strings of her lute, the keyboard of her clavier, murmuring of new songs, of chords and harmonies, of fingering and practice. By the end of the third morning the Countess was huffy and sniffing, and had ceased trying to touch Lythande's hand surreptitiously on the keyboard.

"On the morrow, Lady, I must depart," Lythande said. That morning the curious pull of the enchanted lute had begun to make itself felt, and the magician knew it would grow stronger with every hour.

"Courtesy bids us welcome the guest who comes and speed the guest who departs," said the Countess, and for a final time she sought Lythande's slender fingers.

"Perhaps next year—when we know one another better, dear boy," she murmured.

"It shall be my pleasure to know my lady better," Lythande lied, bowing. A random thought crossed the magician's mind.

"Are you—*Beauty?* If so, Tashgan bade me give you his love."

The Countess simpered. "Well, he called me his lovely spirit of music," she said coyly, "but who knows, he might have called me *Beauty* when he spoke of me to someone else The dear, dear boy. Is it true he will not be coming back?"

"I fear not, madam. His duties are many in his own country now."

The Countess sighed.

"What a loss to music! I tell you, Lythande, he was a minstrel of minstrels; I shall never know his like again," she said, and posed sentimentally with her hand over her heart.

"Very likely not," said Lythande, bowing to take leave.

Lythande moved northward, drawn by curiosity and by the spell of the wandering lute. It was a new experience for the Pilgrim Adept, to travel without knowing where each day would lead, and the magician savored it with curiosity unbounded. Lythande had attempted a few simple unbinding-spells, so far without success; all the simpler spells had proved insufficient, and unlike Tashgan, Lythande did not make the mistake of under-estimating Ellifanwy's spells, when the wizardess had been operating within the sphere of her own competence.

Ellifanwy might not have been able to cope with a were-dragon. But for binding-spells and enchantments, she had had no peer. Every night Lythande attempted a new unbinding-spell, at the conclusion of which the lute remained enchanted and Lythande was racking a brain which had lived three ordinary lifetimes for yet more unbinding spells.

Summer lay on the land north of Old Gandrin, and every night Lythande was welcomed to inn or castle, manor or Great House, where news and songs were welcomed with eagerness. Now and again a wistful matron or pretty housewife, innkeeper's daughter or merchant's consort, would linger at Lythande's side, with a lovesick word or two about Tashgan; Lythande's apparent absorption in the music, the cool sexless voice and the elegantly correct manner, left them sighing, but not offended. Once, indeed, in an isolated farm-stead where Lythande had sung ancient rowdy ballads, when the farmer snored the farmer's wife crept to the straw pallet and murmured, but Lythande pretended to be asleep and the farm wife crept away without a touch.

But when she had crawled back to the farmer's side, Lythande lay awake, troubled. Damn Tashgan and his womanizing. He might have spread joy among neglected wives and lonely ladies from Tschardain to Northwander, for so many years that even his successor was welcomed and cosseted and seduced; and for a time it had been amusing. But Lythande was experienced enough to know that this playing with fire could not continue.

And it was playing with fire, indeed. Lythande knew something of fire, and fire elementals—the Pilgrim Ad-ept was familiar with fire, even the fire of were-dragons. But no were-dragon alive could rival the rage of a

scorned woman, and sooner or later one of them would
turn nasty. The Countess had simply believed Lythande
was shy, and put her hopes in another year. (By then,
Lythande thought, surely one of the spells would prove
adequate to take off the enchantment.) It had been a
close call with the farmer's wife; suppose she had tried
fumbling about the mage-robe when Lythande slept?

That would have been disaster.

For, like all adepts of the Blue Star, Lythande cherished a secret which might never be known; and on it
all the magician's power depended. And Lythande's
secret was doubly dangerous; Lythande was a woman,
the only woman ever to bear the Blue Star.

In disguise, she had penetrated the secret Temple
and the Place Which Is Not, and not till she already
bore the blue star between her brows had she been
exposed and discovered.

Too late, then, for death, for she was sacrosanct till
the final battle of Law and Chaos at the end of the
world. Too late to be sent forth from them. But not too
late for the curse.

Be then what you have chosen to seem, so had run
the doom. *Until the end of the world, on that day when
you are proclaimed a woman before any man but myself*
. . . thus had spoken the ancient Master of the Star . . .
*on that day you are stripped of power and on that day
you may be slain.*

Traveling northward at the lute's call, Lythande sat
on the side of a hill, the lute stripped of its wrappings
and laid before her. If for a time this had been amusing,
it was so no longer. Besides, if she was not free of the
spell by Yule, she would be guesting in Tashgan's own
castle—and that she had no wish to do.

Now it was time for strong remedies. At first it had
been mildly amusing to work her way through the
simpler spells, beginning with, "Be ye unbound and

opened, let no magic remain save what I myself place there," which was the sort of spell a farmer's wife might speak over her churn if she fancied some neighboring herb-wife or witch had soured her milk, and working her way up through degrees of complexity to the ancient charm beginning, "Asmigo, Asmago . . ." which can be spoken only in the dark of the moon in the presence of three gray mice.

None of them had worked. It was evident that, knowing of Ellifanwy's incompetence with her last were-dragon, and her success with love-charms (to Lythande, the last refuge of incompetent sorcery) Lythande had seriously underestimated Ellifanwy's spell.

And so it was time to bypass all the simpler lore of spells to bind and unbind, and proceed to the strongest unbinding-spell she knew. Unbinding-spells were not Lythande's specialty—she seldom had cause to use them. But once she had inadvertently taken upon herself a sword spell-bonded to the shrine of Larith, and had never managed to unbind it, but had been forced to make a journey of many days to return the sword whence it had come; after which, Lythande had made a special study of a few strong spells of that kind, lest her curiosity, or desire for unusual experiences, lead her again into such trouble. She had held this one in reserve; she had never known it to fail.

First she removed from her waist the twin daggers she bore. They had been spell-bonded to her in the Temple of the Blue Star, so that they might never be stolen or carelessly touched by the profane; the right-hand dagger for the dangers of a lonely road in dangerous country, whether wild beast or lawless men; the left-hand dagger for menaces less material, ghost or ghast, werewolf or ghoul. She did not wish to undo that spell by accident. She carried them out of range, or what she hoped would be out of range, set her pack with them, then returned to the lute and began the circlings and preliminary invocations of her spell. At last she reached the powerful phrases which could not be spoken save at the exact moment of high noon or midnight, ending with:

"Uthriel, Mastrakal, Ithragal, Ruvaghiel, angels and archangels of the Abyss, be what is bound together undone and freed, so may it be as it was commanded at the beginning of the world; So it was, so it is, so shall it be and no otherwise!"

Blue lightnings flamed from an empty sky; the Blue Star on Lythande's forehead crackled with icy force that was almost pain. Lythande could see the lines of light about the lute, pale against the noonday glare. One by one, the strings of the lute uncoiled from the pegs and slithered to the ground. The lace holding Lythande's tunic slowly unlaced itself, and the strip wriggled to the ground. The bootlaces, like twin serpents, crawled down the boots through the holes in reverse order, and writhed like live things to the ground. The intricate knot in her belt untied itself and the belt slithered away and fell.

Then, slowly, the threads sewing her tunic at sides and shoulders unraveled, coming free stitch by stitch, and the tunic, two pieces of cloth, fell to the ground, but the process did not stop there; the embroidered braid with which the tunic was trimmed came unsewed and uncoiled bit by bit till it was mere scraps of thread lying on the grass. The side seams unstitched themselves, a little at a time, in the breeches she wore; and finally the sewn stitches of the boots crawled down the leather so that the boots lay in pieces on the ground, while Lythande still stood on the bootsoles. Only the mage-robe, woven without seam and spelled into its final form, maintained its original shape, although the pin came undone, the metal bending itself to slip free of its clasp, and clinked on the hard stones.

Ruefully, Lythande gathered up the remains of clothing and boots. The boots could be resewn in the next town that boasted a cobbler's shop, and there were spare clothes in the pack she had fortunately thought to carry out of reach. Meanwhile it would not be the first time a Pilgrim Adept had gone barefoot, and it was worth the wreck of the clothing to be freed of the accursed, the disgusting, the fantastic enchantment laid on that lute.

It lay harmless and silent before the minstrel magician; a lute, Lythande hoped, like any other, bearing no magic but its own music. Lythande found a spare tunic and breeches in the pack, girded on the twin daggers once more (marveling at any spell that could untie the mage-knot her fingers had tied, by habit, on the belt) and sat down to re-string the lute.

Then she went southward, whistling.

At first Lythande thought the fierce pain between her brows was the glare of the noonday sunlight, and readjusted the deep cowl of the mage-robe so that her brow was shadowed. Then it occurred to her that perhaps the strong magic had wearied her, so she sat on a flat rock beside the trail and ate dried fruits and journey-bread from her pack, looking about to be sure she was unobserved except by a curious bird or two.

She fed the crumbs to the birds, and re-slung her pack and the lute. Only when she had traveled half a mile or so did she realize that the sun was no longer glaring in her eyes and that she was traveling northward again.

Well, this was unfamiliar country; she might well have mistaken her way. She stopped, reversed her bearings and began to retrace her steps.

An hour later, she found herself traveling northward again, and when she tried to turn toward Old Gandrin and the southlands the racking queasiness and pain were more than she could bear.

Damn the hedge-wizard who gave me that spell! Wryly,

Lythande reflected that the curse was probably redundant. Turning northward, and feeling, with relief, the slackening of the pain of the binding-spell, Lythande resigned herself. She had always wanted to see the city of Northwander: there was a college of wizards there who were said to keep records of every spell which had ever wrought its magic upon the world. Now, at least, Lythande had the best of reasons for seeking them out.

But her steps lagged resentfully on the northward road.

There was no sign of city, village or castle. In even a small village she could have her boots resewn—she must think up some good story to explain how they had come undone—and in a larger city she might find a spell-candler who might sell her an unbinding-spell. Though, if the powerful spell she had already used did not work, she was unlikely to find a workable spell this side of Northwander and the college of wizards.

She had come down from the mountain and was traversing a woody region, damp from the spring rains, which gradually grew wetter and wetter underfoot till Lythande's second-best boots squelched and let in water at every step. At the edges of the muck-dabbed trail were soggy trees and drooping shagroots covered in hanging moss.

I cannot believe that the lute means to lead me into this dismal bog, thought Lythande, but when, experimentally, she tried to reverse direction, the queasiness and pain returned. Indeed, the lute *was* leading her into the bog, farther and farther until it was all but impossible to distinguish between the soggy path and the mire to either side.

Where can the accursed thing be taking me? There was no sign of human habitation anywhere, nor any dwellers but the frogs who croaked off-key in dismal minor thirds. Was she indeed to sup tonight with the frogs and crocodiles who might inhabit this dreadful place?

To make matters worse, it began to drizzle—though it was already so wet underfoot that it made little difference to the supersaturated ground—and then to rain in good earnest.

The mage-robe was impervious to the damp, but Lythande's feet were soaked in the mud, her legs covered with mud and water halfway to the knees, and still the lute continued to lead her farther into the mire. It was dark now; even the mage's sharp eyes could no longer discern the path, and once she measured her length on the ground, soaking what garments remained dry under the mage-robe. She paused, intending, first to make a spell of light, and then to find some sort of shelter, even if only under a dry bush, to wait for light and sunshine and, perhaps, dry weather.

I cannot believe, she thought crossly, *that the lute has in sober truth led me into this impassable marsh! What sort of enchantment is that?*

She had come to a standstill, and was searching in her mind for the most effective light-spell, wishing that she, like Eirthe, had access to a friendly fire-elemental to supply not only light but heat, when a glimmer showed through the murky darkness, and strengthened momentarily. A hunter's campfire? The cottage of a mushroom-farmer or a seller of frogskins or some such trade which could be carried on in this infernal sloshing wilderness?

Perhaps she could beg shelter there for the night.*If this infernal lute will permit.* The thought was grim. But as she turned her steps toward the light, there was the smallest of sounds from the lute. Satisfaction? Pleasure? Was this, then, some part of Tashgan's appointed rounds? She did not admire Ellifanwy's taste, if the old sorceress had indeed set this as a part of the lute's wandering.

She plodded on through the mire at such a speed as the sucking bog underfoot would allow, and after a time came to what looked like a cottage, with light spilling through the window. Inside the firelight was almost like the light of a fire-elemental, which came near to searing Lythande's eyes; but when she covered them and looked again, the light came from a perfectly ordinary fire in an ordinary fireplace, and by its glow Lythande saw a little old lady, in a gown of bottle-green, after the fashion of a few generations ago, with a white linen mutch covering her hair, pottering about the fire.

Lythande raised her hand to knock, but the door swung slowly open, and a soft sweet voice called out, "Come in, my dear; I have been expecting you."

The star on Lythande's brow prickled blue fire. Magic, then, nearby, and the little old lady was a hearth-witch or a wise-woman, which could explain why she made her home in this howling wilderness. Many women with magical powers were neither liked nor welcomed among mankind. Lythande, in her male disguise, had not been subjected to this, but she had seen it all too often during her long life.

She stepped inside, wiping the moisture from her eyes. Where had the little old lady gone? Facing her was a tall, imposing, beautiful woman, in a gown of green brocade and satin with a jeweled ulrolot in the satiny dark curls. Her eyes were fixed, in dismay and disbelief, on the lute and on Lythande. Her deep voice had almost the undertone of a beast's snarl.

"Tashgan's lute! But where is Tashgan? How did you come by his instrument?"

"Lady, it is a long story," Lythande said, through the burning of the Blue Star which told her that she was surrounded by alien magic, "and I have been wandering half the night in this accursed bog, and I am soaked to the very skin. I beg of you, allow me to warm myself at your fire, and you shall be told everything; there is time for the telling of many long tales before the final battle between Law and Chaos."

"And why should you curse my chosen home, this splendid marsh?" the lady said, with a scowl coming between her fine-arched brows, and Lythande drew a long breath.

"Only that in this—this blessed expanse of bog and marsh and frogs I have becomes drenched, muddied, and lost," she said, and the lady gestured her to the fire.

"For the sake of Tashgan's lute I make you welcome, but I warn you, if you have harmed him, slain him or taken his lute by force, stranger, this is your last hour; make, therefore, the best of it."

Lythande went to the fire, pulled off the mage-robe and disposed it on the hearth where the surface water and mud would dry; removed the sodden boots and stockings, the outer tunic and trousers, standing in a linen under-tunic and drawers to dry them in the fire-heat. She was not too sure of customs this near to Northwander, but she surmised that the man she appeared to be would not, for modesty's sake, strip to the skin before a strange woman, and that custom of modesty safeguarded her disguise.

Lythande could—briefly, when she must—cast over herself the glamour of a naked man; but she hated doing it, and the illusion was dangerous, for it could not hold long, and not at all, she suspected, in the presence of this alien magic.

The lady, meanwhile, busied herself about the fire—in a way, Lythande thought as she watched her out of the corner of her eye, better fitted to the little old lady she had first appeared to be. When Lythande's under-tunic stopped steaming, she hung the outer clothing to dry over a rack, and dipped up soup from a kettle, cut bread from a crusty loaf, and set it on a bench before the fire.

"I beg of you, share my poor supper; it is hardly

worthy of a great magician, as you seem to be, but I heartily make you welcome to it."

The vows of an Adept of the Blue Star forbade Lythande to eat or drink in the sight of any man; however, women did not fall under the prohibition, and whether this was the little old hearth-witch she had first surmised, or whether the beautiful lady put on the hearth-witch disguise that she might not be easy prey for such robbers or beggarly men as might make their way into the bog, she was at least woman. So Lythande ate and drank the food, which was delicious; the bread had the very texture and scent she remembered from her half-forgotten home country.

"My compliments to your cook, lady; this soup is like to what my old nanny, in a far country, made for me when I was a child." And even as she spoke, she wondered; *is it some enchantment laid on the food?*

The lady smiled and came to sit on the bench beside Lythande. She had Tashgan's enchanted lute in her arms, and her fingers strayed over it lovingly, bringing small kindly sounds. "You see in me both cook and feaster, servant and lady; none dwells here but I. Now tell me, stranger with the Blue Star, how came you by Tashgan's lute? For if you took it from him by force, be assured I shall know; no lie can dwell in my presence."

"Tashgan made me a free gift of the lute," Lythande said, "and to my best knowledge he is well, and lord of Tschardain; his brothers perished, and he returned to his home. But first he must free himself of the enchantment of the lute, which had other ideas as to how he should spend his time. And this is the whole of the tale, lady."

The lady sniffed, a small disdainful sniff. She said, "And for that, being a little lord in a little palace, he gave up the lute? Freely, you say, and unforced? A minstrel gave up a lute enchanted to his measure? Stranger, I never thought Tashgan a fool!"

"The tale is true as I have told it," said Lythande. "Nor is the lute such a blessing as you might think, Lady, for in that world out there beyond the—the blessed confines of this very marsh, minstrels are given less honor than lords or even magicians. And freedom to wander whither one wills is perhaps even more to be desired than being at the mercy of a wandering lute."

"Do you speak with bitterness, minstrel?"

"Aye," said Lythande with heartfelt truth, "I have spent but one summer wandering at the behest of this particular lute, and I would willingly render it to anyone who would take its curse! Tashgan had twelve years of that curse."

"Curse, you say?"

The lady sprang up from the bench; her eyes glared like coals of fire at Lythande, fire that curled and melted about her with sizzling heat; fire that glowed and flared and streamed upward like the wings of a fire-elemental. "Curse, you say, when it brought Tashgan yearly to my dwelling?"

Lythande stood very still. The heat of the blue star was painful between her brows. *I do not know who this lady may be, or what*, she thought, *but she is no simple hearth-witch*.

She had laid aside her belt and twin daggers; she stood unprotected before the anger and the streaming fire, and could not reach the dagger which was effective against the creatures of enchantment. Nor, she thought, had it come yet to that.

"Madam, I speak for myself; Tashgan spoke not of curse but of enchantment. I am a Pilgrim Adept, and cannot live except when I am free to wander where I will. And even Tashgan could not linger as long beneath your gracious roof and accept your hospitality as long as his heart might desire; and I doubt not he found that a kind of curse."

Slowly the fire faded, the streamers of blue dimming

out and dying, and the lady shrank to a normal size and looked at Lythande with a smile that was still arrogant but had a kind of pleased simper to it.

In the name of all the probably nonexistent Gods of Old Gandrin, what is this woman? For woman she is, and like all women vain and greedy for praise, Lythande thought with scorn.

"Be seated, stranger, and tell me your name."

"I am Lythande, a Pilgrim Adept of the Blue Star, and Tashgan gave me this lute that he might return to become Lord of Tschardain. I am not to blame for his folly, that he willingly forwent the chance of beholding again your great loveliness." And even as she spoke Lythande had misgivings, could any woman actually swallow such incredible flattery? But the woman—or was she a powerful sorceress?—was all but purring.

"Well, his loss is his own choice, and it has brought you here to me, my dear. Have you then Tashgan's skill with the lute?"

That would not take much doing, thought Lythande, but said modestly that of this, only the Lady must be the judge. "Is it your desire that I play for you, Madam?"

"Please. But shall I bring you wine? Tashgan, dear boy, loved the wine I serve."

"No, no wine," Lythande said. She wanted her wits fully about her. "I have dined so well, I would not spoil that taste in memory. Rather I would enjoy your presence with my mind undimmed by the fumes of wine," she added, and the lady beamed.

"Play, my dear."

Lythande set her fingers to the lute, and sang, a love-song from the distant hills of her homeland.

> *A single sweet apple clings*
> *to the top of the branch;*
> *The pickers did not forget*
> *But could not reach;*

Like the apple, you are not forgotten,
But only too high and far from my hands.
I long to taste that forbidden sweetness.

Lythande looked up at last at the woman by the fire. Well, she had done a foolish thing; she should have sung a comic ballad or a tale of knightly and heroic deeds. This was not the first time she had seen a woman eager for more than flirtation, thinking Lythande a handsome young man. Was that one of the qualities of the enchantment of the lute, that it inspired woman hearers with desire for the player? Judging by what had happened on this journey, she would not be at all surprised.

It grows late," said the Lady softly, "time for a night of love such as I often shared with Tashgan, dear lad." And she reached out to touch Lythande lightly on the shoulder; Lythande remembered the farmer's wife. A woman rejected could be dangerous.

Lythande mumbled "I could not presume so high; I am no Lord but a poor minstrel."

"In my domain," said the lady, "minstrels are honored above princes or lords."

This was too ridiculous, Lythande thought. She had loved women; but if this woman had been Tashgan's mistress, she would not seek among women for a lover. Besides, Lythande was not happy with the thought of Tashgan's leavings.

The *geas* she was under was literal; she might reveal herself to no *man. I am not sure this harpy is a woman*, Lythande thought, *but I am certain she is no man*.

"Do you mock at me, minstrel?" the woman demanded. "Do you think yourself too good for my favors?" Once again it seemed that fire streamed from her hair, from the spread wings of her sleeves. And at that moment Lythande knew what she saw.

"Alnath," she whispered, and held out her hand. Yet nothing so simple as a fire-elemental; this was a were-dragon in full strength, and she remembered the fate of Ellifanwy.

Lady," she said, "you do me too much honor, for I am not Tashgan, nor even a man. I am but a humble minstrel woman."

She bowed her head before the flames suddenly surrounding her. Were-dragons were always of uncertain temper; but this one chose to be amused; flames licked around Lythande with the gusting laughter, but Lythande knew that if she showed the slightest fear, she was doomed.

Calling up the memory of the fire-elemental, Lythande made a clear picture in her mind of Alnath perched on her wrist, flames sweeping gracefully upward. She felt again the sense of kinship she had experienced with the little fire-elemental, and it enabled her to look up and smile at the were-dragon confronting her.

The gusts of laughter subsided to a chuckle, and once again it was woman not dragon confronting Lythande: the little hearth-witch. "And did Tashgan know your sex—or did he expect you to take over his round in all things?"

Lythande said ruefully "The latter, judging by the instructions he gave me,' and the lady was laughing again.

"You must have had a most *interesting* journey here, my dear!"

Lythande's mind suddenly started working furiously, recalling quite clearly the instructions Tashgan had given her. He had definitely been amused about something: yet Lythande was sure he had not known her secret. No, what amused him had been . . . "Beauty!" The lady was regarding her attentively. "By any chance, Lady, was he given to calling you—Beauty?"

"The dear boy! He *remembered!*" The lady was positively simpering.

He certainly did, Lythande thought grimly. *And boyish is a mild description of his sense of humor! Perhaps he thought me as vulnerable to playing with fire as Ellifanwy?* It would have amused Tashgan to send her to share Ellifanwy's fate. Aloud she said, "He asked me to give you his love." Her hostess looked pleased, but Lythande decided that a bit more flattery would probably help. "Of all the sacrifices he made for his throne, you were the one he regretted most. His duty called him to Tschardain." She hesitated slightly, remembering the look in the dragon-woman's eyes at the sight of the lute. "If you would not object, I think this affair would make a splendid romantic ballad." By now the were-dragon was virtually purring.

"Nothing would delight me more, my dear, than to serve as inspiration to art."

"And," Lythande continued, "I would be honored—and I know it would give Tashgan the greatest pleasure—if you would accept this lute as a small token of the devotion we feel toward you."

Flame flared almost to the ceiling; but the were-dragon's face was wreathed in joyous smiles as she gently took up the lute and caressed the strings.

Early the next morning, Lythande took cordial leave of her hostess. As she picked a careful way through the bog she could hear the strumming of the lute behind her. The were-dragon had more musical ability than Prince Tashgan, that was certain, but the ballad that formed in Lythande's mind was not of love bravely sacrificed to duty, but of a wandering were-dragon minstrel and an unexpected guest at the Yule-feast in Taschardain. Making a mental note to spend Yule in Northwander—if not even farther north—Lythande left the bog behind her and went laughing up the northward road.

Introduction to Looking for Satan

One of the rules of the original Thieves World *anthology was that characters were free to write about other people's characters, although with certain restrictions, e.g. no killing off or reforming someone else's character.*

When Vonda, whom I esteem very highly, sent me a copy of this story, it seemed that in essence she had "reformed" Lythande, for in Vonda's original draft, Lythande agreed to return home with Westerly and her crew, in essence giving up her wandering life. This struck me as an almost too-good solution of Lythande's future, but I couldn't see Lythande doing anything so sensible. I conveyed my doubts to Vonda, and she obligingly rewrote the end in a way which made it clear that Lythande was accepting this as a temporary solution to her difficulties in the world where she was.

But when she goes again to roaming, no doubt there will be other adventures in different worlds . . . for the essence of Lythande's magic is that she crosses worlds at will; she can be not only wherever but whenever she chooses. . . .

LOOKING FOR SATAN
BY VONDA N. MCINTYRE

The four travelers left the mountains at the end of the day, tired, cold, and hungry, and they entered Sanctuary.

The inhabitants of the city observed them and laughed, but they laughed behind their sleeves or after the small group passed. All its members walked armed. Yet there was no belligerence in them. They looked around amazed, nudged each other, and pointed at things, for all the world as if none had ever seen a city before. As, indeed, they had not.

Unaware of the amusement of the townspeople, they passed through the marketplace toward the city proper. It was growing dark and the farmers had nearly finished packing their awnings and culling their produce for anything worth saving. Limp cabbage leaves and rotten fruit littered the roughly cobbled street, and bits of unrecognizable stuff floated down the open central sewer.

Beside Wess, Chan shifted his heavy pack.

"Let's stop and buy something to eat," he said, "before everybody goes home."

Wess hitched her own pack higher on her shoulders and did not stop. "Not here," she said. "I'm tired of stale flatbread and raw vegetables. I want a hot meal tonight."

She tramped on. She knew how Chan felt. She glanced back at Aerie, who walked wrapped in her long dark cloak. Her pack weighed her down. She was taller than Wess, as tall as Chan, but very thin. Worry and their journey had deepened her eyes. Wess was not used to seeing her like this. She was used to seeing her freer.

"Our tireless Wess," Chan said.

"I'm tired too!" Wess said. "Do you want to try camping in the street again?"

"No," he said. Behind him, Quartz chuckled.

In the first village they had ever seen—it seemed years ago now, but was only two months—they tried to set up camp in what they thought was a vacant field. It was the village common. Had the village possessed a prison, they would have been thrown into it. As it was they were escorted to the edge of town and invited never to return. Another traveler explained inns to them—and prisons—and now they all could laugh, with some embarrassment, at the episode.

But the smaller towns they had passed through did not even approach Sanctuary in size and noise and crowds. Wess had never imagined so many people or such high buildings or any odor so awful. She hoped it would be better beyond the marketplace. Passing a fish stall, she held her breath and hurried. It was the end of the day, true, but the end of a cool late fall's day. Wess tried not to wonder what it would smell like at the end of a long summer's day.

"We should stop at the first inn we find," Quartz said.

"All right," Wess said.

By the time they reached the street's end, darkness was complete and the market was deserted. Wess thought it odd that everyone should disappear so quickly, but no doubt they were tired too and wanted to get home to a hot fire and dinner. She felt a sudden stab of homesickness and hopelessness: their search had gone on so long, with so little chance of success.

The buildings closed in around them as the street

narrowed suddenly. Wess stopped: three paths faced them, and another branched off only twenty paces farther on.

"Where now, my friends?"

"We must ask someone," Aerie said, her voice soft with fatigue.

"If we can find anyone," Chan said doubtfully.

Aerie stepped toward a shadow-filled corner. "Citizen," she said, "would you direct us to the nearest inn?"

The others peered more closely at the dim niche. Indeed, a muffled figure crouched there. It stood up. Wess could see the manic glitter of its eyes, but nothing more.

"An inn?"

"The closest, if you please. We've traveled a long way."

The figure chuckled. "You'll find no inns in this part of town, foreigner. But the tavern around the corner—it has rooms upstairs. Perhaps it will suit you."

"Thank you." Aerie turned back, a faint breeze ruffling her short black hair. She pulled her cloak closer.

They went the way the figure gestured, and did not see it convulse with silent laughter behind them.

In front of the tavern, Wess puzzled out the unfamiliar script: The Vulgar Unicorn. An odd combination, even in the south where odd combinations were the style of naming taverns. She pushed open the door. It was nearly as dark inside as out, and smoky. The noise died as Wess and Chan entered—then rose again in a surprised buzz when Aerie and Quartz followed.

Wess and Chan were not startlingly different from the general run of southern mountain folk: he fairer, she darker. Wess could pass unnoticed as an ordinary citizen anywhere; Chan's beauty often attracted attention. But Aerie's tall white-skinned black-haired elegance everywhere aroused comment. Wess smiled, imagining what

183

would happen if Aerie flung away her cloak and showed herself as she really was.

And Quartz: she had to stoop to come inside. She straightened up. She was taller than anyone else in the room. The smoke near the ceiling swirled a wreath around her hair. She had cut it short for the journey, and it curled around her face, red, gold, and sand-pale. Her gray eyes reflected the firelight like mirrors. Ignoring the stares, she pushed her blue wool cloak from her broad shoulders and shrugged her pack to the floor.

The strong heavy scent of beer and sizzling meat made Wess' mouth water. She sought out the man behind the bar.

"Citizen," she said, carefully pronouncing the Sanctuary language, the trade-tongue of all the continent, "are you the proprietor? My friends and I, we need a room for the night, and dinner."

Her request seemed ordinary enough to her, but the innkeeper looked sidelong at one of his patrons. Both laughed.

"A room, young gentleman?" He came out from behind the bar. Instead of replying to Wess, he spoke to Chan. Wess smiled to herself. Like all Chan's friends, she was used to seeing people fall in love with him on sight. She would have done so herself, she thought, had she first met him when they were grown. But they had known each other all their lives and their friendship was far closer and deeper than instant lust.

"A room?" the innkeeper said again. "A meal for you and your ladies? Is that all we can do for you here in our humble establishment? Do you require dancing? A juggler? Harpists and hautbois? Ask and it shall be given!" Far from being seductive, or even friendly, the innkeeper's tone was derisive.

Chan glanced at Wess, frowning slightly, as everyone within earshot burst into laughter. Wess was glad her complexion was dark enough to hide her blush of anger.

Chan was bright pink from the collar of his homespun shirt to the roots of his blond hair. Wess knew they had been insulted but she did not understand how or why, so she replied with courtesy.

"No, citizen, thank you for your hospitality. We need a room, if you have one, and food."

"We would not refuse a bath," Quartz said.

The innkeeper glanced at them, an irritated expression on his face, and spoke once more to Chan.

"The young gentleman lets his ladies speak for him? Is this some foreign custom, that you are too high-bred to speak to a mere tavern-keeper?"

"I don't understand you," Chan said. "Wess spoke for us all. Must we speak in chorus?"

Taken aback, the man hid his reaction by showing them, with an exaggerated bow, to a table.

Wess dumped her pack on the floor next to the wall behind her and sat down with a sigh of relief. The others followed. Aerie looked as if she could not have kept on her feet a moment longer.

"This is a simple place," the tavern-keeper said. "Beer or ale, wine. Meat and bread. Can you pay?"

He was speaking to Chan again. He took no direct note of Wess or Aerie or Quartz.

"What is the price?"

"Four dinners, bed—you break your fast somewhere else, I don't open early. A piece of silver. In advance."

"The bath included?" Quartz said.

"Yes, yes, all right."

"We can pay," said Quartz, whose turn it was to keep track of what they spent. She offered him a piece of silver.

He continued to look at Chan but, after an awkward pause, he shrugged, snatched the coin from Quartz, and turned away. Quartz drew back her hand, then, under the table, surreptitiously wiped it on the leg of her heavy cotton trousers.

Chan glanced over at Wess. "Do you understand anything that has happened since we entered the city's gates?"

"It is curious," she said. "They have strange customs."

"We can puzzle them out tomorrow," Aerie said.

A young woman carrying a tray stopped at their table. She wore odd clothes, summer clothes by the look of them, for they uncovered her arms and shoulders and almost completely bared her breasts. It *is* hot in here, Wess thought. That's quite intelligent of her. Then she need only put on a cloak to go home, and she will not get chilled or overheated.

"Ale for you, sir?" the young woman said to Chan. "Or wine? And wine for your wives?"

"Beer, please," Chan said. "What are 'wives'? I have studied your languaage, but this is not a word I know."

"The ladies are not your wives?"

Wess took a tankard of ale off the tray, too tired and thirsty to try to figure out what the woman was talking about. She took a deep swallow of the cool bitter brew. Quartz reached for a flask of wine and two cups, and poured for herself and Aerie.

"My companions are Westerly, Aerie, and Quartz," Chan said, nodding to each in turn. "I am Chandler. And you are—?"

"I'm just the serving girl," she said, sounding frightened. "You could not wish to be troubled with my name." She grabbed a mug of beer and put it on the table, spilling some, and fled.

They all looked at each other, but then the tavern-keeper came with platters of meat. They were too hungry to wonder what they had done to frighten the barmaid.

Wess tore off a mouthful of bread. It was fairly fresh, and a welcome change from trail rations—dry meat, flatbread mixed hurriedly and baked on stones in the coals of a campfire, fruit when they could find or buy it. Still, Wess was used to better.

"I miss your bread," she said to Quartz in their own language. Quartz smiled.

The meat was hot and untainted by decay. Even Aerie ate with some appetite, though she preferred meat raw.

Halfway through her meal, Wess slowed down and took a moment to observe the tavern more carefully.

At the bar, a group suddenly burst into raucous laughter.

"You say the same damned thing every damned time you turn up in Sanctuary, Bauchle," one of them said, his loud voice full of mockery. "You have a secret or a scheme or a marvel that will make your fortune. Why don't you get an honest job—like the rest of us?"

That brought on more laughter, even from the large, heavyset young man who was the butt of the fun.

"You'll see, this time," he said. "This time I've got something that will take me all the way to the court of the Emperor. When you hear the criers tomorrow, you'll know." He called for more wine. His friends drank, and made jokes, both at his expense.

The Unicorn was much more crowded now, smokier, louder. Occasionally someone glanced toward Wess and her friends, but otherwise they were let alone.

A cold breeze thinned the odor of beer and burning meat and unwashed bodies. Silence fell suddenly, and Wess looked quickly around to see if she had breached some other unknown custom. But all the attention centered on the tavern's entrance. The cloaked figure stood there casually, but nothing was casual about the aura of power and self-possession.

In the whole of the tavern, not another table held an empty place.

"Sit with us, sister!" Wess called on impulse.

Two long steps and a shove: Wess' chair scraped

roughly along the floor and Wess was rammed back against the wall, a dagger at her throat.

"Who calls me 'sister'?" The dark hood fell back from long, gray-streaked hair. A blue star blazed on the woman's forehead. Her elegant features grew terrible and dangerous in its light.

Wess stared into the tall, lithe woman's furious eyes. Her jugular vein pulsed against the point of the blade. If she made a move toward her knife, or if any of her friends moved at all, she was dead.

"I meant no disrespect—" She almost said "sister" again. But it was not the familiarity that had caused offense: it was the word itself. The woman was traveling incognito, and Wess had breached her disguise. No mere apology would repair the damage she had done.

A drop of sweat trickled down the side of her face. Chan and Aerie and Quartz were all poised on the edge of defense. If Wess erred again, more than one person would die before the fighting stopped.

"My unfamiliarity with your language has offended you, young gentleman," Wess said, hoping the tavern-keeper had used a civil form of address, if not a civil tone. It was often safe to insult someone by the tone, but seldom by the words themselves. "Young gentleman," she said again when the woman did not kill her, "someone has made sport of me by translating '*frejôjan*,' 'sister.' "

"Perhaps," the disguised woman said. "What does *frejôjan* mean?"

"It is a term of peace, an offer of friendship, a word to welcome a guest, another child of one's own parents."

"Ah. 'Brother' is the word you want, the word to speak to men. To call a man 'sister,' the word for women, is an insult."

"An insult!" Wess said, honestly surprised.

But the knife drew back from her throat.

"You are a barbarian," the disguised woman said, in a friendly tone. "I cannot be insulted by a barbarian."

"There is the problem, you see," Chan said. "Translation. In our language, the word for outsider, for foreigner, also translates as 'barbarian.' " He smiled, his beautiful smile.

Wess held Chan's hand under the table. "I meant only to offer you a place to sit, where there is no other."

The stranger sheathed her dagger, and stared straight into Wess's eyes. Wess shivered slightly and imagined spending the night with Chad on one side, the stranger on the other.

Or you could have the center, if you liked, she thought, holding the gaze.

The stranger laughed. Wess could not tell if the mocking tone were directed outward or inward.

"Then I will sit here, as there is no other place." She did so. "My name is Lythande."

They introduced themselves, and offered her—Wess made herself think of Lythande as "him" so she would not damage the disguise again—offered him wine.

"I do not drink," Lythande said. "But to show I mean no offense, either, I will smoke with you." He rolled shredded herbs in a dry leaf, lit the construction, inhaled from it, and held it out. "Westerly, *frejôjan*."

Out of politeness Wess tried it. By the time she stopped coughing her throat was sore, and the sweet scent made her feel lightheaded.

"It takes practice," Lythande said smiling.

Chan and Quartz did no better, but Aerie inhaled deeply, her eyes closed, then held her breath. Thereafter she and Lythande shared it while the others ordered more ale and another flask of wine.

"Why did you ask me, of all this crowd, to sit here?" Lythande asked.

"Because. . . ." Wess paused to try to think of a way

to make her intuition sound sensible. "You look like someone who knows what's going on. You look like someone who might help us."

"If information is all you need, you can get it less expensively than by hiring a sorcerer."

"Are you a sorcerer?" Wess asked.

Lythande looked at her with pity and contempt. "You child! What do your people mean, sending innocents and children out of the north!" He touched the star on his forehead. "What did you think this means?"

"I'll have to guess, but I guess it means you are a mage."

"Excellent. A few years of lessons like that and you might survive, a while, in Sanctuary—in the Maze—in the Unicorn!"

"We haven't got years," Aerie whispered. "We have, perhaps, overspent the time we *do* have."

Quartz put her arm around Aerie's shoulders, for comfort, and hugged her gently.

"You interest me," Lythande said. "Tell me what information you seek. Perhaps I will know whether you can obtain it less expensively—not cheaply, but less expensively—from Jubal the Slavemonger, or from a seer—" At their expressions, he stopped.

"Slavemonger!"

"He collects information as well. You needn't worry that he'll abduct you from his sitting-room."

They all started speaking at once, then fell silent, realizing the futility.

"Start at the beginning."

"We're looking for someone," Wess said.

"This is a poor place to search. No one will tell you anything about any patron of this establishment."

"But he's a friend."

"There's only your word for that."

"Satan wouldn't be here anyway," Wess said. "If he were free to come here he'd be free to go home. We'd

have heard something of him, or he would have found
us, or—"

"You fear he was taken prisoner. Enslaved, perhaps."

"He must have been. He was hunting, alone. He
liked to do that, his people often do."

"We need solitude sometimes," Aerie said.

Wess nodded. "We didn't worry about him till he
didn't come home for Equinox. Then we searched. We
found his camp, and a cold trail . . ."

"We tried to hope for kidnapping," Chan said. "But
there was no ransom demand. The trail was so old—
they took him away."

"We followed, and we heard some rumors of him,"
Aerie said. "But the road branched, and we had to
choose which way to go." She shrugged, but could not
maintain the careless pose; she turned away in despair.
"I could find no trace. . . ."

Aerie, with her longer range, had met them at each
evening's new camp, even more exhausted and more
driven after searching all day.

"Apparently we chose wrong," Quartz said.

"Children," Lythande said, "children, frejôjans—"

"*Frejôjani*," Chan said automatically, then shook his
head and spread his hands in apology.

"Your friend is one slave out of many. You could not
trace him by his papers, unless you discovered what
name they were forged under. For someone to recognize him by a description would be the greatest luck,
even if you had an homuncule to show. Sisters, brother,
you might not recognize him yourselves, by now."

"I would recognize him," Aerie said.

"We'd all recognize him, even in a crowd of his own
people. But that makes no difference. Anyone would
know him who had seen him. But no one *has* seen him,
or if they have they will not say so to us." Wess glanced
at Aerie.

"You see," Aerie said, "he is winged."

"Winged!" Lythande said.

"Winged folk are rare, I believe, in the south."

"Winged folk are myths, in the south. Winged? Surely you mean . . ."

Aerie started to shrug back her cape, but Quartz put her arm around her shoulders again. Wess broke into the conversation quickly.

"The bones are longer," she said, touching the three outer fingers of her left hand with the forefinger of her right. "And stronger. The webs between fold out."

"And these people fly?"

"Of course. Why else have wings?"

Wess glanced at Chan, who nodded and reached for his pack.

"We have no homuncule," Wess said. "But we have a picture. It isn't Satan, but it's very like him."

Chan pulled out the wooden tube he had carried all the way from Kaimas. From inside it, he drew the rolled kidskin, which he opened out onto the table. The hide was carefully tanned and very thin; it had writing on one side and a painting, with one word underneath it, on the other.

"It's from the library at Kaimas," Chan said. "No one knows where it came from. I believe it is quite old, and I think it is from a book, but this is all that's left." He showed Lythande the written side. "I can decipher the script but not the language. Can you read it?"

Lythande shook his head. "It is unknown to me."

Disappointed, Chan turned the illustrated side of the manuscript page toward Lythande. Wess leaned toward it too, picking out the details in the dim candlelight. It was beautiful, almost as beautiful as Satan himself. It was surprising how like Satan it was, for it had been in the library since long before he was born. The slender and powerful winged man had red-gold hair and flame-colored wings. His expression seemed composed half of wisdom and half of deep despair.

Most flying people were black or deep iridescent green or pure dark blue. But Satan, like the painting, was the color of fire. Wess explained that to Lythande.

"We suppose this word to be this person's name," Chan said. "We cannot be sure we have the pronunciation right, but Satan's mother liked the sound as we say it, so she gave it to him as his name, too."

Lythande stared at the gold and scarlet painting in silence for a long time, then shook his head and leaned back in his chair. He blew smoke toward the ceiling. The ring spun, and sparked, and finally dissipated into the haze.

"Frejôjani," Lythande said. "Jubal—and the other slavemongers—parade their merchandise through the town before every auction. If your friend were in the coffle, everyone in Sanctuary would know. Everyone in the Empire would know."

Beneath the edges of her cape, Aerie clenched her hands into fists.

This was, Wess feared, the end of their journey.

"But it might be . . ."

Aerie looked up sharply, narrowing her deepset eyes.

"Such an unusual being would not be sold at public auction. He would be offered in private sale, or exhibited, or perhaps even offered to the emperor for his menagerie."

Aerie flinched, and Quartz traced the texture of her short-sword's bone haft.

"It's better, children, don't you see? He'll be treated decently. He's valuable. Ordinary slaves are whipped and cut and broken to obedience."

Chan's transparent complexion paled to white. Wess shuddered. Even contemplating slavery they had none of them understood what it meant.

"But how will we find him? Where will we look?"

"Jubal will know," Lythande said, "if anyone does. I like you, children. Sleep tonight. Perhaps tomorrow

Jubal will speak with you." He got up, passed smoothly through the crowd, and vanished into the darkness outside.

In silence with her friends, Wess sat thinking about what Lythande had told them.

A well-set-up young fellow crossed the room and leaned over their table toward Chan. Wess recognized him as the man who had earlier been made sport of by his friends.

"Good evening, traveller," he said to Chan. "I have been told these ladies are not your wives."

"It seems everyone in this room has asked if my companions are my wives, and I still do not understand what you are asking," Chan said pleasantly.

"What's so hard to understand?"

"What does 'wives' mean?"

The man arched one eyebrow, but replied. "Women bonded to you by law. To give their favors to no one but you. To bear and raise your sons."

" 'Favors'?"

"Sex, you clapperdudgeon! Fucking! Do you understand me?"

"Not entirely. It sounds like a very odd system to me."

Wess thought it odd, too. It seemed absurd to decide to bear children of only one gender; and bonded by law sounded suspiciously like slavery. But—three women pledged solely to one man? She glanced across at Aerie and Quartz and saw they were thinking the same thing. They burst out laughing.

"Chan, Chad-love, think how exhausted you'd be!" Wess said.

Chan grinned. They often slept and made love all together, but he was not expected to satisfy all his friends. Wess enjoyed making love with Chad, but she was equally excited by Aerie's delicate ferocity, and by Quartz's inexhaustible gentleness and power.

"They're not your wives, then," the man said. "So how much for that one?" He pointed at Quartz.

They all waited curiously for him to explain.

"Come on, man! Don't be coy! You're obvious to everyone—why else bring women to the Unicorn? With that one, you'll get away with it till the madams find out. So make your fortune while you can. What's her price? I can pay, I assure you."

Chan started to speak, but Quartz gestured sharply and he fell silent.

"Tell me if I interpret you correctly," she said. "You think coupling with me would be enjoyable. You would like to share my bed tonight."

"That's right, lovey." He reached for her breast but abruptly thought better of it.

"Yet you speak, not to me, but to my friend. This seems very awkward, and very rude."

"You'd better get used to it, woman. It's the way we do things here."

"You offer Chan money, to persuade me to couple with you."

The man looked at Chan. "You'd best train your whores to manners yourself, boy, or your customers will help you and damage your merchandise."

Chan blushed scarlet, embarrassed, flustered, and confused. Wess began to think she knew what was going on, but she did not want to believe it.

"You are speaking to me, *man*," Quartz said, using the word with as much contempt as he had put into "woman." "I have but one more question for you. You are not ill-favored, yet you cannot get someone to bed you for the joy of it. Does this mean you are diseased?"

With an incoherent sound of rage, he reached for his knife. Before he touched it, Quartz's short-sword rasped out of its scabbard. She held its tip just above his belt-buckle. The death she offered him was slow and painful.

Everyone in the tavern watched intently as the man slowly spread his hands.

"Go away," Quartz said. "Do not speak to me again. You are not unattractive, but if you are not diseased you *are* a fool, and I do not sleep with fools."

She moved her sword a handsbreadth. He backed up three fast steps and spun around, glancing spasmodically from one face to another, to another. He found only amusement. He bolted, through a roar of laughter, fighting his way to the door.

The tavern-keeper sauntered over. "Foreigners," he said, "I don't know whether you've made your place or dug your graves tonight, but that was the best laugh I've had since the new moon. Bauchle Meyne will never live it down."

"I did not think it funny in the least," Quartz said. She sheathed her short-sword. She had not even touched her broadsword. Wess had never seen her draw it. "And I am tired. Where is our room?"

He led them up the stairs. The room was small and low-ceilinged. After the tavern-keeper left, Wess poked the straw mattress of one of the beds, and wrinkled her nose.

"I've got this far from home without getting lice, I'm not going to sleep in a nest of bedbugs." She threw her bedroll to the floor. Chan shrugged and dropped his gear.

Quartz flung her pack into the corner. "I'll have something to say to Satan when we find him," she said angrily. "Stupid fool, to let himself be captured by these creatures."

Aerie stood hunched in her cloak. "This is a wretched place," she said. "You can flee, but he cannot."

"Aerie, love, I know, I'm sorry." Quartz hugged her, stroking her hair. "I didn't mean it, about Satan. I was angry."

Aerie nodded.

Wess rubbed Aerie's shoulders, unfastened the clasp
of her long hooded cloak, and drew it from Aerie's
body. Candlelight rippled across the black fur that covered her, as sleek and glossy as sealskin. She wore
nothing but a short thin blue silk tunic and her walking
boots. She kicked off the boots, dug her clawed toes
into the splintery floor, and stretched.

Her outer fingers lay close against the backs of her
arms. She opened them, and her wings unfolded.

Only half-spread, her wings spanned the room. She
let them droop, and pulled aside the leather curtain
over the window. The next building was very close.

"I'm going out, I need to fly."

"Aerie, we've come so far today—"

"Wess, I *am* tired. I won't go far. But I can't fly in
the daytime, not here, and the moon is waxing. If I
don't go now I may not be able to fly for days."

"It's true," Wess said. "Be careful."

"I won't be gone long." She climbed out the window
and up the rough side of the building. Her claws scraped
into the adobe. Three soft footsteps overhead, the shushh
of her wings: she was gone.

The others pushed the beds against the wall and
spread their blankets, overlapping, on the floor. Quartz
looped the leather flap over a hook in the wall and put
the candle on the window ledge.

Chan hugged Wess. "I never saw anyone move as
fast as Lythande. Wess, love, I feared he'd killed you
before I even noticed him."

"It was stupid, to speak so familiarly to a stranger."

"But he offered us the nearest thing to news of Satan
we've heard in weeks."

"True. Maybe the fright was worth it." Wess looked
out the window, but saw nothing of Aerie.

"What made you think Lythande was a woman?"

Wess glanced at Chan sharply. He gazed back at her,
mildly curious.

He doesn't know, Wess thought, astonished. He didn't realize—

"I . . . I don't know," she said. "A silly mistake. I made a lot of them today."

It was the first time in her life she had deliberately lied to a friend. She felt slightly ill, and when she heard the scrape of claws on the roof above, she was glad for more reasons than simply that Aerie had returned. Just then the tavern-keeper banged on their door announcing their bath. In the confusion of getting Aerie inside and hidden under her cloak before they could open the door, Chan forgot the subject of Lythande's gender.

Beneath them, the noise of revelry in the Unicorn gradually faded to silence. Wess forced herself to lie still. She was so tired that she felt as if she were trapped in a river, with the current swirling her around and around so she could never get her bearings. Yet she could not sleep. Even the bath, the first warm bath any of them had had since leaving Kaimas, had not relaxed her. Quartz lay solid and warm beside her, and Aerie lay between Quartz and Chan. Wess did not begrudge Aerie or Quartz their places, but she did like to sleep in the middle. She wished one of her friends were awake, to make love with, but she could tell from their breathing that they were all deeply asleep. She cuddled up against Quartz, who reached out, in a dream, and embraced her.

The darkness continued, without end, without any sign of dawn, and finally Wess slid out from beneath Quartz' arm and the blankets, silently put on her pants and shirt, and, barefoot, crept down the stairs, past the silent tavern, and outside. On the doorstep, she sat and pulled on her boots.

The moon gave a faint light, enough for Wess. The street was deserted. Her heels thudded on the cobblestones, echoing hollowly against the close adobe walls.

Such a short stay in the town should not make her uneasy, but it did. She envied Aerie her power to escape, however briefly, however dangerous the escape might be. Wess walked down the street, keeping careful track of her path. It would be very easy to get lost in this warren of streets and alleys, niches and blank canyons.

The scrape of a boot, instantly stilled, brought her out of her mental wanderings. They wished to try to follow her? Good luck to them.

Wess was a hunter. She tracked her prey so silently that she killed with a knife; in the dense rain forest where she lived, arrows were too uncertain. She had crept up on a panther and stroked its smooth pelt—then vanished so swiftly that she left the creature yowling in fury and frustration, while she laughed with delight. She grinned, and quickened her step, and her footfalls turned silent on the stone.

Her unfamiliarity with the streets hampered her slightly. A dead end could trap her. But she found, to her pleasure, that her instinct for seeking out good trails translated into the city. Once she thought she would have to turn back, but the high wall barring her way had a deep diagonal fissure from the ground to its top. She found just enough purchase to clamber over it. She jumped into the garden the wall enclosed, scampered across it and up a grape arbor, and swung into the next alley.

She ran smoothly, gladly, as her exhaustion lifted. She felt good, despite the looming buildings and twisted dirty streets and vile odors.

She faded into a shadowed recess where two houses abutted but did not line up. Listening, she waited.

The soft and nearly silent footsteps halted. Her pursuer hesitated. Grit scraped between stone and leather as the person turned one way, then the other, and, finally, chose the wrong turning and hurried off. Wess grinned, but she felt respect for any hunter who could follow her this far.

Moving silently through shadows, she started back toward the tavern. When she came to a tumbledown building she remembered, she found finger- and toe-holds and climbed to the roof of the next house. Flying was not the only talent Aerie had that Wess envied. Being able to climb straight up an undamaged adobe wall would be useful sometimes, too.

The rooftop was deserted. Too cold to sleep outside, no doubt; the inhabitants of the city went to ground at night, in warmer, unseen warrens.

The air smelled cleaner here, so she traveled by rooftop as far as she could. But the main passage through the Maze was too wide to leap across. From the building that faced the Unicorn, Wess observed the tavern. She doubted that her pursuer could have reached it first, but the possibility existed, in this strange place. She saw no one. It was near dawn. She no longer felt exhausted, just deliciously sleepy. She climbed down the face of the building and started across the street.

Someone flung open the door behind her, leaped out as she turned, and punched her in the side of the head.

Wess crashed to the cobblestones. The shadow stepped closer and kicked her in the ribs. A line of pain wrapped around her chest and tightened when she tried to breathe.

"Don't kill her. Not yet."

"No. I have plans for her."

Wess recognized the voice of Bauchle Meyne, who had insulted Quartz in the tavern. He toed her in the side.

"When I'm done with you, bitch, you can take me to your friend." He started to unbuckle his belt.

Wess tried to get up. Bauchle Meyne's companion stepped toward her, to kick her again.

His foot swung toward her. She grabbed it and twisted.

As he went down, Wess struggled up. Bauchle Meyne, surprised, lurched toward her and grabbed her in a bear hug, pinioning her arms so she could not reach her knife. He pressed his face down close to hers. She felt his whisker stubble and smelled his yeasty breath. He could not hold her and force his mouth to hers at the same time, but he slobbered on her cheek. His pants slipped down and his penis thrust against her thigh.

Wess kneed him in the balls as hard as she could.

He screamed and let her go and staggered away, holding himself, doubled up and moaning, stumbling over his fallen breeches. Wess drew her knife and backed against a wall, ready for another attack.

Bauchle Meyne's accomplice rushed her. Her knife sliced quickly toward him, slashing his arm. He flung himself backward and swore violently. Blood spurted between his fingers.

Wess heard the approaching footsteps a moment before he did. She pressed her free hand hard against the wall behind her. She was afraid to shout for help. In this place whoever answered might as easily join in attacking her.

But the man swore again, grabbed Bauchle Meyne by the arm, and dragged him away as fast as the latter, in his present distressed state, could go.

Wess sagged, sliding down the wall to the ground. She knew she was still in danger, but her legs would not hold her up anymore.

The footsteps ceased. Wess looked up, clenching her fingers around the handle of her knife.

"Frejôjan," Lythande said softly, from ten paces away, "sister, you led me quite a chase." She glanced after the two men. "And not only me, it seems."

"I never fought a person before," Wess said shakily. "Not a real fight. Only practice. No one ever got hurt." She touched the side of her head. The shallow scrape bled freely. She thought about its stopping, and the flow gradually ceased.

Lythande sat on his heels beside her. "Let me see." He probed the cut gently. "I thought it was bleeding, but it's stopped. What happened?"

"I don't know. Did you follow me? Did they? I thought I was eluding one person."

"I was the only one following you," Lythande said. "They must have come back to bother Quartz again."

"You know about that?"

"The whole city knows, child. Or anyway, the whole Maze. Bauchle will not soon live it down. The worst of it is he will never understand what it is that happened, or why."

"No more will I," Wess said. She looked up at Lythande. "How can you live here?" she cried.

Lythande drew back, frowning. "I do not live here. But that is not really what you are asking. We cannot speak so freely on the public street." He glanced away, hesitated, and turned back. "Will you come with me? I haven't much time, but I can fix your cut, and we can talk safely."

"All right," Wess said. She sheathed her knife and pushed herself to her feet, wincing at the sharp pain in her side. Lythande grasped her elbow, steadying her.

"Perhaps you've cracked a rib," he said. They started slowly down the street.

"No," Wess said. "It's bruised. It will hurt for a while, but it isn't broken."

"How do you know?"

Wess glanced at him quizzically. "I may not be from a city, but my people aren't completely wild. I paid attention to my lessons when I was little."

"Lessons? Lessons in what?"

"In knowing whether I am hurt, and what I must do if I am, in controlling the processes of my body—surely your people teach their children these things?"

"My people don't know these things," Lythande said. "I think we have more to talk about than I believed, frejôjan."

The Maze confused even Wess, by the time they reached the small building where Lythande stopped. Wess was feeling dizzy from the blow to her head, but she was confident that she was not dangerously hurt. When Lythande opened a low door and ducked inside, Wess followed.

Lythande picked up a candle. The wick sparked. In the center of the dark room, a shiny spot reflected the glow. The wick burst into flame and the spot of reflection grew. Wess blinked. The reflection spread into a sphere, taller than Lythande, the color and texture of deep water, blue-gray, shimmering. It balanced on its lower curve, bulging slightly so it was not quite perfectly round.

"Follow me, Westerly."

Lythande walked toward the sphere. Its surface rippled at her approach. She stepped into it. It closed around her, and all Wess could see was a wavering figure, beyond the surface, and the spot of light from the candle flame.

She touched the sphere gingerly with her fingertip. It was wet. Taking a deep breath, she put her hand through the surface.

It froze her fast; she could not proceed, she could not escape, she could not move. Even her voice was captured.

After a moment, Lythande surfaced. Her hair sparkled with drops of water, but her clothes were dry. She stood frowning at Wess, lines of thought bracketing the star on her forehead. Then her brow cleared and she grasped Wess's wrist.

"Don't fight it, little sister," she said. "Don't fight me."

The blue star glittered in the darkness, its points sparking with new light. Against great resistance, Lythande drew Wess' hand from the sphere. The cuff of Wess' shirt was cold and sodden. In only a few seconds the water had wrinkled her fingers. The sphere freed her suddenly and she nearly fell, but Lythande caught and supported her.

"What happened?"

Still holding her up, Lythande reached into the water and drew it aside like a curtain. She urged Wess toward the division. Unwillingly, Wess took a shaky step forward, and Lythande helped her inside. The surface closed behind them. Lythande eased Wess down on the platform that flowed out smoothly from the inside curve. Wess expected it to be wet, but it was resilient and smooth and slightly warm.

"What happened?" she asked again.

"The sphere is a protection against other sorcerers."

"I'm not a sorcerer."

"I believe you believe that. If I thought you were deceiving me, I would kill you. But if you are not a sorcerer, it is only because you are not trained."

Wess started to protest, but Lythande waved her to silence.

"Now I understand how you eluded me in the streets."

"I'm a hunter," Wess said irritably. "What good would a hunter be who couldn't move silently and fast?"

"No, it was more than that. I put a mark on you, and you threw it off. No one has ever done that before."

"I didn't do it, either."

"Let us not argue, frejôjan. There isn't time."

She inspected the cut, then dipped her hand into the side of the sphere, brought out a handful of water, and washed away the sticky drying blood. Her touch was warm and soothing, as expert as Quartz's.

"Why did you bring me here?"

"So we could talk unobserved."

"What about?"

"I want to ask you something first. Why did you think I was a woman?"

Wess frowned and gazed into the depths of the floor. Her boot dimpled the surface, like the foot of a water-strider.

"Because you *are* a woman," she said. "Why you pretend you are not, I don't know."

"That is not the question," Lythande said. "The question is why you called me 'sister' the moment you saw me. No one, sorcerer or otherwise, has ever glanced at me once and known me for what I am. You could place me, and yourself, in great danger. How did you know?"

"I just knew," Wess said. "It was obvious. I didn't look at you and wonder if you were a man or a woman. I saw you, and I thought, how beautiful, how elegant she is. She looks wise. She looks like she could help us. So I called to you."

"And what did your friends think?"

"They . . . I don't know what Quartz and Aerie thought. Chan asked whatever was I thinking of."

"What did you say to him?"

"I. . . ." She hesitated, feeling ashamed. "I lied to him," she said miserably. "I said I was tired and it was dark and smoky, and I made a foolish mistake."

"Why didn't you try to persuade him you were right?"

"Because it isn't my business to deny what you wish known about yourself. Even to my oldest friend, my first lover."

Lythande stared up at the curved surface of the inside of the sphere. The tension eased in the set of her shoulders, the expression on her face.

"Thank you, little sister," she said, her voice full of relief. "I did not know if my identity were safe with you. But I think it is."

Wess looked up suddenly, chilled by insight. "You brought me here—you would have killed me!"

"If I had to," Lythande said easily. "I am glad it was not necessary. But I could not trust a promise made under threat. You do not fear me; you made your decision of your own free will."

"That may be true," Wess said. "But it isn't true that I don't fear you."

Lythande gazed at her. "Perhaps I deserve your fear, Westerly. You could destroy me with a thoughtless word. But the knowledge you have could destroy you. Some people would go to great lengths to discover what you know."

"I'm not going to tell them."

"If they suspected—they might force you."

"I can take care of myself," Wess said.

Lythande rubbed the bridge of her nose with thumb and forefinger. "Ah, sister, I hope so. I can give you very little protection." She—*he*, Wess reminded herself—stood up. "It's time to go. It's nearly dawn."

"You asked questions of me—may I ask one of you?"

"I'll answer if I can."

"Bauchle Meyne—if he hadn't behaved so stupidly, he could have killed me. But he taunted me till I recovered myself. He made himself vulnerable to me. His friend knew I had a knife, but he attacked me unarmed. I've been trying to understand what happened, but it makes no sense."

Lythande drew a deep breath. "Westerly," she said, "I wish you had never come to Sanctuary. You escaped for the same reason that I first chose to appear as I now must remain."

"I still don't understand."

"They never expected you to fight. To struggle a little, perhaps, just enough to excite them. They expected you to acquiesce in their wishes whether that meant to beat you, to rape you, or to kill you. Women in Sanctuary are not trained to fight. They are taught that their only power lies in their abiilty to please, in bed and in flattery. Some few excel. Most survive."

"And the rest?"

"The rest are killed for their insolence. Or—" She smiled bitterly and gestured to herself. "Some few . . . find their talents are stronger in other areas."

"But why do you put up with it?"

"That is the way it is, Westerly. Some would say that is the way it must be—that it is ordained."

"It isn't that way in Kaimas." Just speaking the name of her home made her want to return. "Who ordains it?"

"Why, my dear," Lythande said sardonically, "the gods."

"Then you should rid yourselves of gods."

Lythande arched one eyebrow. "You should, perhaps, keep such ideas to yourself in Sanctuary. The gods' priests are powerful." She drew her hand up the side of the sphere so it parted as if she had slit it with a knife, and held the skin apart so Wess could leave.

Wess thought the shaky, uncertain feeling that gripped her would disappear when she had solid ground beneath her feet again.

But it did not.

Wess and Lythande returned to the Unicorn in silence. As the Maze woke, the street began to fill with laden carts drawn by scrawny ponies, with beggars and hawkers and pickpockets. Wess bought fruit and meat rolls to take to her friends.

The Unicorn was closed and dark. As the tavernkeeper had said, he did not open early. Wess went around to the back, but at the steps of the lodging door, Lythande stopped.

"I must leave you, frejôjan."

Wess turned back in surprise. "But I thought you were coming upstairs with me—for breakfast, to talk. . . ."

Lythande shook his head. His smile was odd, not, as Wess had come to expect, sardonic, but sad. "I wish I could, little sister. For once, I wish I could. I have business to the north that cannot wait."

"To the north! Why did you come this way with me?" She had got her bearings on the way back, and while the twisted streets would not permit a straight path, they had proceeded generally southward.

"I wanted to walk with you," Lythande said.

Wess scowled at him. "You thought I hadn't enough sense to get back by myself."

"This is a strange place for you. It isn't safe even for people who have always lived here."

"You—" Wess stopped. Because she had promised to safeguard his true identity, she could not say what she wished: that Lythande was treating her as Lythande himself did not wish to be treated. Wess shook her head, flinging aside her anger. Stronger than her anger at Lythande's lack of confidence in her, stronger than her disappointment that Lythande was going away, was her surprise that Lythande had pretended to hint at finding Satan. She did not wish to think too deeply on the sorcerer's motives.

"You have my promise," she said bitterly. "You may be sure that my word is important to me. May your business be profitable." She turned away and fumbled for the latch, her vision blurry.

"Westerly," Lythande said gently, "do you think I came back last night only to coerce an oath from you?"

"It doesn't matter."

"Well, perhaps not, since I have so little to give in return."

Wess turned around. "And do you think I made that promise only because I hoped you could help us?"

"No," Lythande said. "Frejôjan, I wish I had more

time—but what I came to tell you is this. I spoke with Jubal last night."

"Why didn't you tell me? What did he say? Does he know where Satan is?" But she knew she would have no pleasure from the answer. Lythande would not have put off good news. "Will he see us?"

"He has not seen your friend, little sister. He said he had no time to see you."

"Oh."

"I did press him. He owes me, but he has been acting peculiar lately. He's more afraid of something else than he is of me, and that is very strange." Lythande looked away.

"Didn't he say *anything*?"

"He said . . . this evening, you should go to the grounds of the governor's palace."

"Why?"

"Westerly . . . this may have nothing to do with Satan. But the auction block is there."

Wess shook her head, confused.

"Where slaves are offered for sale."

Fury and humiliation and hope: Wess's reaction was so strong that she could not answer. Lythande came up the steps in one stride and put his arms around her. Wess held him, trembling, and Lythande stroked her hair.

"If he's there—is there no law, Lythande? Can a free person be stolen from their home, and . . . and . . ."

Lythande looked at the sky. The sun's light showed over the roof of the easternmost building.

"Frejôjan, I *must* go. If your friend is to be sold, you can try to buy him. The merchants here are not so rich as the merchants in the capital, but they are rich enough. You'd need a great deal of money. I think you should, instead, apply to the governor. He is a young man, and a fool—but he is not evil." Lythande hugged

Wess one last time and stepped away. "Good-bye, little sister. Please believe I'd stay if I could."

"I know," she whispered.

Lythande strode away without looking back, leaving Wess alone among the early-morning shadows.

Wess returned to the room at the top of the stairs. When she entered, Chan propped himself up on one elbow.

"I was getting worried," he said.

"I can take care of myself!" Wess snapped.

"Wess, love, what's the matter?"

She tried to tell him, but she could not. Wess stood, silent, staring at the floor, with her back turned on her best friend.

She glanced over her shoulder when Chan stood up. The ripped curtain let in shards of light that cascaded over his body. He had changed, like all of them, on the long journey. He was still beautiful, but he was thinner and harder.

He touched her shoulder gently. She shrank away.

He saw the bloodstains on her collar. "You're hurt!" he said, startled. "Quartz!"

Quartz muttered sleepily from the bed. Chan tried to lead Wess over to the window, where there was more light.

"Just don't touch me!"

"Wess—"

"What's wrong?" Quartz said.

"Wess is injured."

Quartz padded barefoot toward them and Wess burst into tears and flung herself into her arms.

Quartz held Wess, as Wess had held her a few nights before, when Quartz had cried silently in bed, homesick, missing her children. "Tell me what happened," she said softly.

What Wess managed to say was less about the attack than about Lythande's explanations of it, and of Sanctuary.

"I understand," Quartz said after Wess had told her only a little. She stroked Wess' hair and brushed the tears from her cheeks.

"I don't," Wess said. "I must be going crazy, to act like this!" She started to cry again. Quartz led her to the blankets, where Aerie sat up, blinking and confused. Chan followed, equally bewildered. Quartz made Wess sit down sat beside her and hugged her. Aerie rubbed her back and neck and let her wings unfold around them.

"You aren't going crazy," Quartz said. "It's that you aren't used to the way things are here."

"I don't want to get used to things here, I hate this place, I want to find Satan, I want to go home."

"I know," Quartz whispered. "I know."

"But I don't," Chan said.

Wess huddled against Quartz, unable to say anything that would ease the hurt she had given Chad.

"Just leave her alone for a little while, Chad," Quartz said to him. "Let her rest. Everything will be all right."

Quartz eased Wess down and lay beside her. Cuddled between Quartz and Aerie, with Aerie's wing spread over them all, Wess fell asleep.

At midmorning, Wess awoke. Her head ached fiercely and the black bruise across her side hurt every time she took a breath. She looked around the room. Sitting beside her, mending a strap on her pack, Quartz smiled down at her. Aerie was brushing her short smooth fur, and Chan stared out the window, his arm on the sill and his chin resting on his arm, his other shirt abandoned unpatched on his knee.

Wess got up and crossed the room. She sat on her heels near Chan. He glanced at her, and out the window, and at her again.

"Quartz explained, a little. . . ."

"I was angry," Wess said.

"Just because barbarians act like . . . like barbarians, isn't a good reason to be angry with *me*."

He was right. Wess knew it. But the fury and bewilderment mixed up in her were still too strong to shrug off with easy words.

"You know—" he said, "you *do* know I couldn't act like that. . . ."

Just for an instant Wess actually tried to imagine Chad acting like the innkeeper, or Bauchle Meyne, arrogantly, blindly, with his self-interest and his pleasure considered above everything and everyone else. The idea was so ludicrous that she burst out in sudden laughter.

"I know you wouldn't," she said. She had been angry at the person he *might* have been, had all the circumstances of his life been different. She had been angry at the person *she* might have been, even more. She hugged Chan quickly. "Chad, I've got to get free of this place." She took his hand and stood up. "Come, I saw Lythande last night, I have to tell you what he said."

They did not wait till evening to go to the governor's palace, but set out earlier, hoping to gain an audience with the prince and persuade him not to let Satan be sold.

But no one else was waiting till evening to go to the palace, either. They joined a crowd of people streaming toward the gate. Wess' attempt to slip through the throng earned her an elbow in her sore ribs.

"Don't push, girl," said the ragged creature she had jostled. He shook his staff at her. "Would you knock over an old cripple? I'd never get up again, after I'd been trompled."

"Your pardon, citizen," she said. Ahead she could see that the people had to crowd into a narrower space.

They were, more or less, in a line. "Are you going to the slave auction?"

"Slave auction? Slave auction! No slave auction today, foreigner. The carnival come to town!"

"What's the carnival?"

"A carnival! You've never heard of a carnival? Well, ne'mind, nor has half the people in Sanctuary, nor seen one neither. Two twelve-years since one came. Now the prince is governor, we'll see more, I don't doubt. They'll come wanting an admission to his brother the emperor—out of the hinterlands and into the capital, if you know."

"But I still don't know what a carnival is."

The old man pointed.

Over the high wall of the palace grounds, the great drape of cloth that hung limply around a tall pole slowly began to spread, and open—like a huge mushroom, Wess thought. The guy ropes tightened, forming the canvas into an enormous tent.

"Under there—magic, foreign child. Strange animals. Prancing horses with pretty girls in feathers dancing on their backs. Jugglers, clowns, acrobats on high wires— and the freaks!" He chuckled. "I like the freaks best, the last time I saw a carnival they had a sheep with two heads and a man with two—but that's not a story to tell a young girl unless you're fucking her." He reached out to pinch her. Wess jerked back, drawing her knife. Startled, the old man said, "There, girl, no offense." She let the blade slide back into its sheath. The old man laughed again. "And a special exhibition, this carnival— special, for the prince. They won't say what 'tis. But it'll be a sight, you can be sure."

"Thank you, citizen," Wess said coldly, and stepped back among her friends. The ragged man was swept forward with the crowd.

Wess caught Aerie's gaze. "Did you hear?"

Aerie nodded. "They have him. What else could their great secret be?"

"In *this* skyforsaken place, they might have overpowered some poor troll, or a salamander." She spoke sarcastically, for trolls were the gentlest of creatures, and Wess herself had often stretched up to scratch the chin of a salamander who lived on a hill where she hunted. It was entirely tame, for Wess never hunted salamanders. Their hide was too thin to be useful and no one in the family liked lizard meat. Besides, one could not pack out even a single haunch of fullgrown salamander, and she would not waste her kill. "In this place, they might have a winged snake in a box, and call it a great secret."

"Wess, their secret is Satan and we all know it," Quartz said. "Now we have to figure out how to free him."

"You're right, of course," Wess said.

At the gate, two huge guards glowered at the rabble they had been ordered to admit to the parade-ground. Wess stopped before one of them.

"I want to see the prince," she said.

"Audience next week," he replied, hardly glancing at her.

"I need to see him before the carnival begins."

This time he did look at her, amused. "You do, do you? Then you've no luck. He's gone, won't be back till the parade."

"Where is he?" Chan asked.

She heard grumbling from the crowd piling up behind them.

"State secret," the guard said. "Now go in, or clear the way."

They went in.

The crowd thinned abruptly, for the parade-ground was enormous. Even the tent seemed small; the palace loomed above it like a cliff. If the whole population of

Sanctuary had not come here, then a large proportion of every section had, for several merchants were setting up stalls: beads here, fruit there, pastries farther on; a beggar crawled slowly past; and a few paces away a large group of noblefolk in satins and fur and gold walked languidly beneath parasols held by naked slaves. The thin autumn sunlight was hardly enough to mar the complexion of the most delicate noble, or to warm the back of the most vigorous slave.

Quartz looked around, then pointed over the heads of the crowd. "They're making a pathway, with ropes and braces. The parade will come through that gate, and into the tent from this side." She swept her hand from right to left, east to west, in a long curve from the Processional gate. The carnival tent was set up between the auction block and the guards' barracks.

They tried to circle the tent, but the area beyond it all the way to the wall was blocked by rope barriers. In the front, a line of spectators already snaked back far beyond any possible capacity.

"We'll never get in," Aerie said.

"Maybe it's for the best," Chan said. "We don't need to be inside with Satan—we need to get him out."

The shadows lengthened across the palace grounds. Wess sat motionless and silent, waiting. Chan bit his fingernails and fidgeted. Aerie hunched under her cloak, her hood pulled low to shadow her face. Quartz watched her anxiously, and fingered the grip of her sword.

After again being refused an audience with the prince, this time at the palace doors, they had secured a place next to the roped-off path. Across the way, a work crew put the finishing touches on a platform. When it was completed, servants hurried from the palace with rugs, a silk-fringed awning, several chairs, and a brazier of coals. Wess would not have minded a brazier of coals herself; as the sun fell, the air was growing chill.

The crowd continued to gather, becoming denser, louder, more and more drunk. Fights broke out in the line at the tent, as people began to realize they would never get inside. Soon the mood grew so ugly that criers spread among the people, ringing bells and announcing that the carnival would present one more performance, several more performances, until all the citizens of Sanctuary had the opportunity to glimpse the carnival's wonders. And the secret. Of course, the secret. Still, no one even hinted at the secret's nature.

Wess pulled her cloak closer. She knew the nature of the secret; she only hoped the secret would see his friends and be ready for whatever they could do.

The sun touched the high wall around the palace grounds. Soon it would be dark.

Trumpets and cymbals: Wess looked toward the Processional gate, but a moment later realized that all the citizens around her were straining for a view of the palace entrance. The enormous doors swung open and a phalanx of guards marched out, followed by a group of nobles wearing jewels and cloth of gold. They strode across the hard-packed ground. The young man at the head of the group, who wore a gold coronet, acknowledged his people's shouts and cries as if they all were accolades— which, Wess thought, they were not. But above the mutters and complaints, the loudest cry was, "The prince! Long live the prince!"

The phalanx marched straight from the palace to the new-built platform. Anyone shortsighted enough to sit in that path had to snatch up their things and hurry out of the way. The route cleared as swiftly as water parting around a stone.

Wess stood impulsively, about to sprint across the parade route to try once more to speak to the prince.

"Sit down!"

"Out of the way!"

Someone threw an apple core at her. She knocked it

away and crouched down again, though not because of the threats or the flying garbage. Aerie, too, with the same thought, started to her feet. Wess touched her elbow.

"Look," she said.

Everyone within reach or hearing of the procession seemed to have the same idea. The crowd surged in, every member clamoring for attention. The prince flung out a handful of coins, which drew the beggars scuffling away from him. Others, more intent on their claims, continued to press him. The guards fell back, surrounding him, nearly cutting off the sight of him, and pushed at the citizens with spears held broadside.

The tight cordon parted and the prince mounted the platform. Standing alone, he turned all the way around, raising his hands to the crowd.

"My friends," he cried, "I know you have claims upon me. The least wrong to one of my people is important to me."

Wess snorted.

"But tonight we are all privileged to witness a wonder never seen in the Empire. Forget your troubles tonight, my friends, and enjoy the spectacle with me." He held out his hand, and brought a member of his party up beside him on the stage.

Bauchle Meyne.

"In a few days, Bauchle Meyne and his troupe will journey to Ranke, there to entertain the Emperor my brother."

Wess and Quartz glanced at each other, startled. Chan muttered a curse. Aerie tensed, and Wess held her arm. They all drew up their hoods.

"Bauchle goes with my friendship, and my seal." The prince held up a rolled parchment secured with scarlet ribbons and ebony wax.

The prince sat down, with Bauchle Meyne in the

place of honor by his side. The rest of the royal party arrayed themselves around, and the parade began.

Wess and her friends moved closer together, in silence. They would have no help from the prince.

The Processional gates swung open to the sound of flutes and drums. The music continued for some while before anything else happened. Bauchle Meyne began to look uncomfortable. Then abruptly a figure staggered out onto the path, as if he had been shoved. The skeletally thin, red-haired man regained his balance, straightened up, and gazed from side to side. The jeers confounded him. He pushed his long cape off his shoulders to reveal his star-patterned black robe, and took a few hesitant steps.

At the rope barrier's first wooden supporting post, he stopped again. He gestured toward it tentatively and spoke a guttural word.

The post sputtered into flame.

The people nearby drew back shouting, and the wizard lurched along the path, first to one side, then the other, waving his hands at each wooden post in turn.

The foggy white circles melded together to light the way. Wess saw that the posts were not, after all, burning. When the one in front of her began to shine, she brought her hand toward it, palm forward and fingers outspread. When she felt no heat she touched the post gingerly, then gripped it. It held no warmth, and it retained its ordinary texture, splintery rough-hewn wood.

She remembered what Lythande said, about her having a strong talent. She wondered if she could do the same thing. It would be a useful trick, though not very important. She had no piece of wood to try it on, nor any idea how to start to try in the first place. She shrugged and let go of the post. Her handprint—she blinked. No, it was her imagination, not a brighter spot that she had touched.

At the prince's platform, the wizard stood staring

vacantly around. Bauchle Meyne leaned forward intently, glaring, his worry clear and his anger barely held in check. The wizard gazed at him. Wess could see Bauchle Meyne's fingers tense around a circle of ruby chain. He twisted it. Wess gasped. The wizard shrieked and flung up his hands. Bauchle Meyne slowly relaxed his hold on the talisman. The wizard spread his arms. He was trembling. Wess, too, was shaking. She felt as if the chain had whipped around her body like a lash.

The wizard's trembling hands moved: the prince's platform, the wooden parts of the chairs, the poles supporting the fringed awning, all burst suddenly into a fierce white fire. The guards leaped forward in fury and confusion, but stopped at a word from their prince. He sat calm and smiling, his hands resting easily on the bright arms of his throne. Shadowy flames played across his fingers, and the light spun up between his feet. Bauchle Meyne leaned back in satisfaction, and nodded to the wizard. The other nobles on the platform stood disconcerted, awash in the light from the boards between the patterned rugs. Nervously, but following the example of their ruler, they sat down again.

The wizard stumbled onward, lighting up the rest of the posts. He disappeared into the darkness of the tent. Its supports began to shine with the eerie luminescence. Gradually, the barrier-ropes and the carpets on the platform and the awning over the prince and the canvas of the tent became covered with a soft gentle glow.

The prince applauded, nodding and smiling toward Bauchle Meyne, and his people followed his lead.

With a sharp cry, a jester tumbled through the Processional gates and somersaulted along the path. After him came the flutists and drummers, and then three ponies with bedraggled feathers attached to their bridles. Three children in spangled shorts and halters rode them. The one in front jumped up and stood balanced on her pony's rump, while the two following did shoulder-stands, braced against the ponies' withers. Wess, who had never been on a horse in her life and found the idea quite terrifying, applauded. Others in the audience applauded, too, here and there, and the prince himself idly clapped his hands. But nearby a large grizzled man laughed sarcastically and yelled, "Show us more!" That was the way most of the audience reacted, with hoots of derision and laughter. The child standing up stared straight ahead. Wess clenched her teeth, angry for the child but impressed by her dignity. Quartz's oldest child was about the same age. Wess took her hand, and Quartz squeezed her fingers gratefully.

A cage, pulled by a yoke of oxen, passed through the dark gate. Wess caught her breath. The oxen pulled the cage into the light. It carried an elderly troll, hunched in the corner on dirty straw. A boy poked the troll with a stick as the oxen drew abreast of the prince. The troll leaped up and cursed in a high-pitched angry voice.

"You uncivilized barbarians! You, prince—prince of worms, I say, of maggots! May your penis grow till no one will have you! May your best friend's vagina knot itself with you inside! May you contract water on the brain and sand in the bladder!"

Wess felt herself blushing: she had never heard a troll speak so. Ordinarily they were the most cultured of forest people, and the only danger in them was that one might find oneself listening for a whole afternoon to a discourse on the shapes of clouds or the effects of certain shelf-fungi. Wess looked around, frightened that someone would take offense at what the troll was saying to their ruler. Then she remembered that he was speaking the Language, the real tongue of intelligent creatures, and no one but she and her friends understood.

"Frejôjan!" she cried on impulse. "Tonight—be ready—if I can—!"

He hesitated in the midst of a caper, stumbled, but

caught himself and gamboled around, making nonsense noises till he faced her. She pulled her hood back so he could recognize her later. She let it fall again as the cart passed, so Bauchle Meyne would not see her from the other side of the path.

The gray-gold furry little being gripped the bars of his cage and looked out, making horrible faces at the crowd, horrible noises in reaction to their jeers. But between the shrieks and the gibberish, he said, "I wait—"

After he passed them, he began to wail.

"Wess—" Chan said.

"How could I let him go by without speaking to him?"

"He isn't a friend, after all," Aerie said.

"He's enslaved, just like Satan!" Wess looked from Aerie's face to Chan's, and saw that neither understood. "Quartz—?"

Quartz nodded. "Yes. You're right. A civilized person has no business being in this place."

"How are you going to find him? How are you going to free him? We don't even know how we're going to free Satan! Suppose he needs help?" Aerie's voice rose in anger.

"Suppose we need help?"

Aerie turned her back on Wess and stared blankly out into the parade. She even shrugged off Quartz's comforting hug.

Then there was no more time for arguing. Six archers tramped through the gate. A cart followed. It was a flatbed, curtained all around, and pulled by two large skewbald horses, one with a wild blue eye. Six more archers followed. A mutter of confusion rippled over the crowd, and then cries of "The secret! Show us the secret!"

The postillion jerked the draft horses to a standstill

221

before the prince. Bauchle Meyne climbed stiffly off the platform and onto the cart.

"My lord!" he cried. "I present you—a myth of our world!" He yanked on a string and the curtains fell away.

On the platform, Satan stood rigid and withdrawn, staring forward, his head high. Aerie moaned and Wess tensed, wanting to leap over the glowing ropes and lay about with her knife, in full view of the crowd, whatever the consequences. She cursed herself for being so weak and stupid this morning. If she had had the will to attack, she could have ripped out Bauchle Meyne's guts.

They had not broken Satan. They would kill him before they could strip him of his pride. But they had stripped him naked, and shackled him. And they had hurt him. Streaks of silver-gray cut across the red-gold fur on his shoulders. They had beaten him. Wess clenched her fingers around the handle of her knife.

Bauchle Meyne picked up a long pole. He was not fool enough to get within reach of Satan's talons.

"Show yourself!" he cried.

Satan did not speak the trade-language, but Bauchle Meyne made himself well enough understood with the end of the pole. Satan stared at him without moving until the young man stopped poking at him, and, with some vague awareness of his captive's dignity, backed up a step. Satan looked around him, his large eyes reflecting the light like a cat's. He faced the prince. The heavy chains clanked and rattled as he moved.

He raised his arms. He opened his hands, and his fingers unfolded.

He spread his great red wings. Wizard-light glowed through the translucent webs. It was as if he had burst into flame.

The prince gazed upon him with silent satisfaction as the crowd roared with surprise and astonishment.

"Inside," Bauchle Meyne said, "when I release him, he will fly."

One of the horses, brushed by Satan's wingtip, snorted and reared. The cart lurched forward. The postillion yanked the horse's mouth to a bloody froth and Bauchle Meyne lost his balance and stumbled to the ground. His face showed pain and Wess was glad. Satan barely shifted. The muscles tensed and slid in his back as he balanced himself with his wings.

Aerie made a high, keening sound, almost beyond the limits of human hearing. But Satan heard. He did not flinch; unlike the troll he did not turn. But he heard. In the bright white wizard's-light, the short fur on the back of his shoulders rose, and he shivered. He made an answering cry, a sighing: a call to a lover. He folded his wing-fingers back along his arms. The webbing trembled and gleamed.

The postillion kicked his horse and the cart lumbered forward. For the crowd outside, the show was over.

The prince stepped down from the platform and, walking side by side with Bauchle Meyne and followed by his retinue, proceeded into the carnival tent.

The four friends stood close together as the crowd moved past them. Wess was thinking, They're going to let him fly, inside. He'll be free . . . She looked at Aerie. "Can you land on top of the tent? And take off again?"

Aerie looked at the steep canvas slope. "Easily," she said.

The area behind the tent was lit by torches, not wizard-light. Wess stood leaning against the grounds' wall, watching the bustle and chaos of the troupe, listening to the applause and laughter of the crowd. The show had been going on a long time now; most of the people who had not got inside had left. A couple of carnival workers kept a bored watch on the perimeter of the barrier, but Wess knew she could slip past any time she pleased.

It was Aerie she worried about. Once the plan started, she would be very vulnerable. The night was clear and the waxing moon bright and high. When she landed on top of the tent she would be well within range of arrows. Satan would be in even more danger. It was up to Wess and Quartz and Chan to create enough chaos so the archers would be too distracted to shoot either of the flyers.

Wess was rather looking forward to it.

She slipped under the rope when no one was looking and strolled through the shadows as if she belonged with the troupe. Satan's cart stood at the performers' entrance, but Wess did not go near her friend now. Taking no notice of her, the children on their ponies trotted by. In the torchlight the children looked thin and tired and very young, the ponies thin and tired and old. Wess slid behind the rank of animal cages. The carnival did, after all, have a salamander, but a piteous poor and hungry-looking one, barely the size of a large dog. Wess broke the lock on its cage. She had only her knife to pry with; she did the blade no good. She broke the locks on the cages of the other animals, the half-grown wolf, the pygmy elephant, but did not yet free them. Finally she reached the troll.

"Frejôjan," she whispered. "I'm behind you."

"I hear you, frejôjan." The troll came to the back of his cage. He bowed to her. "I regret my unkempt condition, frejôjan; when they captured me I had nothing, not even a brush." His golden gray-flecked hair was badly matted. He put his hand through the bars and Wess shook it.

"I'm Wess," she said.

"Aristarchus," he said. "You speak with the same accent as Satan—you've come for him?"

She nodded. "I'm going to break the lock on your

224

cage," she said. "I have to be closer to the tent when they take him in to make him fly. It would be better if at first they didn't notice anything was going wrong. . . ."

Aristarchus nodded. "I won't escape till you've begun. Can I be of help?"

Wess glanced along the row of cages. "Could you—would it put you in danger to free the animals?" He was old; she did not know if he could move quickly enough.

He chuckled. "All of us animals have become rather good friends," he said. "Though the salamander is rather snappish."

Wess wedged her knife into the padlock and wrenched it open. Aristarchus snatched it off the door and flung it into the straw. He smiled, abashed, at Wess.

"I find my own temper rather short in these poor days."

Wess reached through the bars and gripped his hand again. Near the tent, the skewbald horses wheeled Satan's cart around. Bauchle Meyne yelled nervous orders. Aristarchus glanced toward Satan.

"It's good you've come," he said. "I persuaded him to cooperate, at least for a while, but he does not find it easy. Once he made them angry enough to forget his value."

Wess nodded, remembering the whip scars.

The cart rolled forward; the archers followed.

"I have to hurry," Wess said.

"Good fortune go with you."

She moved as close to the tent as she could. But she could not see inside; she had to imagine what was happening, by the tone of the crowd. The postillion drove the horses around the ring. They stopped. Someone crawled under the cart and unfastened the shackles from below, out of reach of Satan's claws. And then—

She heard the sigh, the involuntary gasp of wonder as Satan spread his wings, and flew.

Above her, Aerie's shadow cut the air. Wess pulled

off her cloak and waved it, signaling. Aerie dived for the tent, swooped, and landed.

Wess drew her knife and started sawing at a guy-rope. She had been careful enough of the edge so it sliced through fairly quickly. As she hurried to the next line, she heard the tone of the crowd gradually changing, as people began to notice something amiss. Quartz and Chan were doing their work, too. Wess chopped at the second rope. As the tent began to collapse, she heard tearing canvas above, where Aerie ripped through the roof with her talons. Wess sliced through a third rope, a fourth. The breeze flapped the sagging fabric against itself. The canvas cracked and howled like a sail. Wess heard Bauchle Meyne screaming, "The ropes! Get the ropes, the ropes are breaking!"

The tent fell from three directions. Inside, people began to shout, then to scream, and they tried to flee. A few spilled out into the parade-ground, then a mob fought through the narrow opening. The shriek of frightened horses pierced the crowd-noise, and the scramble turned to panic. The skewbald horses burst through the crush, scattering people right and left, Satan's empty cart lurching and bumping along behind. More terrified people streamed out after them. All the guards from the palace fought against them, struggling to get inside to their prince.

Wess turned to rejoin Quartz and Chan, and froze in horror. In the shadows behind the tent, Bauchle Meyne snatched up an abandoned bow, ignored the chaos, and aimed a steel-tipped arrow into the sky. Wess sprinted toward him, crashed into him, and shouldered him off-balance. The bowstring twanged and the arrow fishtailed up, falling back, spent, to bury itself in the limp canvas.

Bauchle Meyne sprung up, his high complexion scarlet with fury.

"You, you little bitch!" He lunged for her, grabbed

226

her, and backhanded her across the face. "You've ru-
ined me for spite!"

The blow knocked her to the ground. This time
Bauchle Meyne did not laugh at her. Half-blinded Wess
scrambled away from him. She heard his boots pound
closer and he kicked her in the same place in the ribs.
She heard the bone crack. She dragged at her knife but
its edge, roughened by the abuse she had given it,
hung up on the rim of the scabbard. She could barely
see and barely breathe. She struggled with the knife
and Bauchle Meyne kicked her again.

"You can't get away this time, bitch!" He let Wess
get to her hands and knees. "Just try to run!" He
stepped toward her.

Wess flung herself at his legs, moved beyond pain by
fury. He cried out as he fell. The one thing he could
never expect from her was attack. Wess lurched to her
feet. She ripped her knife from its scabbard as Bauchle
Meyne lunged at her. She plunged it into him, into his
belly, up, into his heart.

She knew how to kill, but she had never killed a
human being. She had been drenched by her prey's
blood, but never by the blood of her own species. She
had watched creatures die by her hand, but never a
creature who knew what death meant.

His heart still pumping blood around the blade, his
hands fumbling at her hands, trying to push them away
from his chest, he fell to his knees, shuddered, toppled
over, convulsed, and died.

Wess jerked her knife from his body. Once more she
heard the shrieks of frightened horses and the curses of
furious men, and the howl of a half-starved wolf cub.

The tent shimmered with wizard-light.

I wish it were torches, Wess screamed in her mind.
Torches would burn you, and burning is what you
deserve.

227

But there was no fire, and nothing burned. Even the wizard-light was fading.

Wess looked into the sky. She raked her sleeve across her eyes to wipe away her tears.

The two flyers soared toward the moon, free.

And now—

Quartz and Chan were nowhere in sight. She could find only terrified strangers: performers in spangles, Sanctuary people fighting each other, and more guards coming to the rescue of their lord. The salamander lumbered by, hissing in fear.

Horses clattered toward her and she spun, afraid of being run down. Aristarchus brought them to a halt and flung her the second horse's reins. It was the skewbald stallion from Satan's cart, the one with the wild blue eye. It smelled the blood on her and snorted and reared. Somehow she kept hold of the reins. The horse reared again and jerked her off her feet. Bones ground together in her side and she gasped.

"Mount!" Aristarchus cried. "You can't control him from the ground!"

"I don't know how—" She stopped. It hurt too much to talk.

"Grab his mane! Jump! Hold on with your knees."

She did as he said, found herself on the horse's back, and nearly fell off his other side. She clamped her legs around him and he sprang forward. Both the reins were on one side of his neck—Wess knew that was not right. She pulled on them and he twisted in a circle and almost threw her again. Aristarchus urged his horse forward and grabbed the stallion's bridle. The animal stood spraddle-legged, ears flat back, nostrils flaring, trembling between Wess's legs. She hung onto his mane, terrified. Her broken ribs hurt so badly she felt faint.

Aristarchus leaned forward, blew gently into the stallion's nostrils, and spoke to him so quietly Wess could not hear the words. Slowly, easily, the troll straightened out the reins. The animal gradually relaxed, and his ears pricked forward again.

"Be easy on his mouth, frejôjan," the troll said to Wess. "He's a good creature, just frightened."

"I have to find my friends," Wess said.

"Where are you to meet them?"

Aristarchus's calm voice helped her regain her composure.

"Over there." She pointed to a shadowed recess beyond the tent. Aristarchus started for it, still holding her horse's bridle. The animals stepped delicately over broken equipment and abandoned clothing.

Quartz and Chan ran from the shadowed side of the tent. Quartz was laughing. Through the chaos she saw Wess, tapped Chan on the shoulder to get his attention, and changed direction to hurry toward Wess.

"Did you see them fly?" Quartz cried. "They outflew eagles!"

"As long as they outflew arrows," Aristarchus said dryly. "Hurry, you, the big one, up behind me, and you," he said to Chan, "behind Wess."

They did as he ordered. Quartz kicked the horse and he sprang forward, but Aristarchus reined him in.

"Slowly, children," the troll said. "Slowly through the dark, and no one will notice."

To Wess's surprise, he was quite correct.

In the city they kept the horses at the walk, and Quartz concealed Aristarchus beneath her cloak. The uproar fell behind them, and no one chased them. Wess clutched the stallion's mane, still feeling very insecure so high above the ground.

A direct escape from Sanctuary did not lead them past the Unicorn, or indeed into the Maze at all, but they decided to chance going back; the risk of traveling unequipped through the mountains this late in the fall was too great. They approached the Unicorn through back alleys, and saw almost no one. Apparently the denizens of the Maze were as fond of entertainments as anyone else in Sanctuary. No doubt the opportunity to watch their prince extricate himself from a collapsed tent was almost the best entertainment of the evening. Wess would not have minded watching that herself.

Leaving the horses hidden in shadow with Aristarchus, they crept quietly up the stairs to their room, stuffed belongings in their packs, and started out again

"Young gentleman and his ladies, good evening."

Wess spun around, Quartz right beside her gripping her sword. The tavern-keeper flinched back from them, but quickly recovered himself.

"Well," he said to Chan, sneering. "I thought they were one thing, but I see they are your bodyguards."

Quartz grabbed him by the shirt front and lifted him off the floor. Her broadsword scraped from its scabbard. Wess had never seen Quartz draw it, in defense or anger; she had never seen the blade. But Quartz had not neglected it. The edge gleamed with transparent sharpness.

"I forswore the frenzy when I abandoned war," Quartz said very quietly. "But you are very nearly enough to make me break my oath." She opened her hand and he fell to his knees before the point of her sword.

"I meant no harm, my lady—"

"Do not call me 'lady'! I am not of noble birth! I was a soldier and I am a woman. If that cannot deserve your courtesy, then you cannot command my mercy."

"I meant no harm, I meant no offense. I beg your pardon . . ." He looked up into her unreadable silver eyes. "I beg your pardon, northern woman."

There was no contempt in his voice now, only terror, and to Wess that was just as bad. She and Quartz could expect nothing here, except to be despised or feared. They had no other choices.

Quartz sheathed her sword. "Your silver is on the table," she said coldly. "We had no mind to cheat you."

He scrabbled up and away from them, into the room. Quartz grabbed the key from the inside, slammed the door, and locked it.

"Let's get out of here."

They clattered down the stairs. In the street, they tied the packs together and to the horses' harnesses as best they could. Above, they heard the innkeeper banging at the door, and when he failed to break it down, he came to the window.

"Help!" he cried. "Help, kidnappers! Brigands!" Quartz vaulted up behind Aristarchus and Chan clambered up behind Wess. "Help!" the innkeeper cried. "Help, fire! Floods!"

Aristarchus gave his horse its head and it sprang forward. Wess's stallion tossed his mane, blew his breath out hard and loud, and leaped from a standstill into a gallop. All Wess could do was hold on, clutching the mane and the harness, hunching over the horse's withers, as he careered down the street.

They galloped through the outskirts of Sanctuary, splashed across the river at the ford, and headed north along the river trail. The horses sweated into a lather and Aristarchus insisted on slowing down and breathing them. Wess saw the sense of that, and, too, she could detect no pursuit from the city. She scanned the sky, but darkness hid any sign of the flyers.

Abandoning the headlong pace, they walked the horses or let them jog. Each step jarred Wess's ribs. She tried to concentrate on pushing out the pain, but to do it well she needed to stop, dismount, and relax. That was impossible right now. The road and the night led on forever.

At dawn, they reached the faint abandoned trail Wess had brought them in on. It led away from the road, directly up into the mountains.

The trees, black beneath the slate-blue sky, closed

in overhead. Wess felt as if she had fought her way out of a nightmare world into a world she knew and loved. She did not yet feel free, but she could consider the possibility of feeling free again.

"Chad?"

"I'm here, love."

She took his hand, where he held her gingerly around the waist, and kissed his palm. She leaned back against him, and he held her.

A stream gushed between the gnarled roots of trees, beside the nearly invisible trail.

"We should stop and let the horses rest," Aristarchus said. "And rest, ourselves."

"There's a clearing a little way ahead," Wess said. "It has grass. They eat grass, don't they?"

Aristarchus chuckled. "They do, indeed."

When they reached the clearing, Quartz jumped down, stumbled, groaned, and laughed. "It's a long time since I rode horseback," she said. She helped Aristarchus off. Chan dismounted and stood testing his legs after the long ride. Wess sat where she was. She felt as if she were looking at the world through Lythande's secret sphere.

The sound of great wings filled the cold dawn. Satan and Aerie landed in the center of the clearing and hurried toward them.

Wess twined her fingers in the skewbald's striped mane and slid off his back. She leaned against his shoulder, exhausted, taking short shallow breaths. She could hear Chan and Quartz greeting the flyers. But Wess could not move.

"Wess?"

She turned slowly, still holding the horse's mane. Satan smiled down at her. She was used to flyers' being lean, but they were sleek: Satan was gaunt, his ribs and hips sharp beneath his skin. His short fur was dull and dry, and besides the scars on his back he had marks on his ankles, and around his throat, where he had been bound.

"Oh, Satan—" She embraced him, and he enfolded her in his wings.

"It's done," he said. "It's over." He kissed her gently. Everyone gathered around him. He brushed the back of his hand softly down the side of Quartz's face, and bent down to kiss Chad.

"Frejôjani . . ." He looked at them all, then, as a tear spilled down his cheek, he wrapped himself in his wings and cried.

They held him and caressed him until the racking sobs ceased. Ashamed, he scrubbed away the tears with the palm of his hand. Aristarchus stood nearby, blinking his large green eyes.

"You must think me an awful fool, Aristarchus, a fool, and weak."

The troll shook his head. "I think, when I can finally believe I'm free . . ." He looked at Wess. "Thank you."

They sat beside the stream to rest and talk.

"It's possible that we aren't even being followed," Quartz said.

"We watched the city, till you entered the forest," Aerie said. "We saw no one else on the river road."

"Then they might not have realized anyone but another flyer helped Satan escape. If no one saw us fell the tent—"

Wess reached into the stream and splashed her face, cupped her hand in the water, and lifted it to her lips. The first rays of direct sunlight pierced the branches and entered the clearing.

Her hand was still bloody. The blood was mixing with the water. She choked and spat, lurched to her feet, and bolted. A few paces away she fell to her knees and retched violently.

There was nothing in her stomach but bile. She crawled to the stream and scrubbed her hands, then her face, with sand and water. She stood up again. Her friends were staring at her, shocked.

"There was someone," she said. "Bauchle Meyne. But I killed him."

"Ah," Quartz said.

"You've given me another gift," Satan said. "Now I don't have to go back and kill him myself."

"Shut up, Satan, she's never killed anyone before."

"Nor have I. But I would have ripped out his throat if just once he'd left the chains slack enough for me to reach him!"

Wess wrapped her arms around herself, trying to ease the ache in her ribs. Suddenly Quartz was beside her.

"You're hurt—why didn't you tell me?"

Wess shook her head, unable to answer. And then she fainted.

She woke up at midafternoon, lying in the shade of a tall tree in a circle of her friends. The horses grazed nearby, and Aristarchus sat on a stone beside the stream, combing the tangles from his fur. Wess got up and went to sit beside him.

"Did you call my name?"

"No," he said.

"I thought I heard—" She shrugged. "Never mind."

"How are you feeling?"

"Better." Her ribs were bandaged tight. "Quartz is a good healer."

"No one is following. Aerie looked, a little while ago."

"That's good. May I comb your back for you?"

"That would be a great kindness."

In silence, she combed him, but she was paying very little attention. The third time the comb caught on a knot, Aristarchus protested quietly.

"Sister, please, that fur you're plucking is attached to my skin."

"Oh, Aristarchus, I'm sorry. . . ."

"What's wrong?"

"I don't know," she said. "I feel—I want—I. . . ." She handed him the comb and stood. "I'm going to walk up the trail a little way. I won't be gone long."

In the silence of the forest she felt easier, but there was something pulling her, something calling to her that she could not hear.

And then she did hear something, a rustling of leaves. She faded back off the trail, hiding herself, and waited.

Lythande walked slowly, tiredly, along the trail. Wess was so surprised that she did not speak as the wizard passed her, but a few paces on, Lythande stopped and looked around, frowning.

"Westerly?"

Wess stepped into sight. "How did you know I was there?"

"I felt you near. . . . How did you find me?"

"I thought I heard someone call me. Was that a spell?"

"No. Just a hope."

"You look so tired, Lythande."

Lythande nodded. "I received a challenge. I answered it."

"And you won—"

"Yes." Lythande smiled bitterly. "I still walk the earth and wait for the days of Chaos. If that is winning, then I won."

"Come back to camp and rest and eat with us."

"Thank you, little sister. I will rest with you. But your friend—you found him?"

"Yes. He's free."

"You all escaped unhurt?"

Wess shrugged, and was immediately sorry for it. "I

did crack my ribs this time." She did not want to talk about the deeper hurts.

"And now—are you going home?"

"Yes."

Lythande smiled. "I might have known you would find the Forgotten Pass."

They walked together back toward camp. A little scared by her own presumption, Wess reached out and took the wizard's hand in hers. Lythande did not draw away, but squeezed her fingers gently.

"Westerly—" Lythande looked at her straight on, and Wess stopped. "Westerly, would you go back to Sanctuary?"

Stunned and horrified, Wess said, "Why?"

"It isn't as bad as it seems at first. You could learn many things. . . ."

"About being a wizard?"

Lythande hesitated. "It would be difficult, but—it might be possible. It is true that your talents should not be wasted."

"You don't understand," Wess said. "I don't want to be a wizard. I wouldn't go back to Sanctuary if that were the reason."

Lythande said, finally, "That isn't the only reason."

Wess took Lythande's hand between her own, drew it to her lips, and kissed the palm. Lythande reached up and caressed Wess's cheek. Wess shivered at the touch.

"Lythande, I can't go back to Sanctuary. You would be the only reason I was there—and it would change me. It *did* change me. I don't know if I can go back to being the person I was before I came here, but I'm going to try. Most of what I did learn there I would rather never have known. You must understand me!"

"Yes," Lythande said. "It was not fair of me to ask."

"It isn't that I wouldn't love you," Wess said, and Lythande looked at her sharply. Wess took as deep a breath as she could, and continued. "But what I feel for you would change, too, as I changed. It wouldn't be love anymore. It would be . . . need, and demand, and envy."

Lythande sat on a tree root, shoulders slumped, and stared at the ground. Wess knelt beside her and smoothed her hair back from her forehead.

"Lythande. . . ."

"Yes, little sister," the magician whispered, as if she were too tired to speak aloud.

"You must have important work here." How could she bear it otherwise? Wess thought. She is going to laugh at you for what you ask her, and explain how foolish it is, and how impossible. "And Kaimas, my home . . . you would find it dull—" She stopped, surprised at herself for her hesitation and her fear. "You come with me, Lythande," she said abruptly. "You come home with me."

Lythande stared at her, her expression unreadable. "Did you mean what you said—"

"It's so beautiful, Lythande. And peaceful. You've met half my family already. You'd like the rest of them, too! You said you had things to learn from us."

"—about loving me?"

Wess caught her breath. She leaned forward and kissed Lythande quickly, then, a second time, slowly, as she had wanted to since the moment she saw her.

She drew back a little.

"Yes," she said. "Sanctuary made me lie, but I'm not in Sanctuary now. With any luck I'll never see it again, and never have to lie anymore."

"If I had to go—"

Wess grinned. "I might try to persuade you to stay." She touched Lythande's hair. "But I wouldn't try to hold you. As long as you wanted to stay, and whenever you wanted to come back, you'd have a place in Kaimas."

"It isn't your resolve I doubt, little sister. It's

my own. And my own strength. I think I would not want to leave your home, once I'd been there for a while."

"I can't see the future," Wess said. Then she laughed at herself, for what she was saying to a wizard. "Perhaps you can."

Lythande made no reply.

"All I know," Wess said, "is that anything anyone does might cause pain. To oneself, to a friend. But you cannot do nothing." She stood up. "Come. Come sleep, with me and my friends. And then we'll go home."

Lythande stood up too. "There's so much you don't know about me, little sister. So much of it could hurt you."

Wess closed her eyes, wishing, like a child at twilight seeking out a star. She opened her eyes again.

Lythande smiled. "I will come with you. If only for a while."

They walked together, hand in hand, to join the others.

The awesome spirits of chaos approach
their appointed hour . . .

—— THE ——
Time Raiders

BERNARD KING

The second in a trilogy of masterful invention

27 July AD 869. There was something unnatural, ungodly
about the rag-draped skeleton. The weathered white frame
appeared intact, if fallen in, but the skull was missing . . .

30 April last year. His face was like parchment stretched
across a skull which was no longer his own. His eyes, blue
and too young for his wrinkled, gaunt visage, smiled down
at those scrambling away in their panic before him . . .

The immortal forces of Thule insinuate their warring
passions through time, feeding the flame of mankind's
destiny. And as the shadows lengthen, the powers of
darkness thrill to the fulfilment of their deadly quest. But
their ritual is incomplete and they must steal the ancient
talisman from those who uphold the flickering light –
wherever and who ever they may be . . .

0 7221 4868 2   FANTASY   £3.50

Also by Bernard King in Sphere Books:
THE DESTROYING ANGEL

A selection of bestsellers from Sphere

FICTION

THE LEGACY OF HEOROT	Niven/Pournelle/Barnes	£3.50 ☐
THE PHYSICIAN	Noah Gordon	£3.99 ☐
INFIDELITIES	Freda Bright	£3.99 ☐
THE GREAT ALONE	Janet Dailey	£3.99 ☐
THE PANIC OF '89	Paul Erdman	£3.50 ☐

FILM AND TV TIE-IN

BLACK FOREST CLINIC	Peter Heim	£2.99 ☐
INTIMATE CONTACT	Jacqueline Osborne	£2.50 ☐
BEST OF BRITISH	Maurice Sellar	£8.95 ☐
SEX WITH PAULA YATES	Paula Yates	£2.95 ☐
RAW DEAL	Walter Wager	£2.50 ☐

NON-FICTION

FISH	Robyn Wilson	£2.50 ☐
THE SACRED VIRGIN AND THE HOLY WHORE	Anthony Harris	£3.50 ☐
THE DARKNESS IS LIGHT ENOUGH	Chris Ferris	£4.50 ☐
TREVOR HOWARD: A GENTLEMAN AND A PLAYER	Vivienne Knight	£3.50 ☐
INVISIBLE ARMIES	Stephen Segaller	£4.99 ☐

All Sphere books are available at your local bookshop or newsagent, or can be ordered direct from the publisher. Just tick the titles you want and fill in the form below.

Name _____

Address _____

_____

Write to Sphere Books, Cash Sales Department, P.O. Box 11, Falmouth, Cornwall TR10 9EN

Please enclose a cheque or postal order to the value of the cover price plus:

UK: 60p for the first book, 25p for the second book and 15p for each additional book ordered to a maximum charge of £1.90.

OVERSEAS & EIRE: £1.25 for the first book, 75p for the second book and 28p for each subsequent title ordered.

BFPO: 60p for the first book, 25p for the second book plus 15p per copy for the next 7 books, thereafter 9p per book.

Sphere Books reserve the right to show new retail prices on covers which may differ from those previously advertised in the text elsewhere, and to increase postal rates in accordance with the P.O.